She didn't intend to do it. If she'd thought about it, she wouldn't have stepped near him again. But he was there, she was in his arms, and it became the most natural thing in the world to touch her lips to his.

Meant to be an expression of gratitude, the kiss became much more. Jeff's hands tumbled to her waist, holding her close as his tongue began a slow exploration of the curve of her mouth. The growling of sexual starvation coiled through her, escaping as a moan trapped between their lips. Her nipples hardened into tight, painful peaks as moisture gathered between her thighs. She had to cling to his shoulders as her knees went weak.

Indigo Sensuous Love Stories

Genesis Press, Inc.
315 Third Avenue North
Columbus, MS 39701

ISBN: 1-58571-066-0
Manufactured in the United States of America

First Edition

No Apologies
by
Seressia Glass

Genesis Press, Inc.

ACKNOWLEDGEMENTS

I would like to thank author Susan Grace and her extended family, and my local writers' group for making me feel less like a stranger in a strange land down here in Florida.

To all the readers who enjoyed *No Commitment Required*, thank you. I look forward to hearing from others. You may contact me through my website www.seressia.com, or at P.O. Box 6603, Delray Beach, FL 33482

Prologue

Dear God, please let her be all right.

Angela Davenport sat huddled in a sickly green chair in the waiting room, arms wrapped tightly about herself in a useless quest for comfort. It had been an hour since they had rushed her cousin Shayla from her labor room to surgery. An hour of agony, waiting, wondering, hoping. Praying.

It would be all right, she struggled to reassure herself. Shayla had always been strong and independent, fiercely so. Her cousin knew what she wanted from life and was determined to get it.

Apparently, that meant a child. It had been a big shock to Angela when her career-driven cousin decided to become a mother, choosing the father from profiles at a sperm bank.

Shayla often said she didn't need a man to make her life complete—or a woman either. It had been Shayla's strength that had gotten Angela through her divorce from Richard seven years ago, and helped her cope in the eight months since she'd walked out on the love of her life, Jeff Maxwell.

Her cousin had given her a shoulder to cry on, had convinced her when she waffled that she'd done the correct thing. Then Shayla had completely taken Angela's mind off Jeff with the announcement that she was pregnant.

The indomitable woman was Angela's hero, proof that she could make it by herself if she chose. Being Shayla's Lamaze coach, giggling with her over purchases and giving her opinion on the baby's future had helped to ease her heartache. At least until the sun went down and she returned to her lonely, empty apartment.

Now Shayla was in trouble. The baby was in trouble. Angela had been ejected from the delivery room when Shayla suddenly lost consciousness during a contraction. The not knowing combined with the frantic scurrying of the hospital staff had her gnawing her fingernails to the quick.

Memories assailed her, one coming into sharp focus.

The June afternoon throbbed with sweltering heat. A couple of months past twelve, Angela had started her growth spurt early, becoming all skin and bones. Shayla, a month away from turning thirteen, showed the promise of the curves of womanhood. They sat in a dilapidated swingset rusting beneath the spreading arms of a magnolia tree. Angela had been complaining about yet another thing she had failed to do to make her mother happy.

"I'm glad I don't have a mother," Shayla announced, twisting around so the chains were braided together. It had been two years since Aunt Terrie had dropped her daughter off at her sister's doorstep, and no one had heard from her since.

"Yes you do," Angela told her, watching her cousin spin.

2

"You have mine."

How matter of fact she'd been then, even with her hormones racing out of control. She didn't mind sharing her mother, but her mother obviously couldn't love more than one child at a time, and Shayla was the child she'd chosen to lavish her love and attention on. Angela had long resigned herself to it, even if it still caused her bitterness. She felt like a black Cinderella, never able to do anything good enough to earn the love that should have automatically been hers. And like Cinderella, she hoped for a miracle, a fairy godmother, a prince.

Angela didn't begrudge her cousin the initial attention. She couldn't imagine what it would be like if her father walked out and her mother sent her to live with an aunt. She'd known that Shayla needed to know she was welcome. And Angela had welcomed her cousin, glad to ease the loneliness of being an only child.

'Course she'd thought that after a while, her mother would start paying attention to her again. But Marie never did, unless Angela did something less than perfect—bringing home less than straight-A's, tracking mud into the house. "Really," her mother would exclaim in exasperation, "I expected better of you." Eventually Angela decided no attention was better after all.

It helped that Shayla was just as uncomfortable with Marie's attention as Angela was. For two young girls with fractured relationships with their mothers, it had been easy to ignore the animosity that could have erupted and befriend each other instead. They were now inseparable.

Shayla stopped her swing, digging her new white sneakers into the red Georgia clay. "We don't need mothers," she stated, her voice ringing with determination in the stifling, moist heat. "We don't need nobody. But if I have a daughter when I grow up, I will never leave her. Never."

Angela had believed her then. Shayla was strong, Shayla was determined. Nothing was going to happen to her or her child.

Please let them be all right. Please God, just let them be all right.

"Ms. Davenport?"

Angela shot to her feet as the doctor came toward her. The front of her tunic was stained with blood, and her eyes were tired. "Yes?"

The doctor took a deep breath, then said, "We believe your cousin suffered an amniotic fluid embolism, resulting in a pulmonary embolism."

"P-Pulmonary...b-but she's all right, isn't she? Shayla and the baby are fine, right?"

The doctor shook her head. "We did everything humanly possible to save Shayla without endangering the life of the child. She went into shock, followed by cardiac arrest. We were able to save the baby girl, but your cousin slipped away."

Blood roared through Angela's ears. She saw the doctor's mouth move, but could no longer make out any of the words. The ones she did hear slammed into her like bullets. "Baby girl...everything humanly possible ...I'm sorry ..."

"Oh my God." Her hand clawed at her mouth as she fought for breath. "Oh my God, no."

One

Four months later

"C'mon, Kayleigh, aren't you tired? Auntie's tired."

Angela cuddled the four-month-old closer, stifling a yawn. She'd deliberately cut short Kayleigh's afternoon nap in hope of producing night sleep that lasted more than three hours and thirty-seven minutes, the current record. It had been so long since she'd slept eight hours straight Angela couldn't remember what it was like.

The little girl she called her niece—much easier to say than second cousin—seemed just as determined to remain awake despite the soothing motion of the rocking chair. Her little legs and fists waved angrily, her smooth face mottled red as she fought the inevitable pull of sleep.

"Kayleigh, please. Wouldn't you like a faux fur bottle warmer? How about a Ferrari car carrier? I'll go to FAO Schwartz tomorrow and buy out the baby section. Just let me get more than four hours of sleep."

She quietly sang "Rock-A-Bye", wondering who thought such a violent song would soothe a baby to sleep. Probably the same one who thought knocking coyotes off cliffs was funny. She switched from singing to humming, and was rewarded with a long baby-sized yawn.

Lord, the last four months had been a nightmare of adjustments. Shayla's death still reverberated numbly through her. Her cousin had left a will and a sheath of legal papers that made handling her affairs as simple as the grief would allow. The legal papers she'd reluctantly signed when Shayla was alive had been a godsend, smoothing the procedures of becoming Kayleigh's legal guardian. Without them, Marie Davenport had stood a good chance of taking Kayleigh away from her.

When her mother told her that she'd filed suit for custody of Kayleigh, Angela had been dumbfounded. And hurt by the timing—the day after Shayla's funeral.

She remembered driving to her parent's Grant Park home, the house that had stopped being a home for her years ago. "How could you do this?" she'd demanded, close to tears as she waved the legal notice in the charged air between them.

"How could you think you can raise a child?" her mother asked, thin face pinched in righteous indignation. "You left your first marriage in a shambles, and you lost that young man you had last year. If you can't even keep a man, how can you keep a child?"

The accusation stung, striking into her deepest fears of failure. "I'll learn. I'll do what I have to do."

"I'm thinking of Kayleigh's best interests," her mother replied. "You fly all over the place, work long hours. Are you going to give up your job? And those people you call your friends. That's the wrong influence to expose Shayla's daughter to."

Anger simmered with hurt. "What's wrong with my friends?"

"Do you really need me to spell it out? One friend who doesn't know to stick with her own kind, and another—that Lawrence—in a relationship that goes against the very nature of God. I will not have you raising my grandniece in that type of environment."

Angela pushed aside the pain her mother was an expert at giving, clenching her hands into fists. It was one thing for her to be attacked; she wasn't going to let her friends be disparaged.

"Yvonne and Lawrence are my friends," she ground out. "You have a lot of nerve talking about going against the nature of God, especially when it comes to family. They have been more like a family to me than you ever have!"

Marie took a step back in surprise, and Angela realized it was the first time she'd stood up to her mother. It felt so good that she kept going. "I will fight you on this, every step of the way. Shayla wants—wanted—me to raise Kayleigh. That's what I intend to do. And if I have to drag you into court to prove that to you, then I intend to do it!"

She'd left then, determined to fight, to prove her mother wrong, to do what Shayla wanted her to do. A call to her father revealed that he knew nothing about the action her mother had taken. The next day he called to tell her that the custody suit had been dropped.

The damage had been done though. The chasm between Angela and her mother gaped too wide to be bridged. She wouldn't deny Marie access to her grandniece, and they'd agreed to bi-weekly visits. But one disparaging comment thrown her way and Angela would be out the door, taking the baby with her.

Kayleigh yawned, distracting Angela from the darkness of her thoughts. The infant yawned again before her lashes swept down into slumber. Angela's heart turned over as it always did. "Goodnight, angel."

Carefully she put her young charge to bed, then grabbed the second baby monitor and headed downstairs. This townhouse, though beautiful and spacious with its prime corner lot, couldn't compare to her Buckhead high-rise apartment with its killer view. But there was no way she'd attempt to raise Kayleigh in the singles scene. The Brookhaven community was close enough to the downtown offices to be convenient, and surrounded by enough trees and parks to make it seem far away from city life. Oglethorpe University was nearby, and a lot of the professors seemed to call her neighborhood home. It was expensive, sure enough, but worth it.

She swept through the dining room and entered the kitchen. It was a bright and cheery room, Mediterranean blue and washed oak, filled with appliances that hadn't been turned on since she bought the place three months ago. As a single woman with a large bank account and demanding career, cooking had never been a necessity. Take-out meals were her specialty, and several places around town knew her by name.

Opening the fridge, she surveyed her choices. The freezer bulged with color-coded plastic and cardboard-covered containers. She reached for pink plastic, vented the lid, and popped it into the microwave.

Reheated dinners were a far cry from dining out at Pano's and Paul's or Chops every night, but she found she didn't mind. Lawrence, assistant extraordinaire, lavished her and Kayleigh with the same care, attention, and companionship he'd given to their boss, Yvonne Benjamin, before she got married. Considering him a true friend, Angela wasn't too proud to accept his help. The man knew how to cook and considered it his God-given duty to ensure that she didn't starve. She just wished she could find a heterosexual version him.

The microwave beeped. Rumbles emanated from her stomach as she breathed in the heady aroma of curried chicken. "Lawrence," she whispered, "you are a god."

Taking the container, a fork, and a bottle of water, she retreated to her living room. With a sigh of contentment she flopped on her couch, remote in one hand, microwave dinner in the other. With Kayleigh finally, blessedly asleep, she had a chunk of relative peace. If she ate quickly enough, she might even be able to get two uninterrupted hours of sleep!

Her life had taken a definite turn, she thought, flipping through channels between bites. As vice president of Your Heart's Desire, a seven-year-old local and online lingerie boutique, her dream job had become a reality. In the last few years, her days had been filled with trotting the globe, meeting with textile designers, searching for accessories, organizing publicity for fashion shows, and weighing in on concepts that her best friend and boss, Yvonne Benjamin, turned into fabric works of art. Now with Yvonne concentrating on designing and raising twins and Angela's own surprise entry into parenthood, the world-traveler role now belonged to Lawrence.

Jet-setting wasn't the only thing she'd had to relinquish now that she was guardian to a four-month-old. Her simple knits weren't on the same level with the silk and cashmere she was accustomed to. However, after having Kayleigh ruin her favorite silk blouse with regurgitated baby formula, Angela had quickly discovered the wisdom of wash-and-wear clothing.

Taking a bite of the entrée, she closed her eyes and indulged in her favorite fantasy, imagining herself scrolling through her electronic organizer, gazing at names and numbers she'd been inundated with since her debut in Your Heart's Desire's first fashion show two years ago. Being whisked away to a quaint French restaurant or a weekend in the mountains. Attending plays, concerts, and the ballet on the arm of a different man each night. Deciding whom to bestow her favors on and whom to reject with the critical eye of a connoisseur, enjoying the power that a hardened heart gave her. Finally, irrevocably ridding her system of its addiction to Jeff Maxwell once and for all.

Dream on.

Jeff Maxwell, a man who could make money grow faster than kudzu. A man who could make love with voice alone. A man who at six-two had the innate grace of the basketball player he'd been, possessed skin like milk-chocolate and eyes like molasses, a veritable feast to the senses whenever they were together. A man who gave her the best year of her life.

A man she'd walked away from, because he still loved another woman.

She'd known from the beginning that Jeff had feelings for Yvonne. They'd known each other for more than fifteen years and Yvonne had all but been adopted into Jeff's family. Then Yvonne met Jeff's best friend, Mike Benjamin, and the two fell in love. Jeff had tried to break them up, playing on differences in their race, Mike's checkered past, anything to drive them apart. He'd succeeded, only to put them back together when he realized the depth of their feelings for each other.

Angela had been there through it all, knowing firsthand the pain of unrequited love. But she thought love and happiness had been hers at last, when she and Jeff grew closer after Mike and Yvonne got married. That one glorious year with Jeff had been the happiest of her life. Then Yvonne had the twins.

When visiting hours had ended after Yvonne's delivery, they'd gone back to Jeff's apartment. He'd wanted her, maybe even needed her, but she'd refused. Instead, she went into the bedroom, found a gymbag, and began stuffing her things into it.

Jeff had stood in the doorway, watching, his expression empty. "Why?"

"Why?" She felt her heart crack further. "How you can ask me why? How can you not know why I'm doing this?"

He moved into the room, grabbing her by the shoulders. "If I knew I wouldn't ask. Don't play games with me."

"You think I'm playing games? Well, ain't that the pot calling the kettle black!"

His dark eyes glittered with a powerful, nameless emotion. "What do you want from me?"

"There's only one thing I want from you, Jeff." She faced him. "I want you to look me in the eye and tell me that you don't love Yvonne."

He stared at her for the longest moment, and Angela felt an infinitesimal hope. It quickly died as his hands fell away.

She turned and zipped her bag with shaking hands. She could have hated him in that moment if her heart wasn't hurting so damned much. "I refuse to be second string, Jeff. Not for you, not for anyone. I deserve more than that."

It had taken everything in her to leave. And it hurt her to her soul that he let her go.

The last time she had seen him had been at the twins' baptism, when they were officially named godparents. Godparents who didn't even speak to each other. He'd left soon after, without a word spoken between them, and disappeared.

Reality came rushing back, a vengeful tidal wave. Their relationship had been nothing more than a year-long one-night stand. No talk about the future or the past. Even without that confrontation, the relationship wouldn't have limped along for very much longer. He would have left eventually; she felt that to her bones.

It had been a year since Jeff left town. Try as she might to purge him from her mind, her senses still burned with memory. Her attempts at going out were disasters from the word go. When she was awarded custody of Kayleigh, her remaining prospects evaporated.

A rebounding woman was one thing. A rebounding woman with a newborn was another.

Now she was lonely but never alone. Kayleigh occupied twenty-five of the twenty-four hours in her day. The few scant moments she had for herself were spent eating or sleeping, with eating about to go the way of the dinosaurs. Work was in there somewhere, at the bottom of the totem pole. She wondered tiredly if this was how it would be, the best years of her life devoted to a fragile, needy, innocent life, with only her hand and a steamy novel for company.

A wave of guilt immediately swept her. She didn't resent Kayleigh's presence in her life. And life wasn't all hell. Saturdays were spent with Yvonne Benjamin and her twins, and every other Sunday she suited up in her mental armor and did her familial duty by taking Kayleigh to visit her parents. Unable to stomach more than a few hours with her criticizing mother, Angela kept the visits short. Most of her unwinding time, if it could be called that, she spent in the beautiful house Lawrence shared with his life-partner, Jaime.

Angela had it better than most single mothers did and she knew it. She had the resources to hire a nanny, a cook, and a maid, but she did none of those. The idea of strangers taking care of Kayleigh was anathema to her. From the moment she'd held the orphaned newborn in her arms, Angela had known that she would fight tooth and claw to be Kayleigh's guardian and fulfill the promise she'd made to her cousin. And if that meant being an old maid ...

Appetite gone, Angela sat the food container on the coffee table, then rubbed the aching spot where her heart had been. Apparently it was her night to trip down memory lane, remembering past pain.

Although she'd buried her reactions to the injustices her mother had dealt and continued to hurl at her, the pain she felt over Jeff had yet to dissipate. Even after a year, it still hurt. She reminded herself for the umpteenth time that she had done the right thing by calling it quits with him. It was a bitch to love someone who didn't return the love. She had gone through that with her ex-husband, Richard. It would be a cold day in hell before she did it again.

"Yeah right," she snorted at the television. "Like I have any chance of going through that again. I'd give a nun better odds."

The ringing of the doorbell startled her like a bad omen.

Tossing down the remote, she hurried to the door before the chime could ring again. She wasn't expecting visitors tonight. She knew Yvonne had some of her protégées over, and Lawrence and his life-partner were supposed to be meeting with their lawyer to discuss adoption options.

Her heart gave a delighted jump. Maybe they had some good news. Lawrence had definitely proven over the years that his Y chromosome hadn't obliterated his nurturing spirit.

With the chain firmly in place, she opened the door. Her breath caught in her throat as her world tilted violently. Oh, my God.

"Hello, Angie," Jeff said. "May I come in?"

Two

She was nothing like he'd remembered—and everything he couldn't forget.

The woman looking back at him through the gap created by the door-chain was practically a stranger. Thin, way too thin, with hair cropped close in tiny auburn tendrils that barely brushed the tops of her ears. Deep, dark eyes , eyes he could swim in, seemed huge in the narrow planes of her cinnamon face. The tightening in his loins and her shocked gasp confirmed her identity.

"May I come in?" he asked again, amazed at the casualness of his tone. Inside he seethed with nervous energy.

She continued to stare at him, that lovely mouth working as if she'd lost her voice. Then coldness crept into her eyes, stilling her features. "I don't talk to strangers."

So the gloves were off already. He gave her what he hoped was a deprecating smile. "Then why did you open the door?"

"So I can do this." With a saccharine smile, she very slowly and deliberately closed the door in his face.

Okay, that went better than he thought it would, but it

irked him nevertheless. "Do you feel better now?" he asked through the door.

The door jerked open. Like an avenging angel she stood before him, eyes flashing, hands on hips. "I'll feel a lot better after I do this!" She raised her hand.

His hand shot out, grabbing her wrist. "Do you really want to do this on your doorstep?" he asked, his voice low. He'd come here to apologize, not antagonize. One look at her and his emotions and common sense had taken a one-way ticket to hell.

Dressed for lounging in socks, jeans, and a dark green turtleneck, the casual Angela looked far different from the glamorous, silk and cashmere Angela he remembered. She was different, changed somehow. Not only in looks and style, but something in her eyes, something deep. It disturbed him.

"I don't want to do this at all," she retorted, tugging to free her hand. "I have nothing to say to you!"

"Fine. You can listen instead." He pushed her back into the house.

"No." Her eyes widened with anger, fear, or shock. Whatever it was, she backed away as he inexorably pushed his way into her house. "There's nothing you can say that I even remotely want to hear."

The quaver in her voice struck him, and he released her. "This doesn't have to be uncivilized, Angie," he said, trying to soothe her as he turned to shut the door. "Just hear me out."

She retreated down the short foyer. He followed close behind, barely registering the dark traditional style of the living room they entered and almost crashing into her when she whirled around. "You have the nerve to call me uncivilized, when you just forced your way into my house?"

She went absolutely still, the blood draining from her face. "How did you find out where I live? Oh God, Yvonne gave you my address?"

"I haven't seen Yvonne," Jeff replied. "I got your address from Pops."

"Pops?"

"Yeah, the doorman at your old place. He always did like me."

"Be glad someone still does," she retorted, folding her arms across her chest. He couldn't help following the gesture, couldn't help remembering how she felt, how she tasted.

A restless, reckless mood settled on him. God, he'd missed her. He almost reached for her, but tucked his hands into his pockets instead. "Nice place."

He didn't mean it. This place was nothing like Angela. He knew she loved the view from her apartment and wouldn't have given it up for anything. This two-story brick townhouse with its classic, dark furnishings couldn't compare to the cosmopolitan art-deco digs close to everything she loved about downtown Atlanta. This place looked too permanent, too settled down.

Settled down. His stomach dropped. Was he too late?

Had she met and married someone else while he was gone?

Coming to see her here, unannounced like this, seemed like a good idea on the flight in. Now he realized it for the mistake it was. Just one of many he'd made during the last two years.

What did you think? That she'd wait like a good little girl for you to get your act together?

He shook his thoughts off to find Angela staring at him as if he'd sprouted an extra head. "I like it."

"You liked your old place too. Why did you move?"

Her expression grew colder. "That's none of your business. In fact, nothing in my life is any of your business. Go back to whatever rock you crawled out from under. I don't care. Just go away."

Just like that, his good intentions went out the window. "Why? Am I disturbing your new man?"

Oh, that got to her. Her back popped as she straightened, folding her arms. "And if I said yes?" she taunted.

An abrupt, consuming fury grabbed him. "Then I'd go upstairs and haul his ass out of your bed!"

She blinked in surprise before anger caused her cheeks to blossom. "You have no claims on me, Jeff Maxwell!" she spat. "You lost that right a year ago—if you ever had it!"

That did it. "Oh, you think so?" He smiled, but he felt far from amused. "Let's see about that!"

Needing to teach her a lesson as much as he needed to touch her, he dragged her close, imprinting her body with his own. His lips descended on hers, hard, demanding, full of a year's worth of hunger, of anger, of regret.

When she stiffened, he softened the kiss to feather-weight brushes of lips to lips as memories swept through his blood. She relaxed against him then, pressing against him with an equal hunger.

Someone moaned. He didn't know who, and he didn't care. All that mattered was having her back in his arms again. Angela apparently did care. She pushed away from him, and as he opened his eyes, slapped him. Hard.

The sound was loud in the charged silence of the room. Jeff blinked, then abruptly stepped away from her. What the hell was he doing?

"Damn it, Angie, I didn't mean to do that," he said, angry with himself for losing control. He stepped farther away from her, needing the distance before he did something to earn another slap. "That's not what I came over here for."

She folded her arms across her chest again. Her boiling anger had subsided to a simmer, but it still lurked beneath the surface of her gaze. "Why did you come here?"

He rubbed at his forehead to ease his sudden headache. "I want to apologize to you."

It sounded lame, especially after what had just happened. Angie apparently had the same thought. She made a sound between a snort and a laugh. "My God, you're serious, aren't you? You came all the way back from wherever the hell you were and pushed into my house just so I could listen to you apologize?"

"Yes."

"Then you came a long way for nothing."

He sighed, searching for calm, for the right words to say. The carefully rehearsed speech he'd spent months crafting evaporated. "I know you don't want to hear this, and you won't believe me, but I'm gonna tell you anyway."

Her expression remained hard, but curiosity crept into her eyes. "Tell me what?"

"About that night, the last night we were together."

Her eyes darkened with the same pain that threatened to suffocate him. That night. God, he'd been reliving that night for the past year. Seeing his two best friends so happy with their newborn sons had done something to him. He'd felt so many things: happiness, jealousy, love. And an ache, so pure, so encompassing that he couldn't name it.

He'd wanted Angela to ease that ache. Needed to feel her with him and around him, taking him into her arms and her body. He'd wanted to lose himself in her sweetness and in doing so, hopefully find himself again.

Instead, she'd walked out on him. He remembered asking her what she wanted from him. He would have done anything, given her anything to ease the ache. Except answer the question she'd asked of him.

He could have lied, but they both would have known it for a lie. He did love Yvonne. He loved her then, he loved her now. He'd loved Yvonne for fifteen years, since he'd first seen her after the accident that left her an orphan and nearly paralyzed her. But he wasn't in love with her. He knew now that he never had been.

"A year ago, you asked me to tell you that I didn't love Yvonne."

She flinched, obviously not expecting him to bring it up. "One of my more glorious mistakes. So what?"

"I didn't answer you then, but I'd like to answer you now." He took a deep breath, then plunged ahead. "I love Yvonne, but I'm not in love with her. I never was."

The silence pounded in his ears as she just looked at him. Then a sound too broken to be a laugh escaped her. "You're right, I don't believe you."

"Angie—"

She rounded on him. "I was there, remember? You came to me when you broke her and Mike apart. I should have refused you then, but stupid me, I couldn't stand to see you hurting like that. I thought my love would be enough for you, but it wasn't, was it?"

She answered herself with a shake of her head. "I could blame you and be done, but I was at fault too. I thought my love could help you, could heal you. How stupid could I get? I spent a year beating my heart against the wall you've got around yours. But even I had my limit."

Pain sliced through him, a reflection of the pain he'd caused her. "Angie..."

"When Yvonne and Mike announced her pregnancy, I watched your face. That was the beginning of the end. I knew it and I still fought against it. Up until that day in the delivery room, I fought it."

Her eyes hardened as she glanced at him. "Do you

remember that day, Jeff? Do you remember how you stood there, what you felt as you watched them with the twins? Well I remember. The hunger and the jealousy and the resignation."

She leveled a finger at him, "It was written all over your face for me and everybody else to see."

He closed his eyes, the better to not see the anguish in hers. But she wasn't done. "I told you before, I won't be runner up. I deserve to be first place in a man's heart. And you, you have no idea what you threw away. I loved you, Jeff Maxwell. I loved you in a way that you will never, ever, be loved again."

He stared at her, stunned. "Y-you loved me?"

She stared at him in horror, as if she'd just realized what she'd said. Then she stepped away from him. "Get out."

No, not like this. He reached for her arm. "Angie, please. We need to talk about this—"

"No!" She jerked away from him, her voice rising. "No more excuses, no more apologies, no more words. Just get out!"

She shouted the last, and as soon as she did her face went slack with fear. "Oh God."

A muffled wail swept down the stairs, duplicated by something that sounded like a walkie-talkie. Shocked, Jeff stared at Angela for a heart-stopping second before pushing past her, snatching the talkie off the couch. "What the hell?"

Another wail answered him. No, it couldn't be. Without a word, he dropped the monitor and turned for the stairs.

"Jeff, wait!"

He didn't listen to her, didn't care about anything other than reaching the source of those plaintive cries. Up the stairs, down a hall, to a half-closed door. He hesitated a split-second before pushing it open.

The room was dimly lit, but unmistakable. The smell of baby powder hit him a second before the sight of the crib did. My God, it was.

Forgetting to breathe, he approached the crib and peered inside. A baby, not more than six months old, flailed tiny fists in the air as it wailed for attention.

A baby. His heart dropped, settled, melted. Powerless to do anything else, he reached into the crib, lifting the tiny bawling bundle of humanity.

Shock and anger left him, replaced by wonder and a pure longing. Dimly aware of Angela frozen in place beside him, he cradled the pink-clad baby close in the curve of his left arm, the fingers of his right hand trembling as he reached to stroke her face. "Hello there."

She stopped mid-wail, as if she realized someone new held her. Her eyes popped open, blinking up at him, cries forgotten. When she gurgled in welcome, he fell headlong into love.

Angela finally moved, stretching her hands to him. "Give her to me."

Jeff raised his head, sudden anger surging in him. Angela had a baby. There was no doubt in his mind who the father was, just like there was no way in hell he was about to relinquish his hold on his daughter. "Don't even think about it."

Still cradling the baby close, he stepped away from Angela then settled into the rocker near the window. He drank in the baby's features, committing them to memory. He had a daughter. The knowledge settled into him, curling like a kitten in his heart. Man, it was a wonderful feeling.

She was beautiful, perfectly beautiful in her pink sleeper with three fluffy sheep dancing across the chest. "What's her name?" he asked, smiling as she gave a huge yawn.

Angela folded her arms about her chest, hovering near him. "I want you to leave."

"I bet you do." He had no intention of leaving, not now. Not ever.

He tried to feel anger, but all he felt was a crushing guilt. His father had instilled in him the meaning of duty and responsibility at an early age. He'd disappointed his father once, when he was eleven years old. He prayed his dad wasn't looking down from heaven in disappointment now.

Setting the rocker in motion, he repeated his question, his eyes never leaving the flannel-clad bundle in his arms. "What's her name?"

"Her name's Kayleigh. Now will you please leave?"

Jeff returned his attention to the precious gift in his arms. "Hi Kayleigh," he crooned. "What a beautiful name for a beautiful girl. I bet you want to know who I am, don't you? All right, I'll tell you. I'm your father."

Three

"For the last time, you are not Kayleigh's father."

Angela stood in the center of her living room, her headache elevated to migraine status. She felt more than a little shell-shocked. She'd made repeated denials since Jeff's paternal announcement, but he'd quietly brushed them off until Kayleigh slipped back into slumber.

Her stomach lurched. Two seconds and Jeff had charmed the newborn. It took minutes and pleading before she could get Kayleigh calmed down, yet she'd stopped crying as soon as Jeff picked her up.

The look on his face as he held Kayleigh, the wonder and the joy, should have told her what he'd assumed. Still, she didn't suspect the assumption he'd made until his announcement.

Now they stared at each other from opposite sides of her living room, he in rising anger, she in rising hysteria. Jeff had returned. Jeff was in her house. Why was he here? Why had he come back? Was it really only to ask for her forgiveness?

The year away had made him more gorgeous than she

remembered. Even with the leather jacket covering him, she could see that he was bulkier, more muscular. He wore a mustache now that only enhanced the kissability of his lips.

Yearning pulsed through her, sweet and potent. Dangerous. She pushed it aside and found the anger that always simmered beneath the hurt.

"Did you hear me? You aren't Kayleigh's father."

"I heard you. I just don't believe you."

His harsh tone only made her angrier. "You have no right to be angry with me, Jeff Maxwell," she spat.

"Oh, don't I?" He stopped before her, six-feet-five-inches of angry male, cinnamon eyes blazing in his cocoa face. "You called it quits. You walked out on me. You have a child. And you think I don't have a right to be angry?"

"No, I don't."

The expression on his face called her statement the lie it was. "If I hadn't come back, would you have told me about her?"

"There's nothing to tell," she retorted, determined not to give ground. There was no way she was going to let his anger, justified or not, obliterate the reasons why she should be angry. "Besides, you made it perfectly clear you didn't want to be found. Not that I would have contacted you anyway, if I'd been so unfortunate as to have gotten pregnant with your child."

His eyes flashed and his jaw clenched with the effort to control his temper. "I would have come back if I'd known. I would have been here."

She decided to punish him a little, feeding his disbelief. "Why? So you could tell me to get rid of it?"

He went absolutely still, and Angela knew she'd gone too far with this hypothetical game of what-ifs. When he spoke, his voice was measured with the effort to control his anger. "No matter what you think of me, never think I would have considered that an option. I'd want my child."

"What a good little Boy Scout you are," she said, sarcasm flowing full-steam. Maybe he'd meant the words as reassurance, but they sliced through her nevertheless. For a child he would have stayed. Not for a lover. Not for her. "And then what would you have done? Leave her like you left me?"

He stopped in front of her. "You walked out on me, remember? Not the other way around."

"No, you couldn't leave someplace you've never been, could you?" she asked, bitterness coating every word. "I never had you. You never belonged to me."

"I do now."

Surprised, she took a step back from him. "What?"

"Marry me."

How many times had she dreamed of this moment, when the man she loved would choose her, would ask to share her life forever? But he wasn't asking for her, because of her. That was obvious by the guilt glinting in his eyes, the hard set of his jaw. Even his hands were bunched into fists.

Like a man resigned to his fate, that's how he looked. He wasn't happy to be making the proposal, and she wasn't happy to hear it, not like this. Probably never.

Her heart thumped a painful rhythm in her chest, so hard she was sure he could hear it. "Go to hell."

His smile was twisted. "I've been there. It wasn't fun." He drew closer, his voice dropping to a husky whisper. "Marry me, Angie."

God, that voice had coaxed her to multiple orgasms, made her ignore her head and listen to her heart, made her long for things that just weren't meant. She clenched her hands. "No. Hell no. Not now, not ever."

"Why not?"

"Why not?" Her laugh was frighteningly close to a sob. "You have the nerve to ask me why not?"

She stepped away from him, needing the distance. "Do you think I could be with you now, forever knowing that I was your second choice? The love of your life is unavailable so you decided to settle? I may be a fool, but I'm not stupid."

He crossed the room quickly, hands coming down hard on her shoulders. "Never, ever think that being with you is settling. You're better than that."

"Damn right." She tried to twist free but it was impossible.

"Angie, I don't care if this is a new millennium. I'm Kayleigh's father and I'm going to be a part of her life."

"Will you please get this through your thick head? You are not her father."

He froze, registering her words at last. She watched a terrible stillness settle in his eyes. "You were with someone else when you were with me?"

Siberia couldn't have been more frigid, but Angela was too angry and hurt to care. "What if I was? You were."

His grip tightened. "Don't lie to me, Angie," he all but growled. "Were you with someone else while you were with me?"

It would have been an easy out to lie, to say that she'd played him as he'd played her. Instead she told the truth. "I was physically faithful to you, Jeff, just like you were with me."

"Then Kayleigh is mine."

"No, she isn't."

"I can count, Angie. You told me she's four months old. That means you were pregnant before I left—"

He broke off, stunned. His hand fell away from her as the blood fell from his face. "Oh God, Angie. You were pregnant when I left." He sank to the couch, his head in his hands.

God, she could still feel his pain, still reel from the sadness of it. Why did it hurt him to think of leaving her alone, carrying his child? "Jeff—"

"Is that why?" he interrupted her, his voice raw. "You knew you were pregnant that night Yvonne had the twins. Is that why you tried to make me choose?"

She was incredulous. "Make you choose?"

"Between you and Yvonne." Anger caused his jaw to clench. "You tried to force me to choose, and when I didn't you walked out. Taking my child away from me."

Now she felt guilty. In a way, she had been forcing him

to choose. And he chose wrong.

Her hands clenched into fists. It was time to end this. "Jeff, listen to me. You're not Kayleigh's father."

"How can you keep denying this?" he demanded with exasperation. "Do you really think I'll just go away?"

"Yes," she answered, pain stealing the volume and heat from her voice. "That's exactly what I think you'll do."

She watched him flush, open his mouth to say something, then close it. There really wasn't anything he could say in defense, nothing that she would believe. He had left her once; he would do it again. You keep remembering that, sister girl. Don't go down that road again.

Wanting nothing more than to get him out of her house and out of her life, she pulled a photo album off the coffee table. Finding the pictures she sought, she turned the album to him.

"What's this?" he asked, suspicious.

"Proof. You're not Kayleigh's father because I'm not her mother."

She watched him peruse the photos, images taken at the baby shower she'd thrown for Shayla in the spring. One picture in particular showed her and Shayla standing together, her cousin quite obviously eight months pregnant. "Shayla is Kayleigh's mother?"

"Yes. Shayla didn't know the father's identity. She was artificially inseminated using a donor from a sperm bank."

His brows dipped. "Your cousin, Ms Independent." His voice was indifferent, and Angela remembered that they hadn't gotten along. "If she's Kayleigh's mother, why do you have her?"

"Shayla's dead. She-she died giving birth to Kayleigh."

All at once his temper changed. The photo album fell to the couch as he rose, pulling her into his arms. "God, Angie," he muttered into her hair. "I'm so sorry. I know how close you were."

Don't take his comfort, she thought to herself, forcing her body to remain stiff. You can't afford the price.

"This has got to be hard on you," he continued, his embrace gentle and close, sapping her anger. "You lose your cousin and gain a child the same day. Did you even have time to grieve?"

Grieve. It seemed to be all she'd done for the past year. "The time found me."

"I'm so sorry I wasn't here for you," he muttered, sincerity rumbling in his chest beneath her ear. "I swear to you, I would have been here had I known."

Did it matter? Perhaps she could have handled the loss better, the mind-numbing arrangements, the threatened suit by her mother to take Kayleigh away from her. Maybe it would have been easier, had he been there. Maybe it would have been worse. Either way was immaterial. He hadn't been here, and she'd dealt with it herself.

Reluctantly she pushed away from his embrace. "I'm managing," she informed him. "I'm doing fine by myself."

His gaze was too assessing. "You sound like her. Raising a child alone isn't easy, especially when you're not prepared for it."

She immediately bristled. "Are you saying I can't take care of Kayleigh?" God, he was just like her mother.

"I'm not saying that at all."

"Good. Because I can take care of her. I've been taking care of her for the last four months, and I'll keep on taking care of her!"

"Calm down, Angie," he said, hands up. "There's no need for you to get defensive."

"I'm not being defensive," she retorted, the knowledge that she was being exactly that making her angrier. "I'm merely letting you know I don't need you. We don't need you. So go back to wherever you came from and stay the hell away from me!"

"Fine." He moved to the door. "That's the way you want it? You got it."

As if mindful of the sleeping baby, he quietly opened the door and stepped through before turning back to her. Gone were the tenderness and the burning anger. In their place was a quiet regret that cut her to the core.

"For what it's worth, I am sorry." He closed the door behind himself with a soft click that echoed through her heart like a gunshot.

Four

He could have had a daughter.

The thought still gleamed in his mind, a brilliant star of knowledge. Kayleigh. A beautiful name for a beautiful baby.

Just the thought of the four-month old made him smile through his misery. As soon as he'd seen her, his whole world had changed. This was what he wanted, what he'd been searching for: a family of his own. When he held Kayleigh, he'd felt an unprecedented feeling of right. And as she'd stared up at him with those large brown eyes, as she gurgled at him in welcome, he knew, he just knew, he'd give anything to be a part of her life.

The idea that he wasn't Kayleigh's father was hard to accept. If it had been true, it would have been easier to convince Angela to let him be a part of her life, to allow them to become a family. Even though Kayleigh wasn't theirs, he still wanted to be a part of her life, to be in Angela's life. Now, it wasn't a matter of convincing Angela that they belonged together. It was a matter of fighting and proving.

Guilt still pulsed through him. No matter what, he shouldn't have left Angela. He should have found a way, made a way to answer her question and stay by her. She'd faced her cousin's death and instant motherhood alone, and he alone was to blame.

Would he have been a help to her? he wondered. Back then he'd felt as if he were sinking in quicksand, so many emotions pulling at him that he couldn't breathe. Getting away was the only option, the only thing he could do. He wouldn't have been any good to anyone, and Angie would have ended up hating him even more than she did now.

The idea that she'd once offered her love and he'd thrown it away filled him with quiet desperation. He had to earn that back. In his stupidity he hadn't recognized the gift she'd given him. He wouldn't pass it by again.

The power to make things right rested with him. He'd do what he needed to do. Starting with Yvonne and Michael.

He left his car, walking up the circular drive to the Benjamin house. The imposing stucco structure with its palladium windows and columned portico was large enough to be called a mansion in some people's book. He hadn't been in his friends' home in more than a year, since the baptism of the twins he was godfather to.

Another responsibility he had abandoned. He rang the bell, then hunched his shoulders beneath his jacket against the late October chill and his own guilt. He had missed the boys' birthday, he'd missed Kayleigh being born.

He had no intention of ever missing out again.

The door opened to barking and laughter. Mike stood in

the doorway, a honey-skinned cherub tucked beneath one arm. His eyes widened in surprise, then narrowed.

"So, the prodigal returns, alive and well. And it only took a year."

The barb found its mark. "I want to talk to you—both of you—about that. If you'll let me."

Instead of answering, Mike shifted the child in his arms. "By the way, this is Robbie. Robbie, this is your Uncle Jeff."

Golden eyes ringed with thick dark lashes stared at him from a cheeky, buttery face. Then Robbie turned his tawny curls and buried his face against his father's shoulder.

Jeff felt as if someone had just kicked him in the stomach. "He's beautiful," he managed to say.

"Yeah, he is," Mike replied with obvious fatherly pride. "We like to think the boys got the best of both of us."

He backed out of the doorway. "Well, come on in and meet your other godson again—and face the music."

Jeff followed his high school friend deeper into the Home and Garden meets Rugrats interior. Robbie wriggled out of his father's arms, slid down his leg like a fireman, and toddled in the direction of noise and laughter. "I guess Yvonne's still mad at me?"

Mike's snort was answer enough, but he said, "There's no point in discussing how worried and upset we both were. No point in discussing how Vonne nearly worried herself sick over you when she should have been basking in mother-hood."

"So are you gonna jack me up again?"

"Who me?" Mike tossed a feral smile over his shoulder. "Nah, man, that honor belongs to my lovely wife. And I don't mind telling you, she's been looking forward to it."

As they passed from room to room, Jeff was consciously aware of the difference a year made. There were photographs everywhere. Wedding photos, fashion shows, pictures of friends and family. Even pictures of Yvonne's family, gone nearly twenty years now, were finally and freely displayed. And everywhere there were pictures of the twins, as if the proud parents were determined to document every second of their sons' lives.

Yvonne and three girls were sprawled on the floor, laughing uproariously as the other twin—Reggie, he remembered—chased after the German Shepherd's tail. Vonne had a mini cam in her hands recording the hilarity.

"Hey honey," she called, swinging the camera around. "Who was that at the...oh, my God."

The camera dropped the short distance to the floor, and Jeff realized that she was prettier than he remembered. Her hair was pulled back into a loose ponytail, her caramel face devoid of makeup. She looked radiantly happy.

He became aware of Mike standing beside him as Vonne rose to her feet. "Five seconds to detonation," her husband murmured. "Five."

"You came back."

"Four."

Vonne stopped in front of them. "I can't believe you're really here."

"Three."

Jeff ignored Mike's countdown. "I'm sorry I didn't let you know where I've been, what's been going on."

"Two."

Vonne reached up and he leaned forward, expecting her to embrace him. "You should be sorry. You should be very sorry." Her hands settled around his collar, grabbing handfuls of the sweater tight against his throat.

"Didn't even make it to one," Mike said, amusement rippling through his voice. He made no move to disengage her hands from Jeff's neck.

Jeff grabbed her fingers in his own. She was damned strong. Her gaze locked to his, expressive brown eyes hardened with anger and hurt. Through the blood pounding in his ears he was dimly aware of the teens and the twins staring at them in wide-eyed awe. "Vonne," he gasped.

"Do you have any idea what you put us through?" she demanded, her voice a whip cutting through the gaiety in the room. "Any idea at all?"

Mike stepped forward then, his hand coming to rest on Yvonne's arm. "Sweetheart, the kids."

Her hands remained tight at Jeff's throat for a few heartbeats more. Then she glanced down and stepped back, dropping her hands. "Shanté, why don't you and the girls take the twins upstairs to the playroom? I'll call you when dinner's ready."

Jeff remained silent as the girls—Yvonne's Mentor Atlanta charges—gathered toys and boys. Reggie, in denim coveralls and red shirt to Robbie's yellow, was obviously the extrovert of the two, chattering happily as he was introduced.

The three adults stood in the center of the room, and Jeff was forcibly reminded of the day a little over two years ago, when he had tried to break his friends apart. And succeeded.

"So." Mike's affable voice cut through the tension. "Is this time for champagne or a referee?"

"There's no point in uncorking the bubbly just yet, love," Vonne said sweetly. "Especially since we don't know if he's staying."

If she had crossed the room and kicked him, Jeff didn't think he could feel worse. Hell, he'd known his homecoming wasn't going to be an International Coffee moment. The way he left, like a thief in the night, guaranteed that. At the time, he felt as if he'd had little choice, not if he still wanted his friends to remain his friends. Now he knew it for the cowardly maneuver it had been.

Apologizing and asking forgiveness wasn't going to be easy. Nothing important ever was. But he wasn't going to give up. Ever.

"I'm staying," he announced, planting his feet. "I'm home for good."

"Humph." Vonne folded her arm across her chest, her opinion clear.

He turned to Mike. "Hey man, you gonna help a brother out?"

"Nope. I sleep with her, so she automatically gets my

vote. And just because I didn't jack you up doesn't mean I forgive you."

Jeff's stomach twisted into icy knots. "I know I have a lot of explaining to do," he finally said with a heavy sigh. "I know I've got my work cut out for me. All I'm asking is that you hear me out."

Vonne and Mike exchanged a long look. "Okay," she said with caution. "We'll listen."

Now that the moment was here, he didn't know how to begin. "Married life agrees with you," he said at last. "With both of you."

It was true. Both Yvonne and Mike had been through hell—Yvonne losing her parents and twin sister in an accident that temporarily paralyzed her, Mike being raked through the coals by his first wife before she died violently. Neither one of them had believed love was for them until they met each other. Their happiness was obvious in every photo, every glance, every touch.

As if choreographed, the couple reached out to touch each other, as if they couldn't do anything else. White skin to black skin, blended in the beautiful shades of their children. They shared a glance that would have been painful to witness a year ago. "It definitely does," Mike said quietly. "And we have you to thank for it."

"Me?" Jeff choked. "You're thanking me for your marriage?"

"Yep. Dealing with the bullshit you put us through made us stronger as a couple," Mike said, his big hand bunched into a fist. "I'd like to think we'd be strong anyway, but surviving the hurt you gave us—well, nobody can hurt us like you can. Outside people and their opinions don't matter after that."

"But you keep on testing us, don't you?" Vonne added. "Just when I think we're gonna make it—we're all gonna be all right—you leave."

God, they probably weren't deliberately making him feel more guilt, but he felt as if he was drowning in it anyway. "I had to leave," he said through clenched teeth.

"Had to?" Vonne's brows dipped. "When everything was going right for you and us? Why did you have to leave?"

Don't answer, he thought to himself. Don't hurt them again, you selfish son of a bitch. You've hurt them enough.

"Jeff?"

"I couldn't stand to see you happy."

Yvonne's gasp echoed in the room. Mike took one step forward, sheltering her, then became still, dangerously still.

Conscious of the pain he was unleashing yet again, Jeff strode to the bay window. Leaves swirled by the panes, twirling in the brilliant-colored dance of death. "I was wrong and I know I was wrong," he finally said, his voice strained. "I was wrong for keeping you from meeting each other all those years. I was wrong for breaking you up. I was wrong for hating your happiness."

His fingernails dug into his palms in the effort to keep speaking, to excise the blight on his soul. "I'm not saying that I regret getting you back together. Doing that was one of the better moments of my life. But the hurt and anger and pain—and yeah, even jealousy—were still in me, with nowhere to go. I didn't want to take it out on you, and I certainly didn't want to take it out on Angie."

He released a bitter laugh. "'Course, she knew. She saw it all. Then she left me."

"What?"

"I couldn't give her the answer she wanted. I couldn't tell her that I didn't love you, Vonne. So she walked away from me. I had nothing left, and I knew I had to get out."

"So you ran."

Yvonne's voice was harsh, unforgiving. He didn't dare turn to face her, to see the anger and hurt he knew they both felt. "Yeah, I ran," he told the window. "I thought it was best. I knew I wasn't being fair to either one of you. And I sure as hell wasn't being fair to Angela."

Angie. A cold fist closed around his heart. More than Vonne and Mike, he'd been unfair to Angela, taking everything she offered and giving nothing in return.

He curled one fist against the window frame, resting his forehead against it. "I had to get right with myself. I knew I couldn't do that here, so I left."

"But you came back." Mike's voice was just as hard as his wife's.

"Yeah, I'm back." He took a deep breath and turned around. They stood side-by-side, arms loosely around each other, a united front. Their faces were stony, revealing nothing.

He stretched a hand to them, willing them to understand. "The past is just that, behind me. I want you guys to last beyond the next millennium. I know I have a lot to make up for, but if you'll forgive me, and let me be a part of your lives and my godsons' lives, I swear I'll do whatever I have to do."

Silence descended again. Jeff forced his hands to unclench as anxiety crawled through him. What would he do if his friends didn't forgive him?

Mike detached from his wife and took a step forward. "I know all about needing second chances," he said quietly. "And even needing third chances. If it were up to me, you'd have it. But it's not up to me."

They turned to Yvonne. She stood in the center of the room, her arms folded. "Vonne?"

"You think you can just disappear for a year without a word? Without even an 'I'm still alive' phone call? You think you can drop in after rubbernecking in New York and London and expect a warm welcome?"

"You knew were I was?"

"Of course I knew where you were," she exclaimed. "You think I'd let my best friend, who also happens to manage a good deal of my money, drop off the face of the planet and not try to track you? Please."

Jeff was dumbfounded. "All this time, you knew where I was and you didn't try to contact me?"

"When it was obvious you didn't want to be contacted, that you wanted to be left alone?" Her eyes flashed fire as she advanced on him. "I knew no matter what, you'd let your mother know where you were. Ida kept me up-to-date on everywhere you went, bless her heart. 'Course, I also had a detective watch you for a month to make sure you weren't going to drown in your sorrows or whatever hang-up you had. Then I left you alone, like you wanted."

The temperature in the room rose several degrees as Yvonne's anger burst forth. Jeff's heart sank. "I didn't expect to get this far, but I had to try."

"What's the matter, Jeff? It's not easy to handle so you're gonna take off again?"

"Vonne." Mike's voice was low with warning as he grasped her forearm.

"I want him to know," she said, her voice cracking. "I want him to know how much he hurt us."

"He knows it," Mike insisted. "He knows because he's hurting too." He drew her closer. "Give Jeff his second chance. If you hadn't given me a second chance, I wouldn't be here. And if you think about it, neither would he."

For a stark moment she stared up at her husband. Then her shoulders slumped. "You're right."

Jeff watched the anger drain from her. "I'm sorry for being harsh, Jeff. I understand, I think, why you did what you did. And I do forgive you."

"Thank you," he whispered.

She wiped at her eyes, exhaling a big breath. "Now, let's work on getting you and Angela back together. You do know she's not going to be as easy as me?"

He choked out a mirthless laugh. Boy, did he know. "You think this was easy?"

Agitation settled further on his shoulders, forcing him to pace. "I saw her."

"You did?"

"Yeah. Pops, the doorman at her old building, told me where she was. I went right over. I saw her. Saw Kayleigh."

Yvonne's gaze softened in understanding. "And you must have thought..."

"Of course I thought it," he replied, sitting on the couch, suddenly tired. "The math added up. When I picked Kayleigh up, it just felt right. It was the most perfect half-hour of my life. Then Angela told me about Shayla. It kills me to realize I wasn't there for her."

"It was a bad time," Mike said. "And then when her mother tried to take Kayleigh away..."

Jeff felt his heart stop. "Angela's mother tried to take Kayleigh away from her?"

"We don't know much about it," Yvonne said. "I know Angie and her mother haven't gotten along for a long time. She consulted with Brianne about it, but then the suit was dropped."

Her own mother sued her? Jeff couldn't imagine it. Couldn't imagine that kind of animosity between family members. That was too cold.

Yvonne moved to him, resting her hands on his shoulders. "Stop feeling guilty."

"How do you know I'm feeling guilty?"

She gave him an arch look. "After fifteen years of friendship you think I can't tell? You're hunching your shoulders over like you're bearing the weight of the world."

"Shouldn't I feel guilty?" he wondered. "Shouldn't I be kicking myself and hating myself just as much as Angela hates me right now?"

"I guess it didn't go well?" Yvonne's voice quieted in sympathy.

"It most definitely did not go well. She threw me out. I wasn't exactly being a Boy Scout though."

"Jeff, martyrdom doesn't become you," Vonne said, then softened her words with a smile. "It's gonna take more than a couple of hours to make everything right. But you will make it all right."

Both question and threat threaded her words. "I'm not giving up, if that's what you mean. The only reason I left there tonight without settling things is because Kayleigh was sleeping."

"Good." Her expression grew sly. "You know, we really need to begin preparation for end-of-year reports. And since my CFO has been on sabbatical..."

"Vonne." Mike settled a hand on his wife's shoulder. "We're not going to butt in."

"Of course we aren't." She raised her head to give him a look of wide-eyed innocence that Jeff hoped Mike didn't believe. "This is business. Jeff's been a part of the year-end financial and operational reviews for years, except for the hiccup last year."

"Hiccup?" She'd been close to strangling him for walking away, and now she called it a hiccup?

"So of course I want you on the team this year. We'll start first thing in the morning, eight sharp."

"All right. Will you be here or at the Buckhead store?"

"Gemini Enterprises has corporate offices now," Mike told him. "It's in the same building as BBC."

Jeff gave a mental whistle. The Midtown office building that housed Mike's marketing firm, Better Business Concepts, was some serious real estate. "The boutiques are doing that good?"

"We're all doing that good," Yvonne said with pride. "Our lives and our wallets have survived just fine without you."

"Ease up, sweetheart," Mike said, but his grin stretched wide. "Any more and he'll start to bleed."

"Come on," Yvonne said, rising to her feet and reaching for his hand. "Stay. Get to know the boys and have dinner with us. I cooked."

"You cooked?" The words were out before he could stop himself.

"Well, a lot's changed in the year," she said. "Mike's been a good teacher, and I learned a lot."

"Yeah, you did, once we got away from making doughnuts." They smiled, sharing a private joke.

Jeff decided not to take any chances. "Thanks, but I still need to get settled in, let my mother know I got in okay. I'll take a raincheck. Maybe I can come over one day soon for a guy's night."

"Monday Night Football on the big screen," Mike agreed with a pleased nod. "The boys are already into it."

"Yeah right," Vonne said, smiling. "Into watching their father act the fool is more like it." She gave Jeff a hug. "I'm so glad you came back."

"Me too." He hugged her tightly, briefly, before setting her away.

"Well," she sighed, "I guess I'd better go check on the boys. They've never seen Mommy choke someone before."

Silence as they watched her leave. "Now that my wife and kids are out of the room," Mike said, "I can put my fist to your face."

He seemed a little too eager for it, Jeff thought. "Wasn't Vonne strangling me enough?"

"Nope." Mike cracked his knuckles. "Which is why I'm gonna do you a favor."

Suspicion made Jeff lower his brows. "What kind of favor?"

"I'm going to keep Yvonne from butting in, so you and Angela can work this out for yourselves. Thank me now, because you're probably not going to want to thank me later."

Jeff followed him out to the foyer. "Why are you doing this?" he asked. "Vonne's gonna hit the roof."

"Oh, she'll probably try to make me sleep on the couch or something," his friend blithely answered. "She might even succeed for a couple of hours. But I have my reasons, as they say."

"And they are?"

"The first reason is purely selfish. I want Vonne to stop worrying about you two. Stressing about you has affected her designing, her company, and most importantly, the kids. You're upsetting the happy-ever-after I'm trying to give her, and I don't appreciate it."

Jeff could see the threat howling at him from a mile away. "Reason enough. But I guess there's more?"

"Yeah. Just two more." Mike removed pen and paper from the hall table and began scribbling. "I want you to know what I know, to have what I have. Just not who I have. If Angela's the one who can give that to you, I'm gonna do whatever I can to help it along—like giving you Angie's phone number."

"So much for impartial." Jeff fell back on sarcasm to cover the sudden lump in his throat.

"You think Vonne's gonna be impartial? She's been trying to get you and Angela together since before I came along."

Mike had a point there, Jeff thought. "So what's your last reason?"

Mike's smile was downright malicious as he handed Jeff the paper. "I have a feeling that Angela's gonna put a hurting on you that my fists can't touch. I'm looking forward to it."

He opened the door, hustling Jeff out into the night. "Good luck, man. I got a feeling you're going to need it."

Five

"How are you?"

Angela looked up as her friend and boss set a steaming mug of tea on her desk. The petite and perky thirty-year-old former figure skater looked immaculate and graceful as always, in stark contrast to Angela's five-eleven angular frame. Given the night that she'd had, Angela felt every one of her thirty-three years, as if she suffered an emotional hangover.

Angela seethed with jealousy some days over her friend's personal and professional success. Even though she knew Yvonne more than deserved her happiness, it did nothing to ease her mood.

"I'm just peachy," she said at last. "In fact, I feel so good any moment now I'm going to break into song." She turned a malevolent eye to her boss. "And how can you still wear cashmere with twin boys running around?"

"You're doing that good, huh?" Yvonne's smile was sympathetic. "Somehow I thought you'd be the worse for wear."

Angela grimaced above the rim of her mug. "I guess you

know, huh?"

Yvonne sat in one of the guest chairs. "Yeah. Jeff came to see us right after you saw him, but he wouldn't really talk about it. What happened?"

"The third-most horrible night of my life, that's what happened. We argued. Kayleigh woke up."

"What did you do?"

"I tried to stop him from getting to her, but he just pushed right past me and headed upstairs. As soon as she was in his arms, she stopped crying like she recognized him or something. H-he thought Kayleigh was ours."

"But you told him the truth, didn't you?"

"Of course I did!" Angela's face flamed at the memory of the harsh look he'd given her. "He didn't believe me at first. It was awful."

Awful didn't even begin to describe her experience last night. As she watched Jeff holding the newborn, she'd gone through a wringer of emotions: anger, fear, and another deep, wrenching emotion she didn't dare put a name to.

She pushed her hands through her hair with a sigh that was almost a sob. "He rocked Kayleigh back to sleep as pretty as you please, as if he's been doing it every night for the last four months. God, she didn't even protest when he put her back in the crib. Then we had it out. I slapped him once, I think. And he asked me to marry him."

"Oh my God." Yvonne stared at her, a horrified expression on her face. "He didn't!"

"He did," Angela nodded, feeling her control slip inch by

precious inch. "I told him no."

"You did?"

"Of course I did!" She surged to her feet. "What other sane alternative was there? He wanted to do the honorable thing, to make Kayleigh legitimate. He couldn't be honorable before, but now he can?"

That hurt. Oh God, that had hurt. And it still did.

"What did you do?"

"I grabbed a photo album, showed him photos of me and Shayla during her pregnancy. I told him Shayla was dead, and he actually tried to comfort me. Can you believe that? I was mad as hell at him and he actually tried to make me feel better. So I told him I didn't need him or his comfort. H-he said fine, and left."

That had shaken her more than anything else. The quiet regret and even the hurt she'd seen in his eyes hammered at her. She'd lain awake torn between tears and anger until Kayleigh had awakened for her early-morning feeding.

"Why did you walk out on him a year ago?"

The quiet question shocked the threat of tears away. "He told you?"

"He didn't mean to. It just slipped out."

Angela looked down at the mug still clutched in her trembling hands. She'd never told Yvonne about walking out on Jeff. It had been easier to let her think Jeff did the walking than the other way around.

She looked at her boss and friend. "You know why," she answered, her voice raw. "I tried so hard to make a difference, to make him be happy settling for me—"

"Angie—"

"If our positions were reversed, would you have stayed? Would you have kept beating your head against that wall?"

"Oh Angie, I don't know. Probably not."

Setting her mug down, Angela rose to her feet. "Well, I couldn't. I realized there was always going to be a part of him that belonged to you. He never gave me his heart, but even if he had, I knew I wouldn't have all of it. It was better to face it sooner rather than later."

Yvonne stood. "You probably won't believe this, but I know Jeff was never in love with me."

Angela resisted rolling her eyes. "Of course you'd think that, Vonne. He never told you how he felt until he thought he would lose you."

"Maybe, but I still believe it."

"Why?"

Her boss gave her a level stare. "Because he never proposed to me."

For a moment Angela just stared at the younger woman in shock. Then she shook her head. "The only reason he proposed to me is because he thought he was Kayleigh's father." She snorted. "If you could call it a proposal. It was more like a demand. Of course, he didn't repeat it once he discovered Kayleigh didn't belong to us."

Why, for the love of God, did she sound bitter about it?

"Ah, Angie, I'm sorry," Vonne said, grabbing her hand. "I wouldn't have pushed so hard for you two to be together if

I didn't believe completely in it. I thought—I thought—"

"You thought that being with me would take Jeff's mind off you being with his best friend."

To her credit, Yvonne didn't try to deny it, though her expression grew pained. "Yes, and I know I wasn't the only one. And given how close you two were by the time Michael and I got married, I knew it was the right thing."

"Obviously you and I were the only ones who thought it."

Sighing, Yvonne returned to her seat. "Angie, I wish I could explain my relationship with Jeff. Believe me, I've done nothing but beat myself up over this since he left. It's deeper than brother and sister. When he met me, I was just a couple of months out of the hospital and still using a walker to drag myself around. He saw me at my lowest and loneliest. I think if anything, he's felt like he's been my protector for the last fifteen years. After my uncle died, Jeff and Coach Calhoun were the only men in my life. And when I moved down here to attend college, it was just the two of us, until I started the company and you hired Lawrence as my assistant."

"A day that will live in infamy." Angela couldn't help the wry grin that tugged at her lips.

Yvonne matched her grin. "Hey, you can't help it if your gay-dar wasn't working. I did need him, just not in the way you thought I did. Come to think of it, he and Jeff didn't get along at first."

Angela remembered how tense it had been whenever she'd come to the townhouse to work. "Come to think of it,

Jeff did spend a lot of time there when Law first started working for you. But that just goes to show how jealous he was of any other man having your attention."

She clenched her hands into fists. "Jeff loves you, Yvonne. Whatever type of love it is, it was enough to make him break you and Mike apart, and make him so jealous of what you and your husband have together that he'd rather leave town than see you. What I had to offer never stood a chance."

"What are you going to do?"

She gasped a laugh. "You mean since leaving the country isn't an option? I'm going to stay away from him. The reason I walked out and the reason he stayed away haven't changed in the past year. And no amount of apology is going to change that. Besides, I threw him out last night. I doubt if I'll ever see him again."

Yvonne just shrugged. "Somehow he didn't look like he was going to give up."

The phone buzzed. "Mrs. Benjamin?"

"Yes, Janice?"

"A Mr. Evans has called twice. He's holding on line five."

"Is he now?" Yvonne's grin turned decidedly feral. "Keep him parked there for me, will you? And make sure the Muzak's really bad."

"Of course." Yvonne could hear the smile in her assistant's voice before she disconnected.

Yvonne rose. "Well, I'm off to have a thoroughly

enlightening conversation. You'll be fine for the afternoon meeting?"

"Of course. I'm not going to let my personal life interfere with work."

"Glad you feel that way," her boss said, heading to the door. "Just remember you said that."

With that cryptic comment, Yvonne took her leave, shutting the door behind her. Angela returned to her desk, running her e-mail program as thoughts ran through her mind. Yvonne seemed calmly accepting of Jeff's return. She'd commiserated, sure enough, but for Yvonne not to push for reconciliation seemed more than a little strange. Maybe the pending call with the distributor had taken her mind off it.

Angela sighed, secretly relieved. She knew Yvonne would be rooting for her and Jeff to reconcile, to have the happy-ever-after that she and Mike had. Yvonne wouldn't be above meddling if she thought it necessary.

Reconciling wasn't about to happen. Angela was still angry—angry for giving him an ultimatum, angry for his refusal to accept it, angry for walking away. Angry because he left, angry because he came back.

Angry because his kiss had been like rain on a scorched desert.

A chime signaled the arrival of new e-mail. From Yvonne. About the year-end review. How did her boss move so fast?

Her phone buzzed again as she clicked the electronic file

open. "Yes, Janice?"

"Mr. Lawrence is here for the review procedure."

Already? Angela stifled a groan. She didn't even have time to read the e-mail. Still, nothing like work would get her mind off her issues. "Send him in."

Her door opened. She looked up, smiling, waiting for Law to appear.

The smile faded.

"What are you doing here?"

Jeff, crisp in a charcoal gray suit brightened with an autumn-colored tie, walked into her office. Lawrence followed, wheeling in a cart loaded with files.

"I'm here in an official capacity."

She looked from one man to the other. "What official capacity?"

"Yvonne wants the year-end review drafted and on her desk by December first," Law informed her. "Mr. Maxwell is going to help draft it. Didn't you get the memo?"

"Of course I got the memo," she retorted, more than a little exasperated. "Just now."

"Really?" Law pushed the cart over to the conference table near the window. "I read it first thing this morning. I'll send a note to have the tech gal check out your computer."

This was not happening. Jeff simply stood there, his briefcase in his hand, watching the interaction with an unreadable expression. She forced herself to turn back to Lawrence. "How can we have a year-end review when we haven't even begun the holiday season?"

Law shrugged. "She says to extrapolate from the projections we made based on last year's sales." He turned to go. "It's all in the e-mail."

"And where is our fearless leader?" So I can knock her into next week for not telling me about this.

"She is currently on a conference call reducing a distributor to tears. I actually heard the poor man sob. Do you want me to go interrupt her?"

Angela and Jeff exchanged glances. They both knew that Yvonne rarely lost it, and never without good reason—or rampant hormones.

"Does it have anything to do with the Desire Everyday line?" she asked.

Law rolled his eyes. "Let's just say that Yvonne's heart's desire is to reach out and choke someone."

"All right." Decided, she punched a button on her phone. "Janice?"

"Yes, ma'am?"

Lord, she hated being called ma'am, especially since Janice had a good eight years or so on her. "Hold my calls, except for emergencies and the nursery. Anything else you can forward to Lawrence to handle. Call up central accounting and tell them to get ready to send hard copies if we need them. And remind me when it's one o'clock."

"Yes ma'am."

She disconnected. "Law—"

"I know. Run interference, hold down the fort and keep Yvonne from doing anything drastic."

"No. If you don't want me to do anything drastic, you'll send downstairs for a double mocha latte, a grande cappuccino, and a half dozen bagels. Now."

"Yes, ma'am."

He had the nerve to salute before he left, shutting the door behind him. Jeff had already crossed to her conference table, pulled out his laptop and plugged it into the wall.

She watched him move, all limber and long-limbed, using an economy of movements that would have looked prudish on another man. Watching him move always thrilled her, whether he walked, sweated during a game of horse, or entered into her smooth and sweet...

Shifting with agitation, she crossed to the conference table. "So this is real, and not something Yvonne cooked up specifically to get us in the same room?"

He booted his computer. "Have you ever known Yvonne to play games when it comes to business?"

"You got a point," she acquiesced with a grimace. "I don't know if this is going to work, though."

She surprised herself by admitting it. It seemed to surprise him too, causing him to look up from his computer.

"No matter the mess of our personal lives, we've always worked together well." The cautiousness in his voice let her know that he wasn't any happier to be there than she was to see him.

"You're right," she agreed with reluctance. "We've prepared this report before. We can do it again."

"Absolutely. Pretty soon, we won't be able to think of

anything else. So I'll thank you now."

"For what?"

"For ordering the cappuccino for me."

Her mouth worked for a moment as she realized she had indeed ordered his favorite coffee. "Some bad habits are hard to break."

He didn't rise to the bait. Instead he sat, reaching for a notepad. "Why don't you bring me up to speed while we're waiting for refreshments."

Grateful for his businesslike tone, Angela took the opposite chair and recapped the previous year, beginning with sales figures and ending with the launch of Desire Everyday, the mainstream lingerie line for every woman.

By the time their refreshments arrived, they'd settled into their usual, albeit stilted, routine. She remembered that Jeff took business as seriously as everyone else in their circle. No matter how he was personally, he neared genius level when it came to understanding and making money.

So it surprised her when he stopped working two hours later with a terse, "We need to talk."

"About what?"

"About last night. About us."

Her breath exploded with a frustrated sigh as she pushed away from the table. Just when things were going so well... "Haven't we said all we needed to?"

He gave her a rueful smile but didn't rise to the bait. "We always were thunder and lightning together."

"More like oil and water."

"We were magic together, Angie. Even if you forgot, your body remembers."

Remember? Her body was rejoicing. "It's biological," she retorted, deliberately rude. "Like my reaction to the pizza I had for dinner the other day. I'll get over it."

"Are you sure?" His voice, smooth as warmed brandy, slid over her skin like silk. "I haven't forgotten what we had. Have you?"

He hadn't forgotten? She swallowed. "What we had was a joke, and you know it."

"I don't think so. I never thought so." He flowed to his feet, all catlike grace that made her mouth water. She remembered how it felt to go dancing with him, the sheer joy of feeling him move. The high she received when catching jealous glances thrown their way, all because she was the one going home with him.

His hands skimmed down her shoulders, leaving static electricity in their wake. "I'm not laughing, Angie." He cupped her hands in his, lifting her palms to place a kiss inside. "Are you?"

Laughing? Not even close. She felt like crying from the sheer pleasure that snaked through her at his touch.

"Angie." His voice was pure sin, soft and tantalizing. "I've missed you. It was good between us, you know it was."

"Good?" Shock intruded on her heated senses. "Is that what you think it was? It was so good between us that you stayed in love with another woman?"

He dropped her hands like hot potatoes. "I never cheated on you, Angie. While we were together I was faithful."

She snorted. "Maybe you didn't cheat with your body, but your heart didn't belong to me, did it?"

He winced. Simultaneous glee and regret claimed her at causing him pain. "Maybe my heart didn't belong to you back then, but it didn't belong to Yvonne either."

"I don't believe you. And there's nothing you can say or do to convince me otherwise."

Jeff sat on the couch, putting his head in his hands. He felt more than a little punch-drunk at the moment. Seeing Angie had brought so many things crashing back on him—guilt, anger, desire. Definitely desire. Just thinking about her caused him to stand at attention in his pants. Yet desire didn't make him blind to her anger. If it did, she had a way of making sure he wasn't blind for long.

Realization of just how deeply he'd hurt her settled in his bones. He'd known that she would be furious. But this, this went beyond fury, beyond anger, beyond something that could be balanced by the mere act of forgiveness. What would he do if she didn't forgive him?

He raised his head to find her staring at him from behind the relative safety of her desk. "Look Angie, I'm sorry. I'm sorry I left town. I'm sorry I wasn't here when you lost Shayla. And I'm sorry I didn't give you a reason to have faith in me."

Surprise drove the anger from her face, and she fell into the chair behind her. "What?"

Fisting his hands, he rose to his feet. "I failed you on so

many levels, I don't think I can begin to count them. If I could take it back, I would. Please believe that."

She stared at him, and his heart turned over. The cropped cut of her hair accentuated the almond shape of her mahogany eyes, the high cheekbones beneath cinnamon skin, the slender column of her neck. The burgundy suit draped her slender frame like a benediction, calling attention to the supple length of legs that he'd always enjoyed watching. If not for the cold wariness in her eyes and the weight she'd lost, he would have said that the year had been good to her.

"That's why you came back? To ask for forgiveness?"

"Yes."

Arms folded across her chest. "Then you're going to be disappointed," she retorted. "I'm not a softie like Yvonne. Whatever soft spot I held for you is gone. I'm not going to tell you I forgive you just so you can sleep at night."

She always did have perfect aim with her sarcasm. "If you're trying to get back at me, let me tell you you're doing a damn good job."

"Good," she shot back. "You should hurt. You should feel guilty. You should lay awake at night wondering what you did wrong, wondering why you're not good enough. You should spend each day wondering if the best thing that happened to you passed you by, and if you'll ever get the chance to have it again."

"I already do that, Angie. Every day for the last year." His smile twisted as memory washed over him. She could verbally beat him up, but it couldn't begin to compare to how he'd raked himself over the coals.

Let her stay mad. If she still cared enough to be angry, there was still hope. While there was still hope, there was a chance.

"I don't expect you to forgive me anytime soon," he told her. "But I told Mike and Vonne, and now I'm telling you: I'm not going anywhere."

"Whoop-dee-freakin'-do."

He bit his tongue against a retort. Thunder and lightning. "I'm going to do whatever I can to earn your forgiveness. And I hope I can earn your friendship again. We were good friends before, Angie. I'd like to have that back."

"The only relationship we're going to have is a business one," she shot back. "And once that's done, it's all done."

She readied another retort, but he stopped her with an upraised hand. "Give me a week to earn your friendship back. One week. That's all I'm asking. If you decide that you can't forgive me after that, then I won't bother you anymore."

Blood pounded behind his ears, loud in the silence as he waited for her answer. He was risking a lot, but she had to know how determined he was. Even if she decided against him when the week ended, he had no intention of leaving.

"All right, Jeff," she finally said. "You have your week. But if I decide that I never want to see you again, I expect you to respect that."

"Okay." He released a deep breath at the lie. He would respect it, even if he couldn't accept it. "May I see you tonight? I'd like to offer my help in planning for Kayleigh's financial future—I'll even charge you, if you want," he added, seeing her about to bristle at the idea that she couldn't manage her finances on her own.

Wariness remained in her expression. "Fine. I could use some advice, and I know you're the best. Can you be at the house by 6:30?"

"I'll be there." Not wanting to push his luck, he started gathering his things. "Angie?"

"Yes?"

"Thank you. You won't regret it."

"I already do, Jeff. I already do."

Six

She was out of her freakin' mind.

No other explanation fit. There was no other reason for her to be running about the house, tidying her office, taking out the trash, removing pantyhose from the shower bar in her bathroom. When she found herself reaching for fresh linens for her bed, she had to force herself to take Kayleigh, march down the hall to her office, and sit at her desk.

What was she thinking?

She wasn't, and that was the problem. Her system was still in shock over Jeff's miraculous reappearance. Having to work with him for the next month. Hearing his request for forgiveness.

Thinking that Kayleigh was his, and asking to get married.

Better correct yourself, she thought, booting up the computer. It was more like assuming Kayleigh was theirs and demanding that she marry him. Of course, she noticed how quick that demand was forgotten when she proved Kayleigh's parentage. That was all right with her. She had no intention of marrying Jeff Maxwell, not now, not ever.

Oh yeah? Is that why you were putting clean sheets on the bed?

God she hated that voice. That voice, the purry, hungry voice, was responsible for yielding to Jeff in the first place. That voice was responsible for that year of borrowed bliss she had—and the year of heartache that followed. No, if she listened to that voice, she would welcome Jeff back with open arms—and legs. There was no way in hell she planned to do that.

Nestling the baby against her shoulder, she opened her financial records. Whether she forgave him or not, it wouldn't hurt to let him look over her plans. Jeff Maxwell could turn straw into gold if he set his mind to it. She was determined to fulfill her promise to Shayla and see to Kayleigh's future. If that meant spending the week with Jeff personally, so be it.

She'd give him his week, then she'd tell him to get out of her life.

At six-thirty sharp he arrived, carrying his briefcase in one hand and a long box tucked under his arm. "What's that?"

"A present for you and Kayleigh. May I come in?"

She backed out of the doorway. "You didn't have to bring anything with you."

"I wanted to," he replied, setting his belongings down long enough to shed his coat. He'd changed from the suit into khakis and a burgundy sweater and t-shirt that served to define, not conceal, the muscles of his arms and chest.

God help her.

"Consider it a house-warming present."

"Huh? Oh." Taking the box, she glanced at the picture on the side. "This is a baby swing."

"Yeah." He took the liberty of locking the door before taking the box from her. "I noticed you didn't have one, so I got one for you. From what I understand, babies can't resist falling asleep in them."

"What makes you the expert?"

"I'm the oldest of eight, remember? I was sixteen when my baby sister Trina was born."

No, she didn't remember that. They'd never talked about his family, not enough that she would remember. Just another sign that their relationship wasn't meant to be deeper than sexual.

"Where would you like me to set this up?"

"We might as well do it in my office," she said, shrugging. "I'm there most of the time anyway."

She realized the suggestiveness of her words as soon as they left her mouth. "Uhm, on second thought—"

"All right." To his credit, Jeff didn't so much as lift an eyebrow before following her upstairs to the third bedroom that served as her office.

"You can set it up there, I suppose," she said, pointing to an open place near the portable playpen. "Would you like something to drink?"

"Sure, whatever you have. Did you already eat?" he asked, pulling out a penknife to open the box. "If not, we could order something."

"I could nuke something instead," she offered, discomfited by the surrealism of it all. "Lawrence left me plenty of food."

He looked up with a grin. "So Law's adopted you now?"

She answered his easy smile with one of her own. "He says he has to earn his wings somehow."

"I guess he can use the brownie points," Jeff agreed. "I'll have whatever you have. You can leave Kayleigh with me."

When she hesitated, he added, "I swear on my sainted mother's soul that I will not tuck her under my arm like a football and run out of the house."

She laughed despite the apprehension sneaking through her. "Your mother's not dead. Is she?"

"Nope." He reached for Kayleigh, cradling the baby with a practiced gesture. "Go on," he urged when she didn't move. "We'll be fine."

It wasn't that she didn't believe him, or trust him for that matter, she thought as she headed downstairs to the kitchen. Okay, maybe it was. But she'd never seen Jeff around a baby. She had no idea if he was capable of watching a child. It didn't matter that he was the oldest of eight.

Jeez, there were seven more like him running around?

Lost in thought, she transferred a plastic container from the freezer to the microwave, set the timer, then retrieved a bottle of formula for the warmer. So much about Jeff was a mystery. How could she have spent a year of her life with someone and not know fundamental things about him, like number of siblings? How could she begin to forgive him if she didn't even know him?

She paused, horrified at herself. Good Lord, she was predisposed to forgive him. Twenty-four hours ago he'd arrived to throw her world off kilter and here she was, ready for everything to go back to the status quo.

"Something smells good."

His voice, though quiet, startled her. He stood in the doorway, Kayleigh gurgling happily on his shoulder. The ease with which he held the baby struck through the barriers Angela had erected against him.

Babies knew, didn't they, if people were bad? Granted, Kayleigh had yet to react in a negative way to anyone Angela let hold her, except Angela's mother. Kayleigh had only been around Angela's parents, Law and his partner, and the Benjamins—people Angela trusted with her life. Could she trust Jeff, even if Kayleigh seemed to?

Disconcerted, she retrieved dishes from a cabinet. "It's some kind of chicken and rice dish," she explained. "I never know what Law's going to leave, but I haven't been disappointed yet."

"You know, I think Law missed his calling. He should start his own business looking after professional single women."

"Over my dead body," she retorted, setting places at the whitewashed table in the corner. "He belongs to us, and we're not going to let him go. Besides, he only does this for people he likes."

"And who pay him an arm and a leg," he said wryly, setting the carrier on the tabletop before circling back for the bottle.

"Well, he's worth every penny. But it's more than that."

She placed a pitcher of sweet tea and glasses of ice on the table before retrieving the casserole dish. "Law is mother, brother, and sister all rolled into one. I don't know what I would have done without him."

With gentle movements he laid Kayleigh in her carrier. As if it was the most natural thing in he world, he tested the warmth of her bottle by dribbling some of the formula on his wrist before offering it to her. "Is it hard, taking care of Kayleigh alone?"

The soft concern in his voice made it impossible for sarcasm or lies. "Yes."

She sat down, concentrating on spooning chicken and rice onto their plates. "The first month I was so afraid of doing something wrong, or possibly hurting her. I cut back on work and devoted myself to learning everything I could about being a mother. The second month I was furious with Shayla for dying and leaving Kayleigh to me. Then I felt guilty for feeling angry. I think I cried more than Kayleigh did. The third month I realized that things were getting better, and I wasn't fantasizing about running away nearly as much. This month I actually feel capable of taking care of her, and being good at it."

Heat flushed up her neck and she sat back, eyes to her plate. "That sounds perfectly awful, doesn't it?"

"No." His hand clasped hers. "It sounds like a woman trying the best she can to keep a promise. And it seems to me that you're doing a damn good job of it."

She flushed anew at his praise. "Well, I couldn't do it without Law, though I have to start weaning myself off his help."

"Why?"

"He's got his own life, and it's full. He and Jaime are considering becoming parents themselves, either through adoption or with a surrogate."

Jeff gave a low whistle. "Whoa. That's huge."

"Exactly. And with all the legal and political drama involved, I don't want him distracted with Kayleigh and me. Besides, I need to be able to do this by myself."

The next eighteen years of her life—actually, the rest of her life—would revolve around Kayleigh. Knowing she had to face it alone, it made sense to start getting accustomed to it now.

They ate in a silence that was comfortable if not companionable. Jeff showed a remarkable ability to feed himself and Kayleigh at the same time. Angela could only stare, wondering who this man was and what he'd done with Jeff Maxwell.

He glanced up from cooing at Kayleigh, a slight smile curving his lips. "What?"

"I just never figured you for the domestic type," she confessed, forking her rice with an aimless gesture.

"What? You think it conflicts with my unrelenting bachelorhood?"

As a matter of fact... "Somehow, I don't see you up to your elbows in dirty diapers."

"One day I might surprise you," he said, his grin wry. "You remember I told you I'm the oldest of eight?"

"Yes."

"We're spaced out pretty evenly, about every two years. Momma had some occasional medical problems, and with Pops working all the time, it fell to me to look after everybody."

He slung his napkin over his shoulder, then lifted Kayleigh into place to burp her. "Dad taught me early on that taking care of family is the most important thing a man can do. I wanted to prove to him that I could do it and make him proud of me."

Rewarded with a loud un-baby-like noise, Jeff put the newborn back into her carrier. "So I learned how to make mac and cheese when I was seven, changed my first diaper when I was eight, and tried to drive to the grocery store when I was eleven."

A shocked laugh almost made her spew a mouthful of food. "You didn't!"

"We were out of Froot Loops," he informed her, his tone serious. "No kid should be out of Froot Loops."

"What happened?"

"I put all the kids in the car, buckled in and in car seats and everything. I started the car and put it in gear. Julian pressed the gas and brakes when I told him to. Well, he tried to anyway."

His grin widened. "We got all the way down the drive-way until a telephone pole and a neighbor stopped us."

Angela had a difficult time reconciling the story with the man before her. "Did you get into trouble?"

"Oh yeah." He shifted in his chair. "We lived in one of those neighborhoods where everybody's momma had the right to whoop up on other people's kids. Mrs. Barnes made sure the other kids were all right before she started laying into me with her newspaper. The other kids ran for Dad, and that made it worse."

She spoke softly, not wanting to break the fragile companionship his story created. "Why was that worse?"

"The expression on his face," he replied, just as quiet. "He didn't have to lay a finger on me. Looking at my Dad, I just knew I had failed him. I thought I was doing something good for the family—and having fun while doing it—but I also put the family in danger. It's a lesson I never forgot. I do my best, even now, to make sure I never fail him again."

His mood lightened with another quick grin. "Especially since he's a lot closer to God now."

Sharing his easy laugh, she rose to gather dishes, her mind whirling. She couldn't imagine Jeff taking care of seven brothers and sisters, especially at sixteen. It contradicted everything she'd thought she knew about him. Now she discovered that what she knew about him didn't even dent the surface. How could she have been so wrong?

"Ugh." He made a disgusted sound. She turned to see him holding Kayleigh at arm's length. "Just like clockwork. Do you want me to change her?"

"I'll do it." It was one thing for him to feed her niece a bottle; it would be another thing entirely to have him change a diaper. That would be way too surreal for her to handle.

She stacked their dishes in the sink, scrubbed her hands, then reached for Kayleigh. "Good Lord, girl, what was in that formula?" she asked as the baby started to fret.

She led the way upstairs. "Don't worry, I'll have you cleaned up soon enough. Then you can test drive the swing Uncle Jeff brought you."

Shocked at her words, she almost missed the top step. Jeff caught her before she did serious damage. "Are you all right?"

With his arms wrapped tightly around her and Kayleigh, the front of his body scorched her back from neck to thigh, his forearms just below the rise of her breasts. No, she most definitely wasn't all right. "I'm fine. I think the carpet's loose on the top step."

Slow to let her go, he continued to hover behind her. "I could check it for you."

"No! I mean, no, I'll have someone fix it later."

Her face on fire, she moved down the hallway past the closed door of her bedroom before stopping at Kayleigh's room. "Why don't you go on into the office while I clean her up? You probably noticed that I've already opened the files for you."

His eyes rested on her for a long telling moment before he blinked. "All right. I'll go ahead and get started. Shouldn't take too long to get a good action plan together."

He moved into the office, and she sagged against the wall in relief. Uncle Jeff. That was more than a Freudian slip—that was an entire lingerie counter! Oh, she knew she hadn't played it off in any believable way, but if he didn't mention it, she could pretend that she'd never said it.

"You just forget everything I said about 'Uncle Jeff,' all right?" she muttered to Kayleigh as she laid the baby on the changing stand she'd had built into one wall. "It'll take more than a childhood story and a baby swing to make me forgive him. Much more."

"The plan you had was a good one, but we should be able to get you at least another ten percent from these new numbers," Jeff said, pulling a sheet of figures out of the printer and handing it to Angela.

She leaned in close and he breathed deep, taking her unique scent into his lungs. Need bit into him, fierce and hot and desperate, causing his control to slip a notch. Nothing would wreck the fragile progress he'd made like an unwanted sexual overture.

Watching her peruse his numbers, he had to wonder if it was truly unwanted. Calling him Uncle Jeff—especially when she considered herself to be Kayleigh's aunt—had been an unconscious slip of the tongue. That meant she'd partially forgiven him, or at least had accepted him back into her life.

He glanced over at Kayleigh slumbering and slobbering in her new swing. Want pooled with the desire. The utter domesticity of the night called to him, forcibly reminding him of what he was missing.

At thirty-five, he had everything going for him—health, success, confidence in who he was and what he'd accomplished. But an emptiness filled him, a restless incompletion that he hadn't been able to define until he'd held Kayleigh for the first time.

Family.

"Looks good," Angela said, breaking into his thoughts. "I'll implement this at the first of the year. Thanks for doing this."

"No problem. Do you have any questions?"

"Just one. Where have you been for the past year?"

The question, calm and quiet, took him by surprise. It never occurred to him that she would mention his disappearance and re-emergence, much less be calm about it.

"I was in London and Tokyo for a while, studying the markets there. From spring on I was in New York setting up an office."

"How is that going?" Her eyes never left the monitor as she began to close files.

"Well, you know, people are always skittish when the market fluctuates like it does. But I've managed to gain a handful of new clients."

"So business is good, huh?"

Did she really want to know or was she just making conversation? Unsure, he nevertheless answered, "I can't complain."

"When are you going back?"

Ah-ha. "I'm lucky enough to be able to work out of a suitcase, with my laptop and my cell phone. I'll still maintain the office there to be close to the Street, and I'm planning to keep my offices here. Besides, this is home."

She nodded, but he could almost see the gears spinning in her head. "How many models did you go through while you were away?"

Her voice remained conversational, but she had a death-grip on the mouse. He reached over, loosening her grip, then swiveled her chair around until he saw her eyes. "None."

She snorted. "You expect me to believe that?"

"No," he admitted. "But it's the truth."

The look she gave him would have melted rock. He didn't blame her for doubting him. Before they got together, he'd made a point of only dating women who wanted short-term relationships as much as he did. He'd never flaunted those relationships, but given their circle of friends and social engagements, Angela probably had an unfortunate idea of just how many women he'd gone through.

Still gripping her hand between his, he willed her to understand. "I didn't go away to screw around, Angie. If you believe nothing else, believe that."

"I don't know what to believe about you," she confessed, her voice soft with anguish. "I want to hate you and not hate you at the same time. I want you to leave, but I feel guilty for feeling that way. I feel guilty for being angry at you."

"Angie." He didn't know what to say.

"I worked extra hard to get over you," she continued, the pain evident in her dark gaze. "I even saw other people."

Blood pounded in his ears, bleeding from his heart. He released her hand, rising to his feet. Numbness settled in his bones. Why was he surprised? Why did the knowledge feel like he'd just been stabbed?

"I didn't come back expecting to pick up where we left off." Liar. "I don't even think we should. But I do want to make it up to you. I want to make sure you don't hate me."

She kept her gaze averted. "I think it would be easier if I did. Right now, all I feel is numb inside."

With a slap to her thighs, she rose. "It's late. I need to put Kayleigh to bed, and I have a lot of work facing me tomorrow."

After gathering his things, he followed her downstairs, unease clawing through him. Her lack of anger unnerved him. Had he somehow lost his chance before he even used it? At the door, he made a last bid. "If I arrange a sitter for Kayleigh the day after tomorrow, will you let me take you out?"

"On a date?"

Why did that surprise her? "Yes, on a date. You probably haven't had a night out since Kayleigh came home."

Longing colored her features as she leaned against the doorframe. "No, I haven't, but I didn't expect to. Maybe

Law and Jaime can watch her for me. Where would we go?"

Encouraged, he gave her a smile. "Why don't you let me surprise you? You'll enjoy yourself, I promise."

"I don't think you should be making promises," she said, no heat or censure in her voice. "Let's just take each moment as it comes, all right?"

Did he have a choice? "All right. Goodnight, Angie."

She let him out into the chill night. "Goodnight, Jeff."

Resolution filled him as he walked down the path to his car. One last chance, and he intended to pull out all the stops. He'd give Angela a date to end all dates—one he should have given her a year ago. He'd accept whatever terms she set to be back in her life. For now anyway.

He drove off into the night, his mind filled with visions of family—the one he'd make with Angela and Kayleigh. If he could get her to forgive him.

Seven

"You have the rest of the day off."

Angela frowned as she looked up from a sheath of operational reports. Yvonne stood in the doorway of her office, arms folded across her chest. "What?"

"I said you have the rest of the day off."

Yvonne was pretty lenient as far as bosses went, but even this was a bit much. "Why?"

"I was hoping you'd tell me," the younger woman said, shutting the door before crossing the room to sit on the edge of Angela's desk. "Law buzzed me to say he was off to get Kayleigh and that a car would be picking you up in fifteen minutes."

"Oh my God!" Angela lurched to her feet, flicking her wrist to stare at her watch. "It's not even three o'clock!"

"I know." The younger woman gave her a look of overt curiosity. "Law wouldn't tell me anything except that you were due for a night out."

A night out. She could have slapped herself. "Oh, Lord, I agreed to go on a date with Jeff."

"What?" Yvonne's eyes widened. "You and Jeff out on a

date? A real date?"

"So?"

"Calm down, I don't mean anything by it. Except that I thought you hadn't forgiven him yet, so this whole date thing seems to come straight out of left field."

"I haven't forgiven him," Angela said, biting off the word yet. "I gave him a week to salvage our friendship. This is day three."

"Really? Do you want to talk about it?"

Yvonne looked eager for it, and Angela didn't really blame her. She hadn't shared the happenings of the last couple of days with her boss, and was glad Yvonne hadn't pressed her on it.

"Hey, why haven't you asked me about this before now?" she wondered. "I figured you'd be pleading Jeff's case every spare minute."

"I wouldn't do that. I swore I'd remain neutral. Besides, Michael ordered me not to throw my two cents in."

Angela felt her eyes bulge. "Since when do you take orders from your husband?"

"Since he threatened to withhold sex."

The horror in Yvonne's voice made Angela want to snort with laughter. "That's an empty threat and you know it."

"Oh yeah? He caught me trying to call you last night, and as a result I didn't get any."

Oh. That explained the mood. "If it will make you and your husband feel better, there's nothing to throw your two cents into. We're working on being friends, nothing more."

Buzzing sounded from the phone. "Ms. Davenport?"

"Yes, Janice?"

"Your car is at the front door."

"Thanks. Let them know I'll be down in five."

Yvonne crossed to the window and peered down. "Just friends, my eye. I don't think that limo can make a right turn if its life depended on it."

"Limo?"

Angela's heart began a staccato beat. Fearing the worst, she crossed the room to peer out the window. Even twenty floors up, the white stretch limo stood out visibly against the gray pavement. "Oh God."

"What in the world do you two have planned?" the designer asked, turning to stare at her.

"I don't know!" she almost wailed, wringing her hands. "He asked if he could take me on a date. But if I'd known he was going to do this, I would have said no. At least I think so. Oh, hell—I don't know what I'd do!" She leaned against the window and closed her eyes.

"You could always call it off."

"Are you kidding me? If Jeff wants to throw his money away on a hopeless endeavor, who am I to stop him?"

"Is it?" Yvonne asked.

"Is it what?"

The younger woman's eyes were serious. "Is it hopeless?"

Angela felt her nerves fray even more. "Of course it is." Stalking back to her desk, she retrieved her purse, ignoring the tremor in her hands. "Nothing's going to happen. I can promise you that."

"Angie."

"What?" God, why did she have to sound so defensive?

"Be careful," her boss and friend urged. "I don't want you to be hurt, you know that. But I don't want Jeff hurt either. If there's no chance for a reconciliation, don't drag this out, okay?"

Guilt prodded her to sarcasm. "I thought you were going to butt out."

A painful grimace flashed across the designer's features, intensifying Angela's guilt. "You're right. I promised I'd butt out, and I will. From now on, I'm out of it. I'll see you tomorrow." She turned back to the window.

Feeling worse than the unidentifiable stuff discovered on the bottom of a shoe, Angela grabbed her coat and quit the office, murmuring a good night to her curious administrative assistant before heading for the bank of elevators. The last thing she wanted to do was antagonize her boss, who also happened to be her best friend. This mess between her and Jeff had Yvonne caught in the middle and Angela knew it wasn't an easy position to be in. Besides, she certainly didn't want Yvonne to have to choose between a vice-president she'd known for seven years and a financial officer she'd known for fifteen.

Even if she'd tried to do the same thing to Jeff.

She winced inwardly as heat flooded her cheeks. What a stupid move on her part, trying to force Jeff to chose between her and Yvonne. She should have known she didn't have a chance, not against the kind of history he had with Yvonne.

Did she plan to string Jeff along for the remainder of the week? The vengeful part of her said it was just what he deserved, payment for the way he'd left. While far from being vindictive, Angela still couldn't easily bring herself to forgive and forget.

The elevator ride to the first floor didn't make her thoughts clearer. The limousine filled the view through the windows and the revolving door. She was gripped with the sudden urge to turn tail and run.

Another part of her surged with excitement. Since Kayleigh's arrival in her life, her entertainment had become restricted to cable TV and buying baby products. She looked forward to the night out as she hadn't looked forward in a long time.

Sweeping out the door and past curious onlookers, she approached the driver, who tipped his hat. "Ms. Davenport?"

"Yes."

With a bow, he opened the door for her and helped her inside. The darkened interior made adjusting her vision from bright sunlight difficult. "Jeff?"

No answer. The door closed behind her, plunging her into tinted darkness, but not before she realized she was alone in the expansive interior. Where was Jeff?

Small lights sparked into brilliance along the floor, and a slight sensation indicated the car moving. "Ma'am," the driver's voice sounded from the speaker behind her, "There are champagne and berries in the bar console in front of you to your right."

Berries in late October? Angela opened a shiny compartment to reveal a minute refrigerator and an ice bucket holding a bottle of champagne. Oh no, these weren't berries—these were chocolate-covered strawberries, her absolute favorite. Thousands of questions assailed her mind. She asked two of the most important. "Where is Mr. Maxwell? And where are we going?"

"I believe there is a note beside the ice bucket."

Sure enough, a folded note lay propped against the silver container. She poured champagne into a crystal flute and set it in the holder beside her, put the bowl of strawberries on her right, then grabbed the note. Sitting back, she read Jeff's bold scrawl:

I know you're wondering where I am and where you're going. You'll find out soon enough. In the meantime: Relax.

Relax. There was no way she'd be able to relax now. What was Jeff up to? He had to know this game of seduction wouldn't work. Even if she had forgiven him—which she hadn't—she wouldn't offer more than friendship and she certainly wouldn't offer her body.

She finished one delectable, sweet strawberry, rolling her eyes in ecstasy. With a sip of the champagne she rested her eyes against the cool black leather. Priorities and concerns jockeyed for position in her head. Relax. Let the night unfold. Take each moment as it comes.

Keep her clothes on.

Two out of three ain't bad.

Angela relaxed under the most expert massage she'd ever received in her life. The exclusive spa in the midst of Buckhead surprised and delighted her, and she submitted to the attendant with relish. She'd already gone through the full body mud mask. If she relaxed any further, she'd start to drool.

Hands moved down her back in rhythmic counterpart to the New Age music filtering from overhead. Lord, she hadn't realized how tense she'd been until the masseuse coaxed the knots from her shoulders. How much more relaxed could she get?

She had never been pampered like this in her life. Not even before her wedding to Richard.

Thoughts of her disastrous marriage sapped some of the contentment from her. She'd been nineteen when she met Richard Giles, a senior on the AU campus. He was charming and handsome and older, and her first real boyfriend. Shayla had disliked him intensely, but then Shayla had no desire to ever give her heart and lose herself as her mother had done.

If only she'd listened to Shayla, she'd have saved herself years of heartache and the humiliation of testifying against her husband in federal court. And if she'd listened to Shayla two years ago, she never would have gotten involved with Jeff Maxwell, and gotten her heart broken again.

At least he wanted to make amends. Richard had never believed he'd done anything wrong, never believed that he'd betrayed her trust or the trust of hundreds of people. At least Jeff was trying to apologize for hurting her, even if it took a year for him to get around to it. Richard had never even said the word sorry except to tell her that she was.

"You are tightening up again," the masseuse said.

"I'm sorry," she apologized, trying to force herself to relax. "I was thinking."

"Stop thinking."

Wonderful advice, easier said than done. Then the masseuse took one foot in large, capable hands. On a sigh her thoughts left her as she began to drool.

She arrived at her next destination, manicure and pedicure, more energized than she'd been in months. The decision to relax and enjoy herself was easy to make in these soothing surroundings. Wrapped in a pale blue terry cloth robe, Angela gave serious thought to recommending the place as a corporate retreat. Enjoying the soothing attention veered close to guilty pleasure, making it all the more enjoyable.

Hair and makeup gave her a moment of trepidation, but the stylist assured her of her expertise in handling Black hair. Sure enough, her cropped auburn curls, now streaked with subtle gold highlights, had never looked better.

Gladys, the attendant, led her back to the dressing room. Angela didn't want the magic to end. It amazed her how quickly she'd become addicted to the attention. But surprises were far from over. Instead of the suit she'd worn to work, a garment bag hung on the changing screen, and a Your Heart's Desire shopping bag sat on the floor beside it.

Slowly she unzipped the dress bag, revealing a luxurious fall of turquoise silk, her favorite color and her favorite fabric. It flowed into her hands like a waterfall, and the fabric revealed itself to be a gorgeous floor-length sheath lined in satin, and a matching wrap.

The dress begged her to try it on. She turned to the Desire bag, removing undergarments from the private label, all in her size. Forever addicted to beautiful lingerie, she took her time sliding into the lace, rolling the stockings up her legs.

A knock sounded at the door before she could slip into the dress. "Do you need help with the dress?"

Angela looked at the silken work of art and knew she'd cry if she got one smudge of makeup on it. "Yes, please."

Gladys entered, beaming. "Ah, que buena! A beautiful dress for a beautiful lady!"

Flushing with a mixture of excitement and embarrassment, Angela caressed the dress. "Thank you. You and the spa have been wonderful."

Gladys unzipped the dress and removed it from its hanger. "We take good care of our clients, especially at times like this."

Angela froze. "Times like what?"

The attendant held the dress carefully so that Angela could step into it. "The señor who made the arrangements said to treat you like a princess." She smoothed the skirt before stepping back to do the zipper. "It must be a special occasion, no?"

Special occasion? Angela forced down a sudden lump in her throat. Surely Jeff wouldn't ask her to marry him again—especially after the way she'd refused him the last time. But what other special occasion could there be?

She didn't have a clue. One thing she did know: a lot of money had gone into the evening so far. The day spa was exclusive and expensive. She doubted that an appointment could be had on a day's notice. The limousine, still waiting outside, wasn't cheap either. Why was Jeff doing all this? Was it simply a quest to renew their friendship?

Gladys patted the beaded straps into place on her shoulders, then helped her into her heels. Lastly she draped the matching wrap over Angela's arms. "I told you, just like a princess—oh, wait!" She rummaged through the bag. "There was something else—another gift for you."

She retrieved a large velvet box. Angela's heart began to race. With good reason too, as she discovered when the attendant opened the lid.

Faceted blue and white gems gleamed up at her. Angela stared at the brilliant jewels in wonder. A large emerald-cut blue topaz surrounded with pavé diamonds glided on a gold choker. The pattern was repeated in earrings and a bracelet.

Hand shaking, she removed her own jewelry, then allowed Marie to slip the necklace and bracelet on her before she slipped on the earrings.

"Dios mio!" Gladys breathed, "you must see!"

She guided Angela to the floor-length mirror. Angela gaped at the person in the mirror. A vision in turquoise and topaz, the reflection looked like someone else, someone ready to walk the carpet at the Academy Awards. She felt like a princess; now she knew she looked like one.

"Are you ready, ma'am?"

Reluctant to move, Angela turned away from her reflection. "Ready for what?"

"The señor said for you to be ready for dinner by six," the attendant said, gathering the remainder of her belongings.

She would have frowned if she weren't afraid it would crack her makeup. "And did the señor tell you where we were going for dinner? Or when I would see him?"

"No, but he did leave a message for you."

"What message?"

"Just one word: Relax."

Angela smiled despite herself. Of course he would know she'd be apprehensive. Who wouldn't in a situation like this? Every moment her resolve melted further, endangering her peace of mind and the protective wall around her heart. When the magic of the night ended, would she still have the strength to tell him no?

Eight

Jeff knew the exact moment Angela entered the intimate restaurant. Conversation stopped, as if someone had frozen the moment in time. Every head turned as a beaming waiter escorted her to the center table.

His breath stuck in his throat. A stunning vision of turquoise silk and caramel skin, Angela sat gingerly in the chair the waiter held for her, eyes darting around the room. From a dim corner in the bar, he watched her pick up the single red rose from the setting before her, eyes closing as she inhaled its fragrance, a serene smile playing across her lips. The smile became a laugh when she noticed the notecard previously hidden beneath the rose. It held just one word: Relax.

He signaled the waiter. "A glass of merlot for the lady."

The waiter moved to complete the order and Jeff returned to the highly pleasurable act of watching Angela. Remembering that turquoise was her favorite color, he'd spent twenty-four grueling hours searching for the perfect dress to match the jewelry he'd bought for her months ago, just before her birthday, and never sent. Lawrence had come to the rescue, proving to be worth every penny Yvonne paid him.

The results spoke for themselves. From the sleek cut of her hair that showed the sharpness of her cheekbones, the graceful column of her neck, to the slimness of her waist and the length of legs that seemed to go on forever, she was amazing. Her beauty stole through him like an early morning mist.

Watching her, he felt a sudden, overwhelming anger at himself. How could he have been so stupid to let her go?

The waiter delivered the glass of wine. Jeff watched her ask the man a question, saw the waiter reply and point in his direction. Never taking his eyes from her, Jeff rose from his seat at the bar and approached her. Her smoky eyes widened, hopefully in appreciation of his black tie appearance.

"Hello."

A shy smile appeared and disappeared on her lips. "H-hello."

"You've captured the attention of everyone here," he said, pitching his voice low. "The women wish they were as beautiful as you and the men envy the lucky bastard you plan to grace with your presence."

She dipped her head, and he didn't need more than candlelight to know that she flushed. "Thank you."

"I saw you from the bar," he continued, pretending that this was their first meeting. "I waited to see if someone would approach you. A man would have to be the worst kind of fool to leave you alone."

Her head jerked up at the sudden harshness of his tone, and her smile dimmed. "It happens sometimes," she whispered.

"Mistakes by some can become blessings to others," he replied, injecting teasing into his voice. He gestured to the chair across from her. "May I?"

"Please."

Sitting, he extended his hand. "Jeff Maxwell, very pleased to meet you. And your name?"

Her eyes darkened in momentary confusion before she smiled, taking his hand. "Angela Davenport. Nice to meet you."

"Ms. Davenport. May I be honest with you?"

Wariness stilled her features but she nodded. "I appreciate honesty."

"Then let me tell you, I was starving until I saw you. You are a feast for the eyes, a buffet of beauty, a smorgasbord for the senses—"

Laughter spilled out of her, warm and rich, causing more than a few men to glance enviously in their direction. "Are you always this culinary with your compliments?"

"Not usually, no." He matched her smile. "But your loveliness and food are all I can think about. I think it's natural to put the two together."

"Then maybe we should order before you lose it all together."

On cue, the waiter approached them. "I am Philippe; I will be your waiter tonight," the young man said with a heavy

French accent. Whether it was real or not, Jeff had no idea. "What would the beautiful lady like this evening?"

Angela raised her menu, muttering something that sounded like, "To not wake up from this dream." She then placed her order in flawless French, and he remembered that she made several trips a year to Paris for various trunk shows. Did she still go, now that she had Kayleigh?

Philippe turned to him. "I'll have the same," he said in plain old American, not knowing what Angela ordered. If it proved unpalatable, he'd sneak a trip in to the Varsity later.

Continuing the illusion of a first meeting, he asked, "May I call you Angela?"

"Of course."

"Angela, you look familiar to me. Do you model?"

"Oh no," she protested, "I'm hardly the model type."

"Please. The men in this room can hardly eat their dinner for watching you. And if the guy behind you isn't careful, he's going to be wearing his fo—too late," he added as the gentleman in question spilled his plate into his lap.

"All right, if you don't model, what do you do?"

"I'm vice president of a company called Gemini Enterprises."

"That definitely sounds familiar. A parent company, right?"

"Yes. We have interests in a couple of restaurants and several print shops. Our crown jewel is the Your Heart's Desire boutiques and lingerie line."

"Of course. I was in one of the stores today, buying special things for a special lady." His voice dropped. "I hope she's enjoying them."

"I'm sure she is," she said, shifting in her chair.

He decided to give her a break. "So tell me, what does the vice president of such a diverse company do in a typical day?"

As the evening progressed, they both shared anecdotes about work. It surprised Jeff to realize that although he'd been intimate with Angela for a year, he really knew very little about her. What were her hopes and dreams? What did she wish for more than anything? He vowed to learn the answers to those questions, and if it were in his power, he'd give them to her.

"Seems like your work life is full," he said, staring down at his artistically arranged dinner. He didn't know whether he should eat it or frame it. A trip to the Varsity for a couple of chili slaw dogs, onion rings and a Frosted Orange was a definite necessity. "What do you do for pleasure?"

Her hands froze in the act of slicing into what looked like a Cornish hen. "I-I don't know," she finally answered. "Most of my life is work and taking care of Kayleigh."

Sadness filled her eyes as she laid her silverware down. He dropped the pretense and lifted her hand in his. "I didn't know Shayla well, but I know you two were like white on rice."

"My cousin and my best friend," she said, her voice quiet with a tremor. "Her father left her and her mother when she was seven and her mother had a hard time dealing with that and making ends meet, so she sent Shayla to live with us. I think I was eight or nine and Shay was a year older. We were inseparable, until I met Richard in college."

She fell into silence and Jeff let her have it. He'd known that she'd been married and divorced, but that was about it. "So, Shayla and Richard didn't get along?"

"No."

There was a wealth of information in that one word and enough warning for Jeff to know Angela considered that line of questioning closed. The need to know about the man who'd gotten Angela down the aisle swept him, but he stamped it down. Given that she still didn't know whether to hate him or not, Jeff didn't want to give Angela any ammunition by pressing her.

Even though he'd ended the charade of a first meeting, he couldn't resist saying, "But you and Shayla were good friends still—or again—when I met you."

"You're right," she agreed. "Blood is thicker than water, they say. Shay helped me cope after the divorce, and after you—after last year."

Her free hand stroked the rim of her wineglass. "Shay was strong. Strong, proud and independent, and happier not needing anyone. I wish I could be like her. Maybe I'd be a better guardian to Kayleigh."

"Angie." He tightened his grip on her hand. "You are strong. How can you say you're not? A major responsibility got thrust on you without warning and you didn't run away screaming. You rose to the challenge with flying colors.

Kayleigh's healthy and happy. Shayla knew you'd be a terrific guardian and that's why she chose you."

Her hand trembled in his before she balled it into a fist and pulled free. "We should probably eat before this squab gets cold."

Squab. Of course that's what it was. "Well, I'll admit it's not my mother's fried chicken, but there's no reason to call it bad names."

She laughed, just as he'd intended. "Thank you for this," she said, giving him a smile that could have powered a small city. "I haven't had a night like this for a while. I must admit, I feel kinda guilty about it."

"Why?"

"I've never left Kayleigh with anyone before, not for this long. Do you think she's all right? Do you think Lawrence was able to get her down for her nap? What if he doesn't feed her right? What if—"

He thrust his cell phone into her hands. "He's speed dial two. I'm pretty sure he's waiting for your call."

Law had indeed waited for her call. Judging from the one-sided conversation, he'd lost the bet with his life-partner over how soon she would call.

"They're doing fine," she said, disconnecting and staring at the phone in surprise. "Everything went well. They're getting ready to put her down for the night."

"Does that set your mind at ease or make you worried?"

"I don't know." Her brows furrowed. "I didn't know they were keeping her for the night."

The look she gave him simmered with accusation. He spread his hands. "I figured you wouldn't want to have to wake her—or them—when the night is done."

He could almost see the thoughts speeding through her mind. Had she always been filled with so much distrust or was it his fault that suspicion had become a permanent part of her life?

"Angie, everything will be fine. Remember who's looking after her," he said. "Law is an expert at taking care of women with demanding tastes."

"What a euphemistic way of putting it," she said with a wry grin. "We know we can be bitchy at times."

"But now isn't one of those times, is it?"

"No, now is definitely not one of those times."

"Then are you ready for the next stage?"

"There's more?" She looked incredulous.

"You didn't think it would end with dinner, did you?" Ridiculously pleased with himself, he gave her a grin as he motioned the waiter to bring the check. "It ain't over until the fat lady sings. You know, I've never liked that saying, but it may be appropriate tonight."

"Why?"

"We have one more destination," he announced, pushing away his plate. "Okay, maybe two," he added as his stomach rumbled. "But there is one planned stop."

She gave him an arch look. "As long as it's not illegal, immoral, or gonna cost me money, I'm up for it."

He gave her a grin. "That'll be tough, but I think we can

handle it. Are you ready?"

"Where are we going?"

"Somewhere you can show off that dress."

He gave her the most wondrous night of her life.

After the restaurant, the limousine whisked them away to the historic Fox Theatre for a Broadway musical. One of her favorites, she'd forgotten the production was coming to town, and was amazed that not only did Jeff have tickets for it, he had choice seats and an opportunity to meet cast members afterwards. Then they engaged in a uniquely Atlanta tradition: they joined several hundred other opulently and casually dressed people at the Varsity for trademark chilidogs and Frosted Oranges.

On the drive back to her house, however, she fell into a silent struggle with herself. What should she do? He had gone all out for her, and despite her every wish not to, she was bowled over. It almost seemed as if the past year was some weird dream-sequence, and she and Jeff were still a couple.

Yet they weren't a couple. She wouldn't be wrestling the sudden fit of nerves that danced in her stomach otherwise. Would he expect more than a goodnight at her front door?

The indecision that twisted inside her told her the truth. The night, wonderful as it was, didn't mean anything. Nothing was any clearer than it had been four days ago.

The limo came to a stop in front of her townhouse. A dichotomy of emotion swirled through her: the desire for the night to be over opposing the desire for the night to never end.

The driver opened the door, then helped her out of the car. Jeff followed, slipping his jacket around her shoulders to ward off the chill as they traversed the path to her front door.

She reached up, unclasping the pendant's chain. With overwhelming reluctance she reached for his hand and dropped the chain into his palm. He stared at her in surprise. "Why are you giving this to me?"

"I can't keep it," she said, struggling with the catch on the bracelet.

"Why?"

She paused in her struggle, staring at him in shock. "I have a pretty good idea of how much this set cost you. There's no way in the world I could keep it—it's too much."

"It's not enough," he told her, his breath fogging the late October night. "A night like this is something I should have done for you a long time ago."

A shaft of disappointment sliced through her. "I was right," she whispered. "This was nothing but an elaborate attempt to get forgiveness."

His eyes gleamed as he stared back at her. "Maybe a part of it was," he admitted, capturing her arm when she would have turned away from him. "But I mean what I said. I should have done this a long time ago. You deserve this. Our first date should have been a night like tonight. I know

I can't put a whole year's worth of apologies into one night, but at least I started making a dent."

"So this whole night—all the money you spent—was to assuage your guilt?"

"No." His hands rested on her shoulders. "Angie, listen to me. I did this because I wanted to do something for you, to give you something to make you happy. I wanted to give you Christmas and Valentine's and your birthday all rolled into one."

She bit her lip, indecision sweeping through her. Lord, she wanted to believe him. She needed to believe him. And the jewelry was so wonderful...

He leaned closer to her. "If it will make you feel better, I bought these for your birthday."

Now she knew she didn't believe him. "My birthday was seven months ago, in March."

"I know," he said softly. "March fifteenth, to be exact. I saw these in a display window while I was up in New York and I knew I had to get them for you. Didn't have a clue how I was going to get them to you, or even if I should. But I had to buy them."

He stuffed the chain into her nerveless hand. "Please, Angie. Keep them. Whether you keep them in your jewelry box and never wear them again or throw them away or hock them, it's up to you. They're yours to do what you want. But if you throw them away, please don't tell me."

Staring up at him, his eyes reflecting the green-white glow of the street lamp, she could see that he was serious.

"Okay. I'll keep it."

His smile turned her insides the consistency of watery grits. "Thank you."

She had to clear her throat a couple of times before she could speak. "Thank you, for everything you did for me today. I really needed it."

"That's why I did it." He reached up slowly to cup her cheek, giving her time to move away. She didn't.

Her stomach flopped. What should she do now? What do you do when your ex-lover gives you the best night of your life without sex? "W-would you like to come in for coffee?"

"Yes, but I'm not going to." He stepped away from her. "In the morning I'll stop by Law's to pick up Kayleigh and meet you here. Say about seven-thirty?"

"Who are you, and what have you done with Jeff Maxwell?"

"It's me, Angie," he told her, spreading his hands. "This is who I am."

No. This charming, chivalrous man didn't resemble the Jeff Maxwell she'd spent the past year being furious with. "Then I don't know you."

"There's more to me than what you know, and what I've shown you. Give me a chance to prove that to you."

"You're scaring me."

His smile dropped. "I overdid it, didn't I? Once I started planning this I couldn't stop."

Misery etched his features. Without thought she went to him, cupping his cheeks in her hands. "You didn't overdo it," she whispered. "This night was pure magic. Thank you."

She didn't intend to do it. If she'd thought about it, she wouldn't have stepped near him again. But he was there, she was in his arms, and it became the most natural thing in the world to touch her lips to his.

Meant to be an expression of gratitude, the kiss became much more. Jeff's hands tumbled to her waist, holding her close as his tongue began a slow exploration of the curve of her mouth. The growling of sexual starvation coiled through her, escaping as a moan trapped between their lips. Her nipples hardened into tight, painful peaks as moisture gathered between her thighs. She had to cling to his shoulders as her knees went weak.

Without warning he broke the kiss, holding her at arm's length. His breath came in harsh gasps that colored the air between them. Reluctance stamped the curve of his jaw as his hands lifted from her one finger at a time.

"Go on, Angie," he said, gesturing her to the door. "Watch a movie, take a bath, read a book, or just sleep. That's why Law kept Kayleigh tonight, to give you an uninterrupted night to do whatever you want."

What she wanted was to ease the hunger that continually ate at her soul. She wanted to have one of those sex scenes like you see in the movies—people ripping clothes off each other as they bumped into walls, furniture, and each other in the overwhelming need to be skin to skin. She wanted an orgasm that wasn't generated by her hand or a joy toy.

"Angie."

The hunger in his voice lured her, then knocked some sense into her. More than a little embarrassed, she turned to the door, fumbling with her keys before she managed to open it. Facing him again, she slid his jacket from her shoulders. "T-thank you for a wonderful night."

"Thank you for letting me share it with you," he answered, his voice husky. God, she knew that tone so well, that tone that let her know that glory would soon be hers in his arms.

He turned and walked down the path briskly, as if needing to put as much distance between them as possible. She waited until he reached the limousine before stepping inside, shutting and locking the door.

Leaning against it, she closed her eyes and released a long, slow breath. It didn't help. Her breasts were still painfully tight, her blood close to boiling. She knew she wouldn't be watching a movie or reading a book tonight.

She just hoped the batteries wouldn't die on her.

Nine

"I can't believe you talked me into this."

Angela surveyed herself in Lawrence's floor-to-ceiling mirror. The silver jumpsuit fit closer than skin, showing every unforgiving curve. "I look like a cross between a silver trophy and a TV antenna!"

"More like something out of Priscilla, Queen of the Desert," he cracked, posing next to her in a matching jump-suit.

"Are you implying that I look like a drag queen and you don't?" she asked, one hand straying to her hip.

"Well..."

"Hey, at least my boobs are real."

Law gave her a critical glance. "That's not much to brag about, you know."

She took a swing at him, not really aiming or wanting to hit. The need to get rid of pent-up energy beat at her. Almost a week since her date with Jeff, and she still smol-dered. Only one thing could cure her now, and she didn't want to think about it.

Going out with Lawrence and Jaime for Halloween

seemed like an answered prayer. She'd accepted the invitation weeks ago, knowing that Law would handle the costumes and arrangements. When Law mentioned that they would be going to the party as Patti LaBelle and LaBelle, she had no idea he meant the platform-heels-walking, skintight-jumpsuit and headdress-wearing incarnation of the group.

She frowned at their reflection. "How are people going to know who we are anyway?"

Law patted his perfect black rhinestone-studded beehive. "They'll figure it out when we start singing 'Lady Marmalade.'"

"Hold up." She turned to face him. "I know I didn't just hear you say we're going to sing."

"Well, to be honest, you and me ain't gonna sing," Law answered. "That's Jaime's department. You and I—" he vamped for the mirror— "will just lip-synch the chorus. All right?"

All right? "What have you gotten me into, you sorry excuse for a TV antenna?"

"Children, children, is that the way to play?" Jaime breezed into the room, hooking an arm around Law's waist and giving him a kiss. Law's life-partner possessed the whip-thin build of a runner, shocking red hair, green eyes and freckles. He also had a voice that could out-diva any diva on the planet.

Angela felt a familiar jealousy grip her as she watched the couple. It happened all around her. Starting with Yvonne, the pairing up had progressed to epic proportions. Almost everybody that worked in the boutiques had gotten engaged or married within the past two years. Employment applications flew in left and right because of two important facts: Desire was a great company to work for, and every woman affiliated with the place seemed destined for an engagement ring.

Except for her. She was the odd woman out and she felt it keenly.

"Hey now, that frown does not go with that outfit," Jaime said, detaching himself from Law, then crossing to her. "We're out to have fun tonight, and we're not going to think about anything the least bit negative. The Great White Drag Queen has spoken."

When put like that, how could she refuse an imperial order? She slapped a smile on her face and adjusted her attitude—and the fit of her jumpsuit. "Come on, boys, it's time to trick or treat!"

"Thanks for going with Michael and the twins up to the fall festival party," Yvonne said.

Jeff took the proffered plate of food and set it down before him. "No problem. We snapped plenty of pictures to add to your collection. Whose idea was it to dress the boys like a basketball and a football?"

"Who do you think?" she answered, rolling her eyes at her husband.

"You know, I would have been more than happy to stay here and baby-sit Kayleigh while you went to the party," he said, unfurling a napkin in his lap.

"I know, and I appreciate it." Moving around the table, she uprighted Robbie's sippy-cup and rescued Reggie's bowl from certain disaster. "But you weren't gone long, and Kayleigh's my responsibility."

"'Fess up, sweetheart," Mike cut in, snagging her around the waist and pulling her onto his lap. "You know you appreciated the peace and quiet."

"Absolutely." She gave him a peck before taking her own chair between Robbie's highchair and Kayleigh's swing. "And let me tell you, it was nice to have another woman in the house. We really bonded." She tickled the baby under her chin. "Can you say 'girl power'? Good girl!"

Jeff hid a smile as he caught Mike rolling his eyes. "Where is Angela anyway? I thought she didn't go out much."

"Law and Jaime took her out to a club for a Halloween party," Mike explained as he helped Reggie spoon up mashed potatoes.

"What?" The piece of steak he chewed nearly projectiled out of his mouth. "She's out with Law and Jaime?"

"Yeah," Yvonne answered, as if it wasn't a catastrophic event. "Law's had this planned for a couple of months. I didn't ask him the details, but he said he'd make sure that Angie enjoyed herself."

Jeff stifled a grunt. With Law, making sure Angela

enjoyed herself would stop just short of being arrested.

"What's the matter, old man?" Mike asked with a knowing grin. "You're not jealous, are you?"

"Come on, why would I be jealous?" He stabbed the defenseless pile of potatoes. "I don't have any claims on her. Obviously one date does not a commitment make. I can't expect her to stop her life just because I'm back."

"As long as you realize that, dear," Yvonne said, calmly slicing into her dinner.

Oh, he more than realized it, Jeff thought to himself. He felt the trueness of it with every passing day. Angela's life brimmed with activity. It certainly hadn't dragged to a halt just because he skipped town. Not that he'd expected it to, but the reality of how unnecessary he was for her proved hard to handle.

"Hey, your steak may be a little past medium, but it's not that bad," Yvonne said, snapping him out of his reverie.

"You're right, it's good. Did you cook it?"

"You don't have to sound so surprised," she answered with a wry smile. "Apparently even I can learn how to cook steak."

"Miracles do happen," Mike agreed sagely.

"Keep it up, mister, and the twins won't be the only ones wearing their dinner."

Conversation steered into the relatively safer waters of business and family for the remainder of dinner. The domestic scene before him crept into Jeff's senses. Lots of guys would run away from dealing with year-old twins and the feedings and changings and patience they required. But looking at his friends, looking at their obvious happiness, Jeff knew he'd give anything to have what they had.

With dinner done, Jeff helped Mike clear the table while Yvonne cleaned mashed potatoes from the twin's fingers and cheeks. "Do you two spend a lot of time with Angela or do you just keep Kayleigh for her?" he asked, passing a stack of plates to Mike.

"Hhm," his friend said, setting the plates on the counter before turning on the tap.

"What's 'hhm' supposed to mean?"

"It means I'm trying to decide if I should torture you or put you out of your misery."

Jeff winced inwardly. He'd forgotten that Mike could hold a grudge with the best of them. His grudge against his first wife had lasted twelve years and probably would have continued, if he hadn't met Yvonne.

"I think I deserve some slack, man," he said, adding a casserole dish to the pile on the counter. "I'm trying to make things right. Even I know I need all the help I can get."

"Okay." Mike flipped off the disposal but left the tap running. "We don't see nearly as much of Angela as Vonne would like. If there's a reason for it, I don't know what it is. But Angela seems to be completely focused on Kayleigh and work."

While the news cheered him, it also made him uncomfortable. "Is she happy?"

Mike gave the question considerable thought as he

loaded the dishwasher. "I think so, relatively speaking, and given everything that's going on. But Vonne would know better than me."

"I'd know better than you about what?" Yvonne called from the doorway.

"Jeff's pumping me for information on Angela. I told him that's your department."

"It certainly is. But it's—Robbie, you stop that this instant! It's gonna cost ya."

Wariness had him pausing, dirty dishes in hand. Yvonne could be just as ruthless as her husband when she wanted to be. "Cost me what?"

"Even trade. Information for baby sitting."

"That's all? Consider it done." If he could watch his brothers and sisters all those years ago, he could take care of a couple of toddlers.

"Oh yeah, you say that now," Mike laughed. "The boys aren't always as behaved as they were at the Halloween party."

Jeff got a mental picture of two toddler-sized sportsballs wreaking havoc at the subdivision's community center. "That was behaving?"

"Don't worry, Uncle Jeff, we'll break you in easy," Vonne said. "You can start by watching Kayleigh while we bathe the boys. That's definitely a two-adult job."

Jeff returned to the dining room, retrieving the baby from her swing. "We'll be fine, won't we, sweetpea?" She rewarded him with a slobbery gurgle.

"Sure you will." Yvonne plucked Robbie from his high chair while Mike lifted Reggie. "Go bond in the living room. And yell if you need anything."

With Kayleigh in one hand and her swing in the other, Jeff retreated to the living room. Keeping the baby carefully balanced in his arm, he wrestled the swing into position. Instead of strapping Kayleigh in he sat on the couch, the baby balanced on his knees.

"We should probably re-introduce ourselves," he said to the infant. "Last time we met, I made the mistake of telling you that I'm your father. Well, as it turns out, I'm not. That doesn't mean that I'm gonna disappear, or that I love you any less than I did when I first saw you."

Kayleigh stared up at him with wide brown eyes, one fist firmly lodged in her little round mouth. At least she seemed to be listening. "So anyway, I'm not related to you just yet. I'd like to become your Uncle Jeff. But there's a little problem with your Aunt Angela. She's being real stubborn. Now don't get me wrong—I don't blame her for it. Lord knows I shouldn't be as far along as I am with her right now. That doesn't mean that I couldn't use a little help anywhere I can get it. So what do you say? Shall we form an alliance, you and me?"

A baby-sized yawn answered him. "Well, either I have nothing to worry about or I'm in big trouble."

His heart flipped over again as the baby's lashes slowly dipped down. "I can tell that Angie takes good care of you, and loves you very much," he whispered. "But who takes care of her?"

"Law's pretty much adopted her, but you already knew that," Vonne said softly as she entered the room.

"Hey. Where's Mike?"

"Reading the boys a bedtime story. He figured we'd want to talk." She sat beside them. "Is she asleep?"

Jeff looked down at the baby, whose eyes were half-mast. "Just about."

"Do you want me to take her?"

"No, I can hold her." The weight felt good in his arms.

"You're attached to her already, I see," Yvonne noted.

"Of course I'm attached to her. I thought she was mine."

"Convenient, since you seem to be attached to her aunt as well."

He frowned. "What are you getting at, Vonne?"

"I just want to make sure that you're sure. Don't play games with her."

The accusation stung him, especially coming from Vonne. "I don't intend to hurt her or play her. I've told you that."

"Good," she sat back. "She doesn't need that."

He looked down at the sleeping baby in his arms. "Is she happy, Vonne?"

His best friend sighed. "I don't think happy is the right word. She's...accepted where she is right now, and she's making the best of it. But the last few months have been brutal for her."

Guilt made him grimace. "And I didn't help the situation any."

"No, you didn't," Yvonne said, softening her words with a light touch on his arm. "And just as she was getting settled in, you blew back into town. You can't blame her for being upset."

"No I don't. She's got a lot on her plate."

"Right. And let me tell you, babies aren't easy," Yvonne said, a wry smile on her face. "There are days when Michael and I look at each other and go 'what the hell were we thinking?' Then there are moments like this when you don't want to be anywhere else."

He could agree with that. Holding Kayleigh, he couldn't imagine anything more perfect than the sleeping child. But how was it for Angela, balancing her high-powered career with raising a child?

"I know enough about your company to know that Angie's not hurting for money. Why didn't she hire a nanny?"

Vonne rolled her eyes. "Come on, Jeff. Who are we talking about here? Angela's the queen of independent women. She wants to take care of Kayleigh herself, to prove to herself—and maybe even her mother—that she can do it. She wouldn't ask for help unless she had to. But so far she's done fine on her own, even if it's all but made her a hermit."

"And Lawrence and Jaime are doing their best to make sure that doesn't happen."

Yvonne gave him a knowing smile. "It's not that bad. They just went to a costume party at Kaleidoscope."

"Kaleidoscope?"

"Yeah, one of the happening clubs for those with alternative lifestyles."

"Is that French for gay bar?"

"It most certainly is." Yvonne gave him a huge smile. "Don't worry, they won't be out too long."

Worry? Why should he worry? Angela hanging out with two of Atlanta's most notorious partyers? What was there to worry about?

"Is she letting Kayleigh stay the night?"

"No, she'll probably be here in the next couple of hours."

Two hours. He intended to be here when she arrived. "'Vonne, would you mind—"

"Not at all," she interrupted smoothly. "I'd actually be surprised if you left. But you have to listen to me regale you with tales of your godsons' adventures over the last year."

"Deal."

Catching up on his godsons' lives proved to be a pleasant and necessary distraction. Shortly before eleven he heard a car pull into the drive. "I guess that's them," Yvonne said unnecessarily, putting the photo album on the coffee table before rising to her feet. "Here. Let me get Kayleigh ready, and you get the door."

He did as instructed, opening the front door before Angela could ring the bell. At least he thought it was Angela.

"What the hell do you think you're wearing?"

Her brows bunched together. "My Halloween outfit,

silly."

He stared at the silver material that showed every curve of her body. "Jesus, I can count your ribs! What are you supposed to be, a metallic Q-tip or an intergalactic prostitute?"

Hands settled on her hips, a sure sign of trouble. "I don't think it's any of your business, Mr. High-and-Mighty," she said airily. "But we did win first prize. What are you doing here anyway?"

"Mike and Yvonne are my friends too," he reminded her, backing up to let her in. She passed him, giving him a good whiff of bar smoke and alcohol. "Have you been drinking?"

"No. Yes," she answered. "Maybe a couple of glasses of wine."

"Here we are." Yvonne took that moment to reappear, Kayleigh securely strapped into her car seat. "She's been a real sweetheart all night."

Instead of grabbing the handle, Angela wrapped her arms about the carseat. "Thanks, Vonne. I appreciate you doing this for me."

Yvonne crinkled her nose. "Are you okay to drive?"

"Of course I am."

"Of course she's not."

Angela turned to glare at him. "Excuse me?"

"I'm taking you home." He grabbed her forearm, steering her towards the door.

She attempted to snatch her arm free of his grip, still keeping a grip on the carseat. "I don't recall asking you to."

He took her arm in a firmer grip. "You didn't. But I'm

driving you anyway. Thanks for dinner, Yvonne. Tell Mike I'll stop by his office tomorrow morning."

As he steered her down the walk to the passenger side of his car she fought him with every step. "I've told you before I don't need your help, you arrogant, egotistical, son of a bi..."

"Call me whatever makes you happy," he growled, jerking her to a stop. "There's no way in hell I'm gonna let you drive yourself and Kayleigh home after you've been drinking."

For a tense moment she just stared up at him, her dark eyes highlighted by the glitter around them, but revealing nothing. Without a word, she slid into the passenger seat. He kicked himself every step of the way to the driver's side.

She didn't speak as he started the car and pulled out of the driveway. Her back straight as a board, her hands folded just so in her lap, she kept her face straight ahead and carefully blank. No anger or sadness radiated from her, just a quiet resignation that made him feel worse with every inch he drove.

The silence grew unbearable. At the next stoplight, he turned to her, reaching a hand for her cheek. "Angie, I'm sorry—"

"No!" The word was half-plea, half-shriek as she threw up her hands in self-defense.

What the hell? She pressed against the passenger door as if her life depended on it. "Hey, I wasn't going to hit you."

With a strained laugh, she dropped her hands to her lap. "I know that. You-you just surprised me, that's all."

The light changed. He darted her another look before turning his attention back to the road. Her hands were clenched in knots in her lap. "Are you all right? Do you want me to stop for anything?"

"No." Her swallow was audible in the dark interior of the car. "I'm fine. I'm just—ready to be home."

The lie, soft as it was, shamed him. She wasn't all right, and the fault lay with him. He had the feeling that once he dropped her at her door, she would make sure that he never had a chance with her again.

The remainder of the ride passed in silence. As soon as he pulled to a stop before her townhouse, she reached for her seatbelt. He exited quickly, taking Kayleigh from the backseat before she could.

"You can hand her to me," Angela said, her posture stiff with distance. "I won't drop her between here and the front door."

"I know you won't," he sighed, knowing he'd offended her with his high-handed cavalier crap. "Just let me see you both safely in. Please."

"Fine." With a swirl of her coat, she turned and stalked in a very straight line up the walkway to the front door. He followed, knowing each step took her farther away from him. A tightness settled across his chest. He could make this right. He had to make this right.

She opened the door then stepped inside to disable the alarm. With Kayleigh as a shield, he stepped past her, using his elbow to flip the light switch. After setting the baby's carrier on the coffee table, he did a quick survey, wasting time looking for signs of a disturbance the alarm system would have caught.

Angela sat on the couch and watched his every movement, arms folded across the chest of her silver jumpsuit. "For your information, I don't make a habit of going out all the time, staying out all hours of the night, or drinking until I can't stand up. Even before Kayleigh I didn't do that."

"I know that, Angie, and I'm sorry I came off like that." He knelt in front of her, careful not to touch her and set her off. "Please believe that."

Her eyes glittered at him. "You made me feel like I was deliberately endangering Kayleigh," she whispered, her voice raw. "You made me feel like I didn't care."

Involuntarily his hands lifted, hovering in the air between them. He wanted to pull her into his arms, wipe the hurt expression from her face. Instead he reached out, clasping the fists planted on her knees. "Angie, I'm sorry for acting like a Neanderthal. I just couldn't let you drive off knowing you'd had even one drink. If something happened to you and Kayleigh, I wouldn't be able to forgive myself."

Her hands lay unmoving under his. "Why?" she asked, her voice soft. "Because of what happened to Yvonne?"

"No," he answered, barely able to speak above the guilt and responsibility that consumed him. "Because of what happened to Katie Ulster."

"Who?"

She had the right to ask. No one knew about Katie

Ulster and his connection with her. Still on his knees, he moved closer to her before plunging ahead. "Ten or twelve years ago, Mike and I were doing our usual barhopping, womanizing thing. Back then another guy used to hang with us, my cousin Ricky."

She didn't say anything, but he could tell that she listened. "One night Ricky had more to drink than normal, but he seemed fine. I only asked him once if he was okay to drive before I let him drive off. I found out the next morning that he hit someone. Ricky didn't have a scratch, but Katie Ulster wasn't so fortunate.

"It was the night of her bachelorette party. Maybe she'd had too much to drink too, I don't know. I only know that Ricky shouldn't have been driving, shouldn't have swerved into or out of someone's way, shouldn't have sent Katie Ulster to the hospital for two months."

He felt her hand, small, cool, necessary, slide over his. "It's not your fault, Jeff."

"Of course it was," he answered, unable to subdue the harsh self-condemnation in his voice. "I could have prevented Ricky from driving home. That's all I would have had to change. If Ricky hadn't been driving, Katie Ulster wouldn't have been hurt."

"And if it had been you, then what?" she wondered. "You could have been hurt. You said you don't know which one was at fault. What if she was the one who swerved into his lane, and your cousin had enough presence of mind to avoid her? If he hadn't, it's possible they both could have died."

He shook his head, wishing he could explain it to her, wishing he could make her understand. In his blood he knew the accident would have been averted if he'd lived up to his responsibility.

"What happened after that?"

"It took about two months, but Katie made a full recovery." And he'd paid off, anonymously, what bills the insurance company didn't cover.

"And your cousin?"

Muscles along his shoulders bunched. "I haven't seen Ricky in a couple of years," he admitted. "Momma keeps up with everybody; she said he was doing okay."

He could feel her staring at him, and he wondered if she judged him. "You're still mad at him, aren't you?"

"Yes. No. I'm mad at myself. I let him drive away when I knew I shouldn't have. So it's my fault."

One hand pulled free of his, then reached up to graze his cheek. The unexpected gesture shook him, and he had to close his eyes a moment before meeting her gaze.

The smile she gave him soothed with sympathy. "Stop blaming and hating yourself. You aren't Superman. You can't protect everybody."

The truth of her words flowed over him, though his instincts fought it. Maybe I can't protect everybody, he thought. But I have to try.

"I know," she whispered, and he realized he'd spoken aloud.

Turning to her, he framed her face in his hands, unable to find the words he wanted to say. "Angie..."

"I know," she said again. "I forgive you."

Who moved first, he didn't know. The distance closed between them, becoming a kiss of comfort and forgiveness.

Angela deepened the kiss, wrapping her arms about his shoulders in a quest to get closer. She needed to forgive him, but she needed to be forgiven too. Time, distance, and pain melted away as she gave herself over to the joy of holding him, tasting him.

Sensations buffeted her, setting her adrift as those wonderful lips worked their magic on her mouth, her chin, her throat. His hands slid up her arms in a measured caress, brushing against her covered breasts and setting the tips to painful erect pleasure.

One moment she was on the couch, the next she'd slipped off and into in his lap, straddling him. She could feel the bulk of his arousal pressed against her heat, and cursed the barrier of fabric that separated them.

Jeff must have had the same thought. In one smooth motion he reached for her zipper and bared her from neck to navel. Relief had her shuddering; his tongue on her nipple had her moaning aloud.

She arched back, providing better access as the delicious sweeps of his mouth pulled a response from deep inside her. His thumb pressed against the rigid crest of her arousal through the fabric. Instinctively her hips pressed forward, seeking the solace his touch promised. Close, so very close...

Kayleigh's whimper cut through her ardor like a hedge trimmer. "Oh God!" She scrambled back, away from him, struggling with the jumpsuit's zipper. Heat—from embarrassment, not passion—flamed her face.

Laughter, soft and low, stopped her frantic movements. She looked up to see Jeff standing in front of her, Kayleigh in his arms. "You have impeccable timing, princess," he told the baby, chuckling again before kissing her forehead.

When Angela rose to her feet, he handed the infant to her, his expression sobering. "I'm glad she woke up," he admitted. "I didn't mean to go that far. I just wanted—needed—"

"It's okay," she interrupted him, embarrassment gone. The truth of it swept her. "You're still forgiven."

His smile brightened his face from lips to eyes as his hand glided up to her cheek. "Thank you for giving me another chance," he whispered, his lips brushing her forehead. "I'll try to make it worth it."

"K-kay."

His thumb did dangerous things to the nerve endings in her cheek. "Can I spend time with you two ladies tomorrow?"

"Sure."

"Okay. I'll see you then." His lips brushed hers, once, twice, then lingered, curling her toes into the carpet. She had to hold onto his shoulder to keep from tumbling backward with Kayleigh.

By the time the kiss ended, every pore on her body

steamed with heated need. Next thing she knew he was at the door. "Goodnight. I'll see you tomorrow."

Angela locked the door behind him, then sank onto the couch, soothing the baby in an absent-minded gesture. She needed soothing herself. Her entire body still hummed with the desire he'd awakened in her.

Jeff was one hundred percent back in her life—and under her skin. Feeling his lips, his hands, his body, had brought so many memories rushing back—pleasure, joy, ecstasy. Being in his arms felt so right.

And that made it wrong.

Ten

The shrilling of the phone jerked him from a fitful sleep. "H-hello?"

"S-something's wrong with Kayleigh," Angela's sob-filled voice shrieked at him. "S-she won't stop crying and I don't know what to do!"

Abruptly wide-awake, Jeff flung back the covers. He could hear the baby's high-pitched wails in the background. Leaping from bed, he cradled the cordless between his cheek and shoulder and headed for his dresser. "Do you have an emergency number for her pediatrician?"

"I don't know!" she wailed. "He saw her this afternoon and gave me his card, but I don't think it's for emergencies."

"Angie, listen to me." He forced calm into his tone as he pulled open a drawer and retrieved a set of sweats. "Call the pediatrician's office. You'll probably get a recording with the emergency number on it. I'm on my way."

"Jeff—"

"Call the doctor, sweetheart. I'll be there in ten."

"Please hurry."

"I will." After disconnecting, he threw the phone on the

bed and pulled on the sweats, his heart pounding in his chest. Even through the phone, he could tell that Kayleigh's cries weren't hunger or diaper-related.

The last time he'd dealt with a newborn had been his youngest sister, eighteen years ago. He'd been sixteen then and thoroughly disgusted with the obvious proof that his parents still had sex. Trina had been a surprise, and his parents worried about her health even before she was born.

He racked his brain for memories as he left the apartment complex. The only thing that could make a baby wail like that was pain. But what kind of pain? Kayleigh couldn't be teething yet. Was it a fever, an infection of some sort?

God, don't let it be an ear infection. He'd been through one of those himself and wouldn't wish that agony on his worst enemy.

Nine minutes later, Jeff pulled into Angela's neighborhood. Her townhouse blazed with lights. The front door swung open before he could reach it.

Angela's tear-streaked face twisted his heart; Kayleigh's anguished cries raked his soul. He closed his arms around Angela in an unbreakable grip as she crashed into him. "Thank God you're here!"

He kissed her forehead. "It's going to be all right," he reassured her, guiding her back up the walk and into the house. Once inside, he crossed to the ill baby wailing her heart out in her carrier. Tears poured down her red, angry face and her arms and legs flailed in fury.

Her forehead was scalding, he noted. "What did the

doctor say?" he asked Angela.

"He wasn't any help! He remembered us from this afternoon, said to keep to the dosage of the prescription, and to let him know if her fever goes up. Shouldn't we take her to the emergency room instead?"

He reached out with his free hand to brush the tears from her face. "Let's see what we can do first. Did you take her temperature?"

"Y-yes. It hasn't changed."

"And when did you last give her medicine?"

"I was supposed to an hour ago, but I couldn't get her to take it," she admitted, fresh tears leaking from her eyes. She's hurting and it's all my fault!"

"Okay, first of all, calm down. Kayleigh could be picking up on how upset you are. You can't soothe her when you're not calm yourself. It's going to be okay. I won't let anything happen to either one of you.'

She took a deep breath, dashing the tears from her face with both hands. "O-okay."

"Where's her medicine?"

"Upstairs in her bathroom."

He followed Angie upstairs to the bathroom. "Fix the dosage for me," he requested, peeling the damp sleeper from Kayleigh's warm skin.

"Here." Her hand shook as she gave him a dropper filled with medicine.

"Thanks. Okay sweet-thing, we need you to take your medicine. We need you to get all better."

It took a couple of tries, but he managed to get every bit of the dosage into the squirming infant's mouth. "There you go." He turned to Angela. "Did the doctor say what was wrong?" He asked.

"H-he said that it was a really bad cold, that's all." She wrapped her arms around her middle. "But she's been crying nonstop for the last two hours."

"Ah. Do you have one of those aspirators?"

"What?"

"It's usually blue, with a big squeezable bulb on the end, and a skinny end to place in the nose. You use it to clear a stuffy nose."

"Oh-yeah, I have one of those." She hurried across the hall and quickly returned with the soft rubber device.

"Thanks." He hesitated before using it. In his experience, babies didn't take kindly to having the inside of their noses sucked out, even if it was for their own good. In Angela's unnerved state, more shrieks from Kayleigh would do her in—or give him a black eye.

"Angie, why don't you go downstairs and fix a bottle of apple juice for Kayleigh? After I clear her nose, I'm going to start a bath for her. I think it'll help."

"Are you sure?"

"Yeah. Go on."

With one last tear-filled glance at them, she left the bathroom. Jeff sat on the closed john, cradled the squirming baby close and aspirated one nostril. Kayleigh disliked it intensely, if her wail was any indication. He gently wrestled with her to clear the other nostril. After another shriek of outrage, she quieted down.

Breathing a sigh of relief, he crossed to the nursery and laid the baby in her crib, then retrieved the baby tub and returned to the bathroom. He turned the tap to an appropriate temperature before opening the under-sink cabinet in a quest for baby bubble bath.

The cabinet was jam-packed with every baby necessity known to man. Powder, talc, shampoo, oil, cleaner, moisturizer. Q-tips, cotton balls, soap. It looked as if Angela had taken a buggy, started at one end of the baby aisle and scooped two of everything up as she proceeded to the other end.

One of the products happened to be an aromatic bath gel purported to ease congestion. He poured a capful into the bath, turned off the tap, then lifted the basin onto the wide counter. With swift efficient movements he returned to Kayleigh, undressed her, and took her to the bathroom for her bath. She took to the aromatic water immediately, quieting as he ran the sponge over her.

Concentrating on soothing her, he hummed a song that his mother had often sung to him and his siblings. His mind full of easing Kayleigh, he didn't think about Angela's whereabouts until after he'd bathed the quieting infant.

Angela paused in the doorway, her panic arrested by the sight of Jeff bathing Kayleigh. The way he handled her, expert and gentle, the way he crooned to her, natural and low, spread through her like the warmth of sunshine after a hard rain. He was so capable, so sure...

So unlike her.

She must have made some sound, because he glanced up, a slow smile spreading across his face. "Hey, I think she's better."

Not wanting to disrupt the calming influence he'd exerted, she crept closer. Kayleigh did seem to be better. She wasn't nearly as fidgety or irascible. Why hadn't she thought of clearing Kayleigh's nose, of giving her an aromatherapy bath?

"You're good at this," she whispered, unable to speak louder past the lump in her throat.

"I've had lots of practice," he said with a self-deprecating grin. "Watching Momma raise seven other kids, something was bound to stick."

"You'd make a good father." The truth of it, knowing that Kayleigh truly was in capable hands pressed in on her, relieving her.

Jeff gave her a pleased smile. "Do you really think so?"

She gestured with her free hand as if to gather her thoughts in. "I do. It—it just seems to come naturally to you."

"I guess it does," he said, watching Kayleigh grab his finger in her tiny fist. "Momma and Dad were good role models. To me, family is everything. Nothing could make me happier than having a family of my own."

He darted a glance at her before returning his attention to the baby. "What about you? Didn't you and your ex-husband want a family?"

Alarm tightened her stomach. Of course he'd want to know what she thought about having a family. "I did," she finally said, spinning the bottle in her hands. "There just never seemed to be the right time to start one. There was Richard's business and I'd just started with Yvonne. Anyway, maybe I should prove that I can manage with Kayleigh before I even think of having my own family."

Feeling completely unnecessary and totally vulnerable, she sat the bottle beside him on the counter. "I think, you know, in the rush, that I-I forgot to lock the door. I'll be right back."

She turned and escaped, and realizing that she was escaping her shortcomings only made her want to run away all the more. She rushed down the stairs, and so it wouldn't seem like she was a complete liar, actually checked the locks. Balancing on legs that suddenly seemed to have forgotten their primary function, she toddled over to the couch and collapsed on it.

Kayleigh had been in such agony, the cries knifing through her heart. And instead of calling a doctor, as any decent parent would have done, she had called Jeff. Jeff had to tell her to call the pediatrician. Jeff realized that Kayleigh's nose was stuffed, Jeff discovered the power of an herbal bath. And her measly contribution to improving Kayleigh's welfare? Fetching a damn bottle of apple juice.

Unable to breathe, she bent double, wrapping her arms about her knees and burying her head in her lap. It was a position she'd assumed many times before, her instinctive reaction to impending failure. And she was failing.

Her mother was right. She couldn't do it. She just wasn't cut out to be a mother. No instincts kicked in when Kayleigh got sick, no defensive mechanism to protect the baby at all costs. Kayleigh's pained crying and obvious suffering had frozen Angela. God, if she wasn't capable of handling a cold, how was she going to be able to deal with teething or a more serious illness?

"I'm sorry, Shay. I'm so sorry," she whispered into her knees, giving vent to the tears she'd held back for so long. She cried for her losses: her innocence, her first marriage, her relationship with Jeff, her cousin. And she cried for Kayleigh who deserved a mother, not a woman who failed at everything she touched.

"Angie."

She turned away from the sound of his voice, scrubbing the tears away from her cheeks. "Is Kayleigh better?"

"Don't do this to yourself."

"Do what?" She had to force herself to turn around and face him.

He sat beside her on the couch. "Blame yourself."

"I'm not blaming myself," she refuted, then spoiled the declaration by adding, "Blame myself for what? For not knowing how to take care of a child? For being a failure?"

"Angie, you're not a failure."

"Of course I am." Her voice grew hoarse with the effort to staunch tears. "Oh, not at business. Just a failure at the things that matter. I failed to make my mother love me. I failed with my marriage. No matter how hard I tried, I only made it worse. I failed with you because I couldn't love you enough to make you stop loving another woman. I failed to keep Shayla alive, and now I'm failing her daughter."

"Angie—"

Once she started, she just couldn't stop. "Every day I'm paralyzed over some new fear. I'm afraid I'm going to lay her wrong. Pick her up wrong, turn my back at the wrong time. No one's ever needed me the way Kayleigh has, and I can't deal with it."

He took her hands, but she pulled away and shot to her feet, appalled at what she'd revealed to him. "I'm sorry, Jeff," she said, forcing her tone to steadiness with a deep breath. "I should be thanking you for coming to my rescue, not forcing you to listen to me bitch. I'm all right now."

But she wasn't and she knew she wasn't. Tremors shook her, signaling capitulation. If she could simply wait for him to leave, she could then go upstairs, bury her head in her pillow, and bawl her eyes out.

"Angie." He touched her shoulder, turned her around. No fight left in her, she didn't protest as he fit her head to his shoulder and wrapped his arms about her.

For five seconds she thought she would be all right. Then with a sniffle and a shudder, the dam broke. Once begun, the flood wouldn't stop despite her efforts. Through it all, Jeff held her close, anchoring her, running his hand up and down her back in a soothing motion.

She had no knowledge of how long the angst poured from her. When it finished, she felt drained, lighter than she had in months. It felt good.

So did being in Jeff's arms. She pulled back and he let her, though he kept his hands on her waist. His eyes, dark with concern, warded away the chill that had settled on her in her helplessness. She knew at that moment she wanted him to hold her, needed him to kiss her. Needed the comfort and the reassurance, if not the love.

"Angie." He leaned forward, taking the moisture from her cheeks with his own. The profundity of the gesture touched her, changed her. When he shifted, touching her lips with his own, she was ready and willing to receive him.

Simplicity itself, his mouth drew her closer, offering, not taking. There was nothing inherently sexual about the kiss or the way he held her, yet she tingled deep inside nevertheless. She broke away first, resting her cheek against his chest. "Thank you."

His arms tightened around her. "I'm here for you, Angie. You know that, don't you?"

Not really, not for sure, but she didn't want to argue. "Yes."

"Come upstairs and see Kayleigh," he whispered against her ear. "She's sleeping peacefully, thanks to you."

Surprise caused her to draw away from him. "Thanks to me? But you were the one—"

"I couldn't have done it without you," he said, taking her hand and drawing her back up the stairs. "If you hadn't stocked what I needed, Kayleigh would still be uncomfortable."

She allowed herself to be led down the hall to the nursery. He'd dimmed the lights to turn on the lamp that projected revolving stars onto the ceiling and walls. Kayleigh lay sprawled in baby abandon in her crib, her pacifier clutched in one tiny fist.

Relief flowed through her, almost unhinging her knees. Jeff caught her with one arm around her waist, hauling her against the hardness of his chest. "How long have you been up taking care of her?" he demanded.

"Since yesterday," she answered, grateful for the support of his arm. With Kayleigh better, the adrenaline rush of fear drained out of her, leaving her tired. "Or maybe it's been two days. Is it tomorrow yet?"

Jeff did something he'd never done before. He swung her into his arms, then headed out the door and down the hall to her bedroom. Once inside, he deposited her on her bed. "You need to rest," was all he said as he slipped off her shoes then pulled the comforter over her.

Sudden panic had her sitting up. "Are you leaving?"

He paused, halfway between the doorway and bed. "Well, I was hoping...would you mind if I sack out on your couch? I'll leave first thing."

The uncertainty in his voice made her decision easy. "No."

"No? Uh, okay. Then I guess I'll see you sometime tomorrow." He turned to the door.

"Jeff." She was out of bed and beside him in seconds. "I meant you don't need to sleep on the couch. My bed's big enough for both of us."

He stared at her, those dark eyes concerned and searching as they roamed her face. "Are you sure?"

She couldn't be sure about anything anymore. All she knew was that being in Jeff's arms had been the closest thing to peace she'd had in a long time. She wanted to feel that again. "Yes. I'm sure."

"Okay." He turned back to the bed, and she retreated to her bathroom, brushing her teeth. She paused as she slipped her rose-colored sleep chemise over her head. Would Jeff think the silky bit of lingerie an invitation?

She twisted her lips in a wry pout. Like saying he could share her bed wasn't? She'd always loved lingerie, a fact Jeff had certainly known and appreciated before. There was no need to change now. And it was too late to turn back.

"You need this," she whispered to her reflection. "Don't think about it, don't regret it. Just do it."

From the tentative safety of the bed, Jeff watched her step into the darkness of the room. His gut clenched in need. The dim light from the window caught the shiny material she wore, and he belatedly remembered how much she loved lingerie. And how much he loved her in it—and out of it.

She quickly crossed the room, the fabric just skimming the tops of her thighs. His erection grew painful, and he wondered how he'd survive the night without touching her.

The bed dipped slightly as she got in and settled the covers over herself. She lay on her back, stiff, the covers tucked tight under her chin as she stared at the ceiling.

"Turn on your side," he whispered.

"What?" Her voice cracked.

"Turn your back to me."

"Oh...okay." She did as he instructed, keeping several inches between them. He sidled closer, not enough to poke her in the back with his erection, but close enough. His hands settled on her shoulders and she flinched. A definite bundle of nerves. "Relax," he urged her softly, beginning a gentle massage of the knotted muscles in her shoulders.

It took several minutes before she followed his order, her breathing deepening. He had every intention of only massaging her shoulders until she went to sleep, he really did. But the urge to touch the silk draping her curves, the scent of her skin, and her nearness proved too great a temptation.

Unable to do anything else, his hands slid down her back, bunching the short gown in his grip. He began to slide it upward in slow deliberate movements, giving her time to refuse him.

She didn't. Instead, she rose slightly, enabling him to remove the gown completely. The invitation fired his senses and he took full advantage of it.

Angela thought she would die when Jeff wrapped his arms around her, pulling her snug against him. The length of his arousal pressed against her instead of inside her like a firebrand. How could she have forgotten that he preferred to sleep as naked as the day he was born?

His left hand, hot, possessive, slipped from the pulse pounding at the base of her throat to tease one nipple then the other, sweet plucking that resonated deep inside her. His right hand slid over the curve of her hip, seeking and finding the soft folds that hid the rigid knot of pleasure.

She was wet, so wet and ready for him. She could feel it as his fingers delved into her, stroking her, an artist brushing at the canvas of her arousal. Another moan tore from her.

"That's it," he coaxed, his voice husky with desire as his hips thrust against her. "Sing for me baby."

Sing she did, uncontrollable moans and sighs as his fingers stroked, circled, teased, pleased. His lips fastened to the curve of her neck between her ear and shoulder, his tongue tracing lazy circles in her heated skin.

She melted against him, opening, flowing in a stream of desire. Her hand gripped his hip, anchoring to reality as she pushed forward against his hand, backward against his erection. His breath stuttered against her ear, and the pressure of his hand increased, pulling a response from her.

Ecstasy gathered momentum. Spiraling upward, the pleasure exploded from her with a gasp, a rushing waterfall of sensation so glorious, so delicious, it was almost perfection.

Long moments later she settled back to earth. Breathless, she turned to him. "Did you...finish?"

With a chuckle he pressed lightweight kisses to her lips her throat. "No, but it still felt good." His erection pressed between them, hard, heated flesh.

She reached down, wrapping her hand around him. She

wanted it, wanted him, inside. Now. "Please," she whimpered, knowing she was begging, too frenzied to care. "Please."

"Baby, I can't." Jeff's voice roughened with agony. "I need you so bad, I wouldn't be able to stop in time. I didn't bring any protection with me."

God, she hadn't thought of that. She was glad he did. "Maybe I have some, from when you and I..."

She raised herself to her elbows then flicked on the light. Squinting against the glare, she opened the drawer of the nightstand. Maybe she still had condoms from the last time she and Jeff were together. A year ago. Lord, when did condoms expire? Had she dumped them out when she packed for the move?

"What's this?"

Jeff reached across her, removing her joy toy from the drawer. She snatched it back from him. "I was celibate. I never said I was a saint."

"Hhm," his lips grazed her shoulder, and she paused her frantic search of the drawer, eyes closing in pleasure. "Maybe I could watch sometime."

"Jeff!" Shocked, she gave a snort of laughter.

"All sorts of thoughts have been running through my head since our date," he admitted, his breath sliding over her shoulder as he grazed up the nape of her neck. "I've tortured myself with fantasies of doing all sorts of things to you and with you. Playing Tic-Tac Toe on your stomach with chocolate sauce. Making sundaes with whipped cream and strawberries on your breasts. Sipping champagne from your belly button. Drizzling syrup across your thighs, taking my time licking it off."

"Jeff."

His name broke on her lips as she melted back into her pillow. "Check the other drawer."

He rolled to his left. After a moment, he started to laugh. Did she leave another toy on that side? "What is it?"

"I told you Lawrence was trying to earn his wings." He showed her a box of condoms with a sticky note attached. Thought these might come in handy. Law was scribbled on it in screaming red ink.

"Somehow I don't think this is on the list of what angels are supposed to earn wings for," she said, unable to resist stroking a hand down his chest as he ripped open the box. My God, abs like those were only seen in magazines.

He sucked in a breath as her hand skimmed over first one nipple then the other. "Why not?" he asked, his breath ragged as he retrieved one shiny packet and tossed the box on the nightstand. "This—" he reached over, cupping her breast— "is as close to heaven as a man can get while alive."

He readied himself then rose above her, kneeing her legs apart. She reached for the lamp, but he clamped down on her wrist. "Leave it," he growled, "so I know this isn't a dream."

Her nipples hardened into painful peaks as he lowered himself enough to kiss her. His sheathed arousal pressed close to her, making her restless for fulfillment. Their lips met, tongues dancing in a simulation of the ritual as old as time. She nipped his bottom lip, arching against him in blatant invitation. They groaned in unison as their nipples brushed together. It seemed as if their whole bodies were kissing.

"Now," she whispered.

All at once he surged into her, hard and deep. She arched again, a low sigh of pleasure bubbling from her at being filled at last. He kept her wrists pinned above her head, so she wrapped her legs around his waist, settling him deeper with an appreciative groan.

"Christ, Angie," he breathed, muscles shaking with the effort to keep still. "You feel so damn good."

"So do you..." Her breath stuttered away as he slowly withdrew until just the tip remained inside, then just as slowly flowed back in to the hilt. He repeated the sensuously measured stroke once, twice, three times until she commenced a constant moan.

The light, the room, everything dimmed around her as Jeff continued his erotic assault, shortening his retreat and advance to build a cresting wave of desire. Eyes locked to his, she rode the wave, matching the pace he set, chanting appreciation with each thrust.

He released her hands suddenly, reaching down to lift her hips. She pulled him to her, wrapping arms and legs about him, their mouths imitating the movements below. Nothing mattered save reaching that glorious plane of ecstasy. He drove into her hard, as hard as she rose to meet him, colliding in a frenzied dance. "Yes, oh God, yes... "

Ecstasy burst upon her, launching her like fireworks into an exploding freefall. She dimly felt Jeff surge against her once more, a harsh sound tearing from him as he found his own release.

Her last coherent thought was never wanting to awaken from this dream.

Eleven

Angela refused to awaken from the most erotic dream of her life.

She lay in the center of a pile of pillows, an ocean breeze washing over her heated skin. Her dream lover kissed her hello with an insistent pull at one breast, then the other, while his hand blazed down her belly to the juncture of her thighs. Questing fingers sought her center, found it, made it weep in sheer delight. Diving, thrusting, curving into the secret lagoon. One brush, one thorough stroke sent her spiraling up from the depths of slumber to wakefulness, to the sublime pleasure beyond.

It took a long while to drag her eyes open. Her dream lover sat beside her on the bed, grinning at her with a sensual twist of lips that had her stomach clenching in renewed need. "Good morning."

She realized that she lay sprawled and naked on her bed like a woman who had just been thoroughly...oh, wait. She had.

A blush crept up her cheeks and she reached for the covers. "Morning." She looked at the sunlight spilling into the room. "What time is it?"

"Eight-thirty."

"Eight-thirty? Oh my God!" Heedless of her nakedness, she leapt out of bed. "I'm late—I can't believe I'm late! I have to call Yvonne, the pediatrician. Kayleigh—why didn't Kayleigh wake me up? Oh God, is something wrong—"

She crashed into six-feet, five-inches of male muscle and bounced off, slightly dazed.

"Angie." His arms gripped her shoulders. "Calm down. Kayleigh is fine despite her cold. She's had her morning bottle and diaper change and is safely tucked in her crib." He nodded to the monitor on the nightstand. "I already called Lawrence and cleared your staying home with Kayleigh if that's what you want to do. And the pediatrician's office called to confirm the appointment for eleven a.m."

He'd taken care of all that? "Why didn't you wake me?"

The dark molasses of his eyes softened as he cupped her cheek. "Because you needed the rest, especially since you slept through the phone and Kayleigh waking up."

His hands slipped down, cupping her bare buttocks. "Now please take pity on me and go take a shower before I throw you back on the bed."

Jeff hid a smile as her eyes widened in surprise before she broke away from him and sprinted for the bathroom. He enjoyed the view until she slammed the door behind her, then went to gather Kayleigh and head downstairs to make breakfast.

Securing Kayleigh in her swing, he flipped the radio on

then began to rummage in the fridge for breakfast fixin's. Eggs, cheese, fresh vegetables and fruits, all neatly arranged. He recognized Law's handiwork and grinned. Maybe he'd go out and buy Law a set of wings himself, he thought as he set supplies on the counter to prepare omelets. Law deserved them, especially for last night.

He closed his eyes as the memory of Angela's anguish washed over him. Never, ever did he want to hear that kind of helpless fear in her voice again. Never wanted to see that look of despair as she talked about her perceived failures.

How in the hell could she think of herself as a failure? Angela had overcome her divorce, her cousin's death, instant motherhood, her mother's attempts to take Kayleigh. She'd endured and persevered. If that wasn't success, what was it?

God, the need to comfort her had been overwhelming, as overwhelming as the need to touch her, taste her, take her. Even though it had been a year, he knew that they'd never had a night together like last night. Hopefully it heralded the first of many nights together.

Waking up next to her gave him a sense of rightness he hadn't felt in a long time. Taking care of Kayleigh while Angela caught up on her sleep made it easy to create the fantasy of family. He didn't care if it lacked machismo; it felt good to be needed. He'd always been the champion, the defender, the protector. Being the oldest of eight, it came naturally to him. Even now, it was the only way he knew to be.

Going off to college had been a wrenching experience.

Guilt had beat at him relentlessly, knowing in his gut that he should have been home taking care of the family as he'd always done, even when his father still lived. The ease with which his brothers and sisters had gotten along without him had unnerved him.

Then Mike's first wife had been killed in college, and Jeff was there for his best friend. When Mike buried his hurt beneath a what-the-hell player attitude, Jeff was right there with him. The rebellious, responsibility-free years had been exhilarating for a while, but he quickly became restless.

So it had been something of a godsend when Yvonne decided to move to Atlanta in an effort to leave her painful past behind. Relinquishing his position as her protector when she fell in love with Mike, as the one she chose to turn to, proved more than difficult two years ago. He'd reacted badly then, out of misguided fear of losing Vonne, using everything from Mike's player past to the stresses of interracial relationships to break them apart. That fear had even convinced him, for a little while, that he was in love with Yvonne.

God, even after helping mend what he'd tried so hard to destroy, he'd felt so lost. Angela had been a lifeline, and their year together had been wonderful. He'd wanted Angela to need him. Hell, he'd even asked her what she wanted from him. But she tended towards independence like her cousin, not wanting or needing anyone for anything, always keeping him at arms' length.

Things were different now. They had to be after last

night. Angela had needed him. She'd called him for help and he'd given it, comforting her and Kayleigh. Hopefully in the process he'd shown her that he could be depended upon, that he would be there when she needed him.

He was determined to let her know in no uncertain terms that he was here to stay. He'd cleared the first hurdle. Angela'd let him back into her bed. It would be just a matter of time before she let him back into her heart. Their futures were combined now.

The idea kept him smiling and humming until Angela finally appeared. One look at her told him that she regretted their night together.

For one thing she'd chosen to dress all in black—jacket, blouse, pants, shoes. For another she avoided eye contact with him as if he didn't exist. She went straight to the swing and lifted Kayleigh into her arms, checking for herself how the baby fared.

"She's fine," he felt the need to reassure her. He poured a cup of coffee, fixed it to her liking, and held it out. "Here."

With Kayleigh balanced on one hip she came toward him, reaching for the cup. Their hands met, then their gazes. Just a brief glance before hers skittered away. "Thanks."

She retreated—an appropriate word—to the breakfast table. "Was she fussy?" she asked, holding the baby like a shield before her. "Did she take her bottle okay?"

"Her fever's down," he answered, sliding the second omelet onto a plate and bringing both to the table. "She didn't finish all of her bottle, but she got a good bit of it down.

I think she's a lot better."

"You should have woke me up," she insisted, placing Kayleigh in her carrier. "You didn't have to do all this."

Did she mean fixing breakfast or all of it? "You were exhausted," he pointed out. "Besides, I wanted to do this for you."

Angela felt her heart leap into her throat at his quiet words. She didn't think she could handle this. Jeff here, in her house, taking care of Kayleigh, fixing her breakfast. Leaving his mark on her skin, her senses, her heart.

Every rule she'd made to protect herself against this lay in tatters. Fear and desperation had compelled her to call him last night, hoping that he would come riding to her rescue.

Rescue her he did, with his confidence and comfort. God, his comfort. He'd given it and she'd taken it, greedily, again and again. Three or four times, each more tender than the last.

Where the hell had her willpower gone? How easily she'd relinquished control—her common sense, her niece, her body. The seeming familial perfection of the situation would have given her fits of hysteria if she weren't so damn scared. What was supposed to happen now? And how could she protect her heart?

"Angie."

"What?" Her voice sounded like cotton crammed her throat.

"Please don't do this."

"Do what?" she asked, knowing it was stupid but wanting to stave off the confrontation for as long as possible.

"Don't regret this. Don't make our time together seem like a bad thing."

"I shouldn't have let it happen," she said past the sudden lump in her throat. Her appetite nonexistent, she pushed her plate away and concentrated on holding back tears. "I should have let you sleep on the sofa like you wanted."

The light dimmed in his eyes, and she knew she'd hurt his feelings. "Why? We both needed each other last night. You think I'm going to walk away now? You think I got what I wanted so now I'll just leave?"

She looked at the butchered remains of her breakfast. So many things scared her right then. Her reaction to him, his motives for wanting her, her weakness, and her gift for failure.

"Listen to me, Angie." He reached for her hand. "I'm here. I'm not going anywhere. And I'm not going to hurt you."

"You can't make that kind of promise, Jeff," she managed to say, her throat squeezed tight. "Nobody can."

For a long moment his hand lay on top of hers. Then he pulled it back, and it felt as if he pulled away emotionally as well.

"Jeff—"

"All I want is a chance," he interrupted. "Whether we end as friends, go back to where we were before, or move beyond it, I want us to take that chance. I want you to take that chance. It's up to you."

"All right." She didn't know whether she meant it as an acknowledgment or agreement.

He relaxed by visible degrees, finally giving her a smile. "Will you do something for me?"

The quiet question had her freezing in place, coffee mug to her lips. She was instantly wary. "Do what?"

"I'd like a favor. Don't answer right away; just think about it."

"Think about what?" She couldn't keep the suspicion from her voice.

His smile dimmed. "I want you and Kayleigh to spend Thanksgiving with me and my family."

"Oh." She didn't know what to make of his offer. Holidays ceased being fun a long time ago, thanks to her mother. Even two years ago, when she and Jeff were supposedly together, they'd spent Thanksgiving and Christmas apart. She and Shayla had treated holidays as days off that they spent anywhere but home, especially since her parents often went on cruises. Thanksgiving shopping and parade-watching in New York City, skiing in Colorado, sunning in Puerto Vallarta—all were preferable to staying home alone or spending time with Marie Davenport.

What would it be like, she wondered, to be part of a big family gathering? Like the Cosby Show? Food, family, football, and fun? She was tempted, so very tempted.

But why would Jeff invite her now? He hadn't invited her two years ago, when they were as officially a couple as could be claimed, which should have been a clue to her about the life-span of their relationship. But if lack of invitation meant lack of commitment then, what did receiving an invite mean now? She suddenly felt as if she stood atop a large precipice, staring into a foaming whirlpool far below.

"Angie."

He reached out again, clasping her hand in his. "You're over-thinking this. I'm not asking you to saw off your arm. You told me your parents are cruising in Cozumel until just after the holiday, and I just thought that you and Kayleigh might enjoy yourselves. And you can trade baby horror stories with my sister and sisters-in-law."

He leaned closer. "The family is mostly harmless until we get a spades game together. Then we're worse than a wrestling show."

A smile quirked her lips. "Now that would be something worth seeing."

"Then you'll come?"

She took a deep breath, then jumped. "Yes. We'll come."

"I can't do this!"

"Of course you can," Lawrence soothed her, Kayleigh balanced expertly on his knee. "It's just Thanksgiving, not state dinner at the White House."

Angela gave him a baleful look. "You're not helping.

And quit bouncing her like that. You'll make her throw up."

"She won't throw up on me," Law boasted. "Will you, girl? Of course not, my little princess wouldn't do that." His voice trailed off into cooing baby conversation that made Angela roll her eyes.

"This is a big deal. I've never met his family before." She threw a sweater on the bed and reached into the closet for another. "What about this?"

He barely gave it a glance. "Too glitzy."

"This?"

"Is your name 'Sister Angela'?"

"Ooh." She threw the blouse on the floor. "Why are you even here?"

"I'm asking myself the same thing," Law admitted. "I left my perfectly fine man and a baking turkey to help a thirty-two-year-old woman decide what to wear for Thanksgiving dinner. It must be for moral support."

"You call this moral support?" She threw a hand up, gesturing at the disaster area that used to be her bedroom. "Jeff is going to be here in—oh my God, in fifteen minutes—and I'm still standing here in my underwear."

"I noticed."

"Lawrence!"

He rose, tucking Kayleigh under one arm. "Hey, I'm gay, not blind. Besides, I designed that cami set." He tugged on one strap. "Why the freak out? You never had a problem with what to wear before."

"Well, this is different."

Law's glance conveyed his understanding. "This means a lot to you, doesn't it?"

"No, it doesn't."

Even if she couldn't translate his look, she could translate his snort. "Oh all right," she admitted, exasperated. "Of course it's a big deal."

She rubbed her arms with a nervous gesture. "The last time Jeff and I were together, spending the holidays as a couple didn't even come up. Shay and I did our annual trip to New York for the parade and shopping. At Christmas I was so exhausted from dealing with the stores, I couldn't deal with going anywhere or doing anything. I think Jeff and I exchanged presents Christmas night and then we spent New Year's Eve together. We never even talked about our families to each other."

Law shook his head. "I don't get y'all. You're so into each other, yet you don't know a thing about each other."

"See?" Angela felt her lips curve into a smile although she didn't feel the least bit humorous. "Like I've been trying to tell you and that match-making boss of ours, what Jeff and I have is nothing more than—" she broke off, staring at Kayleigh. "It's nothing more than S-E-X."

"Well, if that's all, then you certainly don't need to impress his mother." Kayleigh balanced on one hip, Lawrence surveyed the wreckage of her closet. "How many people are going to be there?"

"With us, there'll be thirteen adults and five kids."

"The black Brady Bunch, huh? Well, I don't think you

can go wrong with comfortable jeans and a sweater. Course, if you'll be too nervous to get your eat on, you can wear your really tight jeans."

Angela could feel her stomach churning higher. "I am nervous, but I'm not going to wear tight jeans. If I don't eat, his mother will think I'm uppity. And if I wear those jeans, his mother will know I'm uppity."

"You? Uppity?"

Only the fact that he held Kayleigh kept her from hitting him. "Lawrence Brendan Williams, you get out of my house this instant!"

"Okay, okay, don't turn all Momma-in-the-hood on me. What's Thanksgiving like with the Maxwell clan?"

"Jeff told me that it's real casual. They always play touch football before dinner, which is usually about three. Then it's cards and football before dessert and decorating the Christmas tree."

"That's downright Norman Rockwellian," Lawrence said after a low whistle.

"I know," Angela said, thrusting her legs into a pair of black jeans, frowning over the loose fit. "I don't know if that's reassuring or terrifying."

He handed her an aqua cashmere turtleneck, her power color. Lord knows she could use every mental support she could get. In the week since Jeff had issued the invitation she had vacillated between thinking it was a good thing to it being a recipe for disaster. She wanted to know more about Jeff and his family. She was almost desperate to know what made him tick.

And if that meant submitting herself to the Grand Inquisition, so be it.

"Have I not been feeding you?" Lawrence asked, giving her a critical glance. "Or are you trying to become a super-model?"

"I'm taking care of a five-month-old, or have you forgotten that bundle of joy hanging on your hip?" Angela shoved the hem of her turtleneck into the top of her jeans. "Who has time to eat?"

"Especially when your free time is spent having S-E-X."

"Law!" Embarrassment had her suddenly close to tears.

"Hey, hey, what's this?" Law put Kayleigh in her carrier as Angela sat on the bed, covering her face with her hands. Arms went around her. "Hey, I'm just teasing you."

"But you're right. Oh God, you're so right. I shouldn't be doing this. There are so many reasons why I shouldn't be doing this."

"Name one."

She rolled her eyes. "There's the biggest one, right there," she said, pointing at Kayleigh. "My time should be devoted to her, not myself."

"Angie, Kayleigh is an important part of your life, but you can't deny yourself the opportunity to live. Shayla wouldn't want you to do that."

"I don't know," she whispered. "Shayla seemed so bound and determined to go through it alone."

"Angie," Law's voice was low. "Forgive me for pointing

out the obvious, but you're not Shayla. You don't have to go through life alone."

She put the heel of her hand to her mouth to staunch the sob that threatened to break. "But I'm not alone, am I? She's always going to be a part of my life. She's going to always come first. Every decision I make, I have to consider Kayleigh first."

"You could give her up."

It was all she could do to keep her jaw from hitting the floor, she was so shocked. "What?"

"Don't look so surprised," he said with uncharacteristic snappishness. "You know you've thought about it more than once. How easy would you have it if Kayleigh weren't in your life? Didn't your mother try to take her off your hands?"

Anger had her clenching her fists. "Kayleigh is not something you hand off like an old sweater." Defensively, she picked the infant up, cradling her on her shoulder. "I'm not giving her up. Not for anyone, certainly not for Jeff."

"I don't recall him asking you to."

"He hasn't," she admitted. "He wants to be a father to Kayleigh. Or at least he did."

"And why is that a bad thing?"

"It's not." She hesitated.

"The look on your face says otherwise."

"I don't know about him, Law. I don't trust him, his apology, or his reasons. I don't know why he's here, why he's with me."

"Ask him."

"I can't ask him that." The very idea had her heart pounding in her chest.

"Why not?"

"Because I don't want to know."

"Women." He rolled his eyes.

"That's a sexist comment, surprising coming from a man who used to do drag shows."

"Hey, I still have a Y chromosome in here somewhere. I can tell you, it makes men do stupid things sometimes. Even I need things spelled out occasionally."

Angela began shoving the mound of clothing back into her closet. "I'm beginning to think I'm losing my mind. I make decisions every day that affect hundreds of people and millions in profit without a second thought. But I'm terrified of this dinner, of making a mistake."

"With Jeff?"

"With Jeff. With Kayleigh. With my heart."

The words hung in the air between them. Law gave her a look full of sympathy. "You've fallen in love with him again, haven't you?"

"No," she denied, a trembling hand wiping tears from her eyes. "I never fell out of love with him. I never stopped loving him, even when I hated him."

"Then tell him."

"I can't." She shook her head, more tears spilling down her cheeks. "Not until I know he loves me for me, and not because Kayleigh needs a father or because he can't have Yvonne. I need to hear the words from him, believe them.

And right now I can't do anything else. I can't make the first move."

"Angie, Angie." Law clucked his tongue as he grabbed a tissue from the nightstand and dried her cheeks. "I don't blame you for not wanting to lay everything on the line. For what it's worth, I agree with you."

That surprised her. "You do?"

"Of course. I know this isn't easy for you, not by a long-shot. But I do have some advice, if you want it."

"No thanks."

"Too bad." He picked up Kayleigh's carrier. "You're going to get it anyway."

She followed him downstairs, gathering her composure with every step. She flopped onto the couch, blowing her bangs from her forehead. "All right, O great gay swami. Dispense your nuggets of wisdom."

"I'm keeping my nuggets to myself."

She just looked at him.

"Okay, maybe not completely to myself. But here's my advice: relax."

"Relax?" She could feel her eyes bulging. "Are you kidding me? This is your sage advice?"

"No, I'm not, and yes, it is." He placed the baby carrier on the coffee table. "Relax and be yourself. It's Thanksgiving dinner with thirteen adults and a handful of kids. There's nothing formal about it. Take each moment as it comes, and enjoy yourself."

He retrieved the baby bag and set it next to Kayleigh. "I

think Jeff used up his quota of stupidity over the last two years; it won't take him long to smarten up. Besides, isn't this the time of year for miracles?"

He pulled out his keys, then gave her a kiss on the forehead. "I better get back to my boo and my bird. I'm wishing you good luck, but I don't think you're going to need it."

"Thanks, Law. You always know what to say."

"I do, don't I? I guess that makes me a cunning linguist."

"Oh, you!"

With a laugh, she pushed him out the door then returned to the couch, her mind whirling. She settled back with a sigh. If she'd had any sense, any shred of intelligence at all, she would have said no to Thanksgiving dinner, and no to the ecstasy she found in Jeff's arms. She should have said no the first time, the eighth time—hell, even last night.

God! It had been a long and lonely year. He was right, her body had remembered the joy he could bring her. By the light of day it scared her senseless. But at night she threw her brain and propriety out the window, giving in to pure unbridled satisfaction.

She could get used to this, she knew. She could give in to the fantasy Jeff created and gave life to each day. Every morning he would arrive, sharing breakfast with her and Kayleigh before chauffeuring them to work and nursery. The process was repeated after work, with dinner at home, or out. There was never a shortage of sitters for Kayleigh, with Law and Yvonne leading the pack, wanting to give them time alone together. They didn't call in those offers often; though unspoken, she enjoyed it when they worked together to prepare Kayleigh for bed, and as he'd never turned down the offer, Angela felt Jeff enjoyed it as well.

One thing that surprised her was that he never assumed they'd end up in bed together. Despite the need she saw when she looked at him, he waited for her invitation. And even though she wanted it badly, he never stayed the full night since Kayleigh's illness.

He was so different from the Jeff she knew—or thought she knew. Thoughtful, considerate from the first, showering Kayleigh with gifts and offering to watch the baby while Angela spent some quality time alone.

Thoughtful. Attentive.

Dangerous.

The door chime had her heart leaping into her throat. With a quick glance at Kayleigh, Angela went to open the door. Jeff was dressed in jeans, sneakers and a rugby-style shirt beneath his leather jacket. "Thank God."

He frowned. "What is it? Is something wrong with the baby?"

"No, nothing's wrong." She stepped back, allowing him to enter. "I'm just glad you're in jeans."

He gave her a thorough kiss hello after shutting the door. "I'm planning on major flag football. I do have sweats in the car for dinnertime. Momma throws down when it comes to holiday spreads."

His gaze traveled slowly from her jeans-clad legs, resting long enough on her turtleneck to cause her nipples to tighten in reaction. "I'm glad you're in jeans too," he said, his voice husky. "Very glad."

"D-don't look at me like that," she stammered, heat creeping up her neck. "We don't have time for that right now."

"I'll always have time for you, Angie."

The words rang with such sincerity that her breath caught. The look in his eyes gave further truth to his words, causing her heart to flutter like a trapped butterfly. "Thanks," she whispered, not knowing what else to say. Law's words rang in her mind. Maybe it was a time for miracles. Maybe it was time to hope.

Twelve

Jeff drummed his fingers on the steering wheel as they whizzed down the highway south of Atlanta.

"Where do your parents live?" Angela asked, turning back from checking on Kayleigh.

"It's just my mother now, but Catrina and Jason still live at home until they finish college. We bought her a place on the Southside."

"We?"

"The older kids—me, Cassie, Justin, and Julian—bought her a new place about eight years ago. We should be there in another fifteen minutes or so."

She turned the radio to a hip-hop station. "Do all the boys' names start with J?"

"You noticed that, huh?" He gave her a quick smile. "The boys are all J's and the girls are all C's. There's me, then Julian, Cassandra, Justin, Caitlyn, Jonathan, Jason, then Catrina."

"Oh God," she groaned. "I'm not going to be able to remember everybody."

Keeping his left hand firmly on the wheel, he reached out

with his free hand to clasp hers. "No one will expect you to. Not on the first visit anyway. Cassandra is right after me, and she goes by Cassie. She's the most outgoing of us all. Caitlyn is more quiet, she's the pediatrician, remember?"

When she nodded, he continued, "She goes by Lyn. Catrina is the baby of the family at eighteen, and we call her Trina. Julian is the next oldest son after me, and he can be stuffy at times. If you think I'm uptight, wait 'til you meet him."

"I don't think you're uptight," she told him. "Quite the opposite, actually."

Was that a good thing? He wondered. Probably not, considering the hard time he continued to have convincing her that he was in it for the long haul.

He darted a quick glance at her. "I guess I'll have to do a better job convincing you of how responsible I can be."

She was silent, so he went on. "You'll probably recognize Justin when you see him, and Jonathan is the youngest son, still at home until he gets his degree."

"Okay, so that's ten adults. Who are the others?"

"Jules' wife Natalie, Cassie's husband Sam, and Lyn's fiancé Peter. I think Trina may have an exchange student friend staying over the holidays with her."

A groan answered him. "I can do this. I'm vice president of a multi-million-dollar firm. I fly all over the world and speak three languages. I can do this."

"Of course you can," he assured her, lifting her hand to his lips for a quick kiss. "They'll welcome you with open arms. And if all else fails, just let Kayleigh become the center of attention. She probably will be anyway."

The hand clasped in his, closed into a fist. "What did you tell your family about us? I mean, about me and Kayleigh?"

He exited the highway and merged onto the street before answering. "Momma knows everything of course. Everybody else just knows I'm bringing someone to dinner."

What he didn't tell her was how big a deal her presence would be. Of course Mike had been over all the time in high school, and his mother had all but adopted Yvonne when she moved here. But there was one unspoken rule that he and his siblings adhered to: no one brought a date to holiday family gatherings unless they were serious. Cassie had done it with Sam, Jules had followed with Natalie, and they'd met Lyn's fiancé at the Fourth of July gathering.

Now he was bringing Angela.

His family would take Angela's visit as a sign—exactly what he wanted them to think. They would try to put Angela at ease, but they would all be extremely interested in the first woman he'd ever brought to meet the family. And somewhere between hello and dessert, his mother would take Angela aside for a heart-to-heart talk. It would either go well or it wouldn't. Jules' first fiancé hadn't fared well, and they'd broken up before the next family gathering. The first guy Cassie brought home didn't even make it past him and his brothers.

A knot twisted in his stomach. Angela was strong and

gentle, kind and acerbic. She would hold her own, but if talk turned to the future, what would she say? Sure, she'd let him back into her life, and into her bed, but he still wasn't in her heart. There was a strong possibility that their fledgling relationship would end tonight.

His hands bunched into fists. He couldn't let that happen. Angela was meant for him. He knew it. He'd convince his family, and he'd convince her.

"Jeff, you plan on breaking my hand?"

Chagrined, he released her. "Sorry about that."

"You know, you might have broken it. Maybe we should stop by a hospital and have it examined."

He laughed. "You're not getting out of this that easily. Just be yourself and have a good time."

Slowing, he turned the car into a gated subdivision. He heard Angela's audible swallow. "You guys bought your mother a house here?"

"Yeah." Rolling down the window, he punched a code into the control box and waited for the gate to swing open. He drove through, taking a right. "Momma deserved it. She and Dad worked hard to provide for us, and she worked even harder after he died. Giving her a house and coming home for the holidays is the least we can do."

"Your mother must be very proud of all of you."

"She is," he answered truthfully. "And if you give her a moment, she'll tell you just how proud she is. Our parents urged us to be the best we could be; we couldn't do anything else but honor that."

"It sounds like you have a wonderful family."

"Don't get me wrong, we're not 'The Cosby Show.' We fought like cats and dogs, but if anyone messed with one of us, they messed with all of us."

"You family must be very important to you."

He heard the wistfulness in her voice and it pulled at him. "Family is the most important thing there is," he whispered. "I'd do anything for my family." And I want you to be part of it, he thought to himself.

He parked the car by the mailbox, then came around to help her out. Her mouth dropped open as she stared up at the house. "Oh my God."

A sigh of pride sifted from him as he stood beside her, gazing up at the impressive house. Maxwell Manor, they called it: a three-story brick with columns, a sweeping, land-scaped yard, and palladium windows. The running joke was that they'd lose the kids inside during a game of hide and seek.

"It's formal and informal," he reassured her as he opened the rear door, handing her the diaper bag before turning to retrieve a sleeping Kayleigh. "Momma always had a way with turning a house into a home. She could host a state dinner or a barbecue without batting an eye."

With Kayleigh in her carrier in one hand, he reached for Angela's with the other and started up the sloping driveway. The garage doors were down and four other cars and an SUV filled the drive. "Looks like the gang's all here."

Angela began to drag her feet, lagging behind him. "Are

you sure I can't convince you to take me home?"

"Trust me," he said, pulling her closer. "You'll enjoy yourself. None of my brothers and sisters bite anymore."

She swallowed audibly. "Anymore?"

"I'm teasing you, Angie." He reached out, kissing her. "Just relax."

"Okay." She gave him a tremulous smile. "Will you kiss me again?"

"Absolutely."

"Hey! Cut that out!"

Jeff jumped away from her and turned to the door. Justin stood in the doorway, smiling. "Hey, man," he said to Jeff, offering his fist for a tap. He then gave Angela that slow look that all men use when they're undressing women in their minds. "Momma said you were bringing a date, but she didn't say it was Miss America."

Irritation had Jeff frowning, and it didn't help that Angela was smiling back at his brother as if she'd never been complimented before.

"Lay off for one day, will ya?" He turned to Angela, bringing her to the door. "Angie, this is my second younger brother, Justin. Justin, this is Angela. And this," he held up the carrier, "is Kayleigh."

For once, Justin was speechless. It only lasted a moment. "You been holding out on us."

Angela stepped forward. "Kayleigh isn't—"

"And what if I was?" Jeff interrupted her, giving his brother a hard look.

Justin threw up his hands. "Okay, your turn to chill, unless you can back that talk up."

Jeff took a step forward. "Oh I can back it up, believe me. Just like I always have."

"Is that testosterone in the air, or just a bunch of bull?"

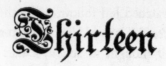

Thirteen

Angela watched as a slender woman with shoulder-length micro-braids shoved Justin out of the way. "You two could at least let people in before you start laying it on." She stuck out her hand to Angela, her grin quick and easy. "I'm Cassie."

Shifting the diaper bag, Angela took the proffered hand with relief. "I'm Angela."

"Welcome to the madhouse, also known as Maxwell Manor. "I see you've met Justin. You'll discover that the Maxwell men are all like that. Ooh. And who's this?"

Angela answered before Jeff could. "This is my niece, Kayleigh."

Cassie took the carrier from Jeff. "Take the hormones out back, boys. The others already have the ball out. I'll take Angela around and get Kayleigh settled with the rest of the little people."

A frisson of fear skittered down her back. It must have been written all over her face, because Jeff touched her arm and asked, "Are you cool with this?"

Most definitely not, but she nodded anyway. "Go on, I'll

see you later."

As she watched Jeff follow his brother down a hallway, Angela wondered if it would be rude to turn and bolt. Before she could suit thought to action, Cassie threaded her arm through Angela's, effectively imprisoning her.

"You'll have to excuse the men, and I use that term loosely." Cassie gave her a wry grin. "They have this rivalry over who can make more money for the family. But it probably had a lot to do with the way Justin was looking at you."

"Oh my God." Angela clapped a hand to her forehead. "That was Justin Maxwell, the lead singer of Knightfall."

"In the flesh. I guess you've heard of them?"

"Heard of them? They're the best thing since Boys II Men. No wonder Jeff said I'd recognize him."

"Then I guess I'd better warn you right now, we're a family of over-achievers." Cassie led her deeper into the spacious home. "You got Jeff and his mutual funds, Justin and his band. Julian's an orthopedic surgeon, Lyn's a pediatrician, and Jon plays baseball. Jason's going to law school, and Trina's in her freshman year at Spelman."

The acid in Angela's stomach kicked into high production. "I probably don't want to know, but what do you do?"

Cassie laughed. "My husband Sam and I have a veterinary practice, and I do pet portraits on the side."

Yep, she was definitely at the wrong party, Angela thought. She made a grab for the handle of the baby carrier. "Excuse me, I'll just be leaving now."

"Oh no you don't." Cassie gave her a gentle push the last

few steps down the hall. "Being vice-president over at Gemini Enterprises is nothing to sneeze at. Besides, five minutes here and you'll think we've all just been voted off an island."

Right. This family probably had the collective income of a third-world country. Where did she fit in?

"Give us a chance," Cassie pleaded. "Momma's dying to meet you."

"She is?" Angela heard her voice rise an octave or two before cracking.

"Of course. Jeff's never brought anyone to a family gathering before, so we're all curious about you."

Turn around, Angela thought to herself. Just grab the baby and run. She won't tackle you if you're holding Kayleigh. You can just kill Jeff later.

"Cassie?" a feminine voice called. "I just saw Jeff. Is his lady friend with you?"

"Yes, Momma. We'll be right there." Cassie's free hand locked on Angela's elbow, dragging her forward into an airy, two-story room. Five women sat on sage-colored furniture. A boy and girl, no more than eight, played checkers while two toddlers played keep-away with a ball in the center of the floor.

Every one of them swiveled their heads to face her as she and Cassie entered the room. She froze, resisting the urge to flee. Damn Jeff for leaving her to face this alone!

"This is Angela," Cassie said, giving her another subtle push. "And this is Kayleigh. Angela, from left to right are my baby sister Trina, her friend Paula, my sister-in-law Natalie, and my sister Lyn. And this gorgeous woman is our mother, Ida."

Angela forgot the other women in an instant as she focused her attention on the Maxwell matriarch. "Hello, ma'am."

Ida Maxwell looked to be in her mid-fifties, tall and round with gorgeous salt-and-pepper hair framing bright brown eyes in a laugh-lined face. "If you remember everyone's names, you get a prize," the older woman said with a gentle smile. "I gave birth to half of them, and even I have difficulty keeping them straight."

Sitting, Ida patted the vacant spot beside her on the couch. Angela placed the diaper bag on the floor before taking her designated place as Cassie set the carrier on the marbled coffee table. Ida peeked in on Kayleigh, who was beginning to stir at last. "May I?"

Like she was going to say no? Angela nodded. "Of course."

Jeff's mother unfastened the straps with deft hands, lifting the baby out of the carrier. Angela had stressed over Kayleigh's outfit even more than she had her own. She'd settled on a burgundy velour jumper and a white turtleneck printed with a falling leaf pattern, thermal undies, booties, too many blankets and a white lace headband. She looked adorable. Like an Eskimo, but adorable.

"What a precious little girl. What did you say her name is?"

"Kayleigh," she answered, sitting beside the older woman. "She's five months now—almost six, actually."

Once she started talking, she couldn't stop the flood. "She's my niece—actually my cousin's daughter. I'm her guardian. Her mother died giving birth to her."

A chorus of sympathetic sounds filled the air. One of the women, tall and slender, approached them and plucked Kayleigh from Ida's lap. From the way she examined Kayleigh, Angela assumed she was the pediatrician, Lyn.

"Instant motherhood can't be easy," she said at last, "but it looks as if both of you have adjusted well."

"Thanks. But there are days when I want to scream."

"I dreamed of escaping to a desert island, especially after Demetrius was born," Cassie said, pointing to the preschooler. "And let's not even talk about teething."

The older woman next to Cassie nodded. "It was the same for me when I had Junior," she said, indicating the older boy. "Calgon couldn't take me away often enough. And fair warning: the two's really are terrible."

"That's enough y'all," Ida cut in with a laugh. "You'll scare the poor girl half to death."

"Too late," Angela sighed. Laughter rewarded her.

"Now don't let them fool you," the matriarch said, "they adore their children. And if you noticed, both of them had another. Of course, I had eight, but I wouldn't recommend that to anyone these days. Do you want children of your own?"

What a loaded question. In the warmth of the living

room, Angela believed in the power of family and the creation of dynasties. She had even dreamed of it, during the brief heydays of her marriage to Richard and even during the year with Jeff. Now, fumbling through the motherhood experience with Kayleigh, she doubted she had what it took to be a supermom.

"Momma," the youngest woman exclaimed, "I thought we were going to wait until after dinner to start the Inquisition!"

Breakfast threatened to leave Angela's stomach the same way it had arrived. "She's kidding, isn't she?"

"Of course she is," Cassie hastened to assure her, then spoiled it by adding, "we were going to ply you with alcohol first."

The men arrived then, seven of them trooping in from the back of the house. All were stunning. Four of them had Jeff's ball-player height, one looked like he could stop a freight train with his bare hands, and the last, with his black hair and blue eyes, looked as if he'd stepped out of the pages of International Male.

Jeff came to perch next to her on the arm of the couch. "Has the Grand Inquisition started yet?"

His teasing manner and his presence relaxed her. "No, I think we're waiting for the truth serum to be delivered."

"Momma?"

"Oh, Jeff, we weren't that bad," his mother protested.

Really?" a huge bear of a man asked. "When Cassie brought me home for the first time, I felt I was lucky to leave with my skin intact." He gave Ida a big smack on the forehead to soften his words.

She swatted at him. "Sam, you know my boys gave you a worse time than I did."

"True, but it was worth it." He turned to Angela, sticking out a hand that could grip a basketball with little problem. "I'm Sam, Cassie's better half."

"Excuse me?"

"I mean other half." He gave Angela a wink before turning to placate his wife.

Jeff looped an arm about Angela's shoulders. "We didn't hurt Sam nearly as much as we should have," he confided. "He may be a vet, but he's built like a Mack truck."

He gestured to the other men. "This is Lyn's fiancé Peter, who made the grade at the Fourth of July gathering. You met Justin, behind him is Jonathan and baby brother Jason. And the straggler who doesn't know how to smile is Julian."

Angela committed each name to memory as best she could. Cassie and Sam were going to be easy. So would Peter. Justin she knew, but she had a feeling she would confuse Jason and Jonathan, who looked as if only a year separated them. And Jeff was right. Julian didn't seem capable of smiling until he sat next to his wife.

"Jeff didn't tell us you have a daughter," Julian said, his eyes flicking from her to Kayleigh to Jeff.

So much for waiting for dinner. "No, I don't suppose he would have," she said evenly, more than ready to get the interrogation over and done.

"Kayleigh is Angela's niece," Julian's wife—Natalie—said, putting a hand on her husband's knee. "Angela's her guardian."

That answer didn't seem to mollify him in the least. "So how long have you two been dating?"

Why did he have to make it sound like something dirty? "Jeff and I have known each other for about seven years," she replied, not really answering his question. She wasn't sure that what she and Jeff were doing could be called dating. "He serves as the unofficial CFO of the company I work for."

"Oh yeah," Trina said. She turned to her friend. "It's that lingerie shop we went to last week—Your Heart's Desire."

"I remember her," Justin cut in. "The owner used to be over all the time. What's her name?"

Angela felt her shoulders tighten. "Yvonne Benjamin."

"Oh yeah," the singer nodded. "Cute little thing. How's she doing?"

"She's doing fine," Jeff answered. His voice was calm, but she could feel the tension in his arm. "She married Mike Benjamin two years ago. They've got year-old twin boys now. I think you were on tour, which is why you missed the wedding."

"I know y'all were just friends and all," the youngest man—Jason—said, "but we always thought y'all would get married."

Stomach dropping to her knees, Angela answered before

Jeff could. "So did a lot of people."

"Yvonne was and always will be a good friend," Jeff said evenly. "But she and Mike belong together."

"Mrs. Maxwell," Angela said, standing, "would you mind if I put Kayleigh's bottles in the refrigerator?"

"Of course not. Jeff, why don't you show Angela the way?"

"Sure." He rose, touching her elbow to guide her, but Angela stepped away from him, covering the move by reaching for Kayleigh's bag. As she followed him away from the awkward silence she heard Trina say, "Way to go, dip-weed. You're about as subtle as a freight train."

The kitchen was like the other parts of the house she'd seen: large, airy, and right out of HGTV. Delicious aromas filtered from the stainless steel oven, filling her with a persistent longing for home and hearth.

Angry with herself, she set the diaper bag on the gray marble island, unzipped it with a vicious gesture, then began pulling bottles out. Hands covered hers. "Angie I'm sorry"

"For what?" She spun away from him to open the fridge. She took advantage of its stuffed-to-the-gills interior to conceal her flaming cheeks. "There's nothing to apologize for."

"My brother's big mouth for one thing," he said, his voice sounding right behind her. A hand appeared over her shoulder, holding another bottle. "I know he upset you."

"I'm not upset," she lied through her teeth, shutting the gleaming door harder than she intended. "There's nothing to be upset about. Everybody assumed you were going to marry

Yvonne. Even I did."

He caught her by the shoulders. Anger flared in her, then sputtered away as she regarded the distress in his soft brown eyes. "What can I do to convince you, once and for all, that I'm not in love with her?"

"Stop trying to convince me."

He stepped back from her as if she'd offended him. Maybe she had, if the expression on his face was any indication.

"Look, let's just forget about it, okay?" She spread her hands. "It's Thanksgiving—food, family, and football. Let's just enjoy it and not think about the other stuff."

It took a long moment before he nodded. "Deal. One condition though."

Condition? "What sort of conditions?"

"I want a kiss."

"Right now?"

"Right now." The look on his face dared her to argue. He leaned against the marble and oak island, holding out his arms. "Come here."

One kiss couldn't hurt, and it would prove there were no hard feelings, she thought, moving into his embrace with a cautious glide.

She had reason to be cautious. His hands settled on her hips, fitting her between the hard muscles of his jeans-clad thighs. Lips claimed hers in an implacable melding, pure seduction sweeping over her senses like steam in a sauna.

Yielding to the silent magic of his mouth, she leaned

against him, opening her lips for the conquest of his tongue. In answer, his hands plunged into her back pockets, cupping her buttocks to bring her flush against his rising hardness. If she knew nothing else, she knew he desired her. At the moment, that was perfectly all right.

"Hey! No public displays of affection!"

Cassie's amused voice cut through the heat clouding Angela's senses. Particularly her common ones. Flushing, she broke away from Jeff, putting the island between them.

"Cas, you've got rotten timing," Jeff groused. "Besides, we're not in public."

"You're right." She jumped into her husband's startled arms, braids swinging, and laid a long one on the dazed man. "Now, if we're all through showing off, the Maxwell ladies have accepted the touch football challenge." She paused, giving them both a lascivious look. "Unless there are other games you'd rather play?"

"N-uh, no," Angela said, flushing again. Playing football seemed the perfect answer. Lord knows she needed to go outside and cool off. Anything was preferable to thinking about the force of Jeff's kiss and what had precipitated it.

She soon discovered that touch football was not as gentle as the name implied, given how seriously the Maxwells took it. Julian bowed out, keeping his mother and the kids company on the glassed-in portion of the deck. Jeff and Justin captained each team, and Jeff made sure she was first chosen.

It was a perfect day for Thanksgiving. There had been

enough cool days in October to turn leaves brilliant gold and lustrous copper and every shade in between, and they swirled in the sunlight and the soft breeze like African rhythm dancers. Thin clouds striped the afternoon sky

The Maxwells played fiercely and energetically, cheering and jeering in good-natured competition. Angela gave herself over to the game, knowing Kayleigh was in good hands with Ida Maxwell. She sprinted across the large backyard, waving her hands wildly to signal Jeff that she was open. He saw her and launched the ball into the air.

It could have been a highlight reel. The football sailed toward her, growing larger in her vision with each heartbeat. She threw herself in the air, rewarded by the solid thump of the ball to her chest.

She landed amid whoops and hollers then turned, preparing to run for glory. Without warning something large and hard slammed into her, sending her crashing to the ground, dead weight smothering her.

It took a moment for her dazed senses to recognize Justin staring down at her, his light brown eyes filled with concern. "Are you all right?"

All right? She couldn't seem to catch her breath. Not only was he solidly built, he was gorgeous as well. What do you say when the lead singer of the hottest R&B group around asks if you're all right while lying on top of you? Anybody got a camera?

One moment Justin was there, the next he seemed to be halfway across the yard. Jeff stood over her, hands clenched into fists. It didn't take a mind reader to see that he was extremely pissed off.

"Did he hurt you?" He clearly hoped the answer would be positive.

"No," she answered, reaching for his outstretched hand. "Just knocked the wind out of me."

"You sure?" He helped her to her feet, turning her this way and that as if to determine for himself that she was unharmed. Once accomplished, he set her aside and strode to Justin.

"What the hell do you think this is, Extreme Wrestling?" he demanded. "You could have seriously hurt her!"

"Hey man, it wasn't intentional," Justin protested, dusting himself off.

Jeff stepped forward, and Angela had the certainty that he intended to hit his brother. Anxiety and embarrassment twisted inside her. This wasn't the impression she wanted to make on Ida Maxwell.

She caught his arm. "Jeff, please. I'm okay. Let's not make this an international incident."

The anger in his eyes smoldered a moment longer. He closed his eyes slowly, and just as slowly opened them again. "All right."

"Everybody come wash up," Ida called. "Dinner's just about ready."Angela kept her eyes to the ground, the better not to see everyone staring at her. Who could blame them? On this day of family and food, she'd almost caused two brothers to get into a fight. It couldn't get any worse than this.

Could it?

Fourteen

It could get a lot worse, Angela discovered.

Dinner began just like the Thanksgiving meals she'd seen on television. As head of the family, Jeff gave the blessing, an eloquent speech about family and fellowship. Then everyone went to town on the spread: a whole ham, the largest turkey she'd ever seen, sweet potato casserole and candied yams, collard greens, giblet gravy, dressing, green bean casserole and so many other things. She could swear she heard the table creaking as if it were one dish away from breaking in half.

All in all, the feasting unfolded as a rowdy, raucous affair unlike anything she'd ever witnessed. Everyone seemed to be talking and laughing at once even as they cleaned their plates.

Angela picked at her food, feeling out of place. Thanksgiving with the Maxwells was a far cry from the stilted holiday meals she'd had growing up. Once she reached high school, so many things had stopped. Sunday school, holiday dinners, birthday cakes. Only Christmas remained a big deal in the Davenport home, and thanks to her father.

How many times had she dreamed of being part of a big

family, of celebrating holidays in style? Too many times, too many years to count. Seeing this now, included yet separated, made her uncomfortable. This wasn't hers. This would never be hers.

"Too much, huh?"

Angela turned to Cassie, seated on her left. "What?"

Cassie leaned towards her. "The phenomenon known as Maxwell Mayhem. We never learned how to sit still, much less be quiet. It can be overwhelming to people who haven't been around us."

"I've never been through anything like this before," she admitted. "Holidays just weren't a big deal when I was growing up, and after I got married, we never—" She broke off, revealing more than she'd intended.

Cassie caught it anyway. "You were married before?"

"Yes. I was young. It didn't work out. I got divorced."

"Oh, Angela." Cassie reached over and grabbed her hand. "I would say I'm sorry, but I'm not."

Expecting empty sympathy, Cassie's words surprised her. "Why?"

"Because if you were still married, you wouldn't be here with my brother."

How true. "Don't read too much into this, Cassie," she suggested. "We've tried this once and it didn't work. Our friendship is barely rebuilt. Jeff and I are a long way away from anything else, if ever."

Just the mention of his name had Angela looking down the length of the table towards him. Jeff sat near the kids' table, and he'd turned to joke with his nephew and niece about something. As usual, he had Kayleigh balanced on his knee, one arm wrapped securely around her.

His love for Kayleigh was so obvious everyone thought he was her father. A bittersweet smile twisted Angela's lips. If only his feelings for her were just as obvious, one way or another.

Her gaze drifted over the table, then skidded to a stop as Julian caught her eye. He wasn't smiling. In fact, he frowned. He'd been nothing but distant and downright rude since he'd met her. Why didn't he like her? She hadn't done anything to him—she didn't even know the man. Why was he looking at her as if she were a lab experiment gone wrong?

Did it matter? a small voice inside her whispered. Of course not. Whether any member of Jeff's family liked her or not was immaterial. She probably wouldn't see any of them again. The idea depressed her further. It would have been nice to have Cassie for a friend.

As dinner wound down, Ida rose, beginning to pick up plates. Angela jumped up with her. "I'll help," she volunteered, feeling the need to offer more than her appetite to the day.

"Thank you." Ida surveyed her family. "The rest of you scatter. Angela and I can take care of this. I know you're dying to start the spades game, and break in that new pool table in the basement."

Angela gathered the ravaged remains of several dishes and followed Ida into the kitchen. They worked in a companionable silence for a moment, Angela following the other woman's directions to retrieve storage containers and bags. She was so lost in her thoughts that she squeaked when Ida finally spoke.

"You know, this is supposed to be the time when I submit you to the third degree. But I'm not going to do that."

That so surprised Angela that she almost dropped a container of yams. "You aren't? Why?"

Ida gave her a gentle smile. "Because I know you aren't ready for that, and I realize you have more questions than I do."

Angela concentrated on stacking one storage container on top of another. It dismayed her that Ida could read her so easily. But the older woman was right. She wasn't ready for this. She doubted she ever could be. And she did have questions zooming through her mind like frenzied mosquitoes. One made it to her lips.

"Are you surprised that Jeff didn't marry Yvonne?"

"I suppose I should be, but I'm not," the matriarch said, rinsing a dish in the sink before placing it in the dishwasher. "I remember when we first met her at the wedding all those years ago. She and Jeff connected immediately. Of course, you know all this, since you work with her."

"I know they've been close for fifteen years," Angela replied, the admission sticking in her throat. "I don't know why they never got together."

"Because she didn't love him that way."

"That I do know. But Jeff seemed to have a difficult time

accepting it."

"Really?" Ida smiled as she ripped a sheet of foil. "Then why did he never propose to her?"

"Because—" Angela clamped her mouth shut. Yvonne had said the same thing, but Angela had dismissed it as a ploy to make her feel better. Ida just confirmed that it wasn't a deception. Why had Jeff never asked Yvonne to marry him? Why? Especially if he was in love with her, right?

His mother moved beside her. "I'm sure you've noticed that Jeff is extremely protective. All my children are, especially when it comes to family. Jeff learned it early, being the oldest. By the time he met Yvonne, being protective was as natural as swimming is to a fish. He couldn't not protect. I'd like to think that becoming an honorary Maxwell helped Yvonne through the darkness she suffered, but it was mostly her friendship with Jeff and her own strength that helped heal her."

Ida put the last of the leftovers into the refrigerator. "Of course, that protective streak gets my boy into trouble sometimes, like when he tried to break Mike and Yvonne up."

"Are you saying that Jeff broke them up because he was feeling protective of Yvonne?"

"Yes. I know that Mike had a good track record with the ladies. What do you young people call it? Being a player. That boy had a lot of hurt and anger in him when his first wife died, and he took it out on the female population—quite well from what I understand. So when Jeff discovered that Mike and Yvonne were seeing each other, it stands to reason that his protective instinct kicked in. It wasn't easy for Jeff trying to choose between his two best friends, but he didn't want Yvonne to be another casualty of Mike's revenge. He knew Mike would probably land on his feet, but Yvonne..." she trailed off.

Angela knew what Ida meant to say. After losing her entire family, it wasn't easy for Yvonne to learn to love again. She'd protected her heart for years until Mike Benjamin came along.

Ida poured herself a cup of coffee. "Of course, love had other plans for those two, thank goodness. If Jeff had known before how deeply they loved each other, he wouldn't have broken them up."

"But he did break them up," Angie felt compelled to point out.

"And put them back together again," Ida insisted. "Believe me, I'm not excusing what he did. Once he realized how they belonged together, he did everything in his power to help them."

"I remember," Angela said, her voice quiet. "But I also remember when Yvonne had the twins, how he reacted then."

Bitter memories welled inside her. "Did he tell you that we were together, the year after Mike and Yvonne got married?"

"I know." Ida's voice seemed to lose the permanent smile it carried.

"And you know why he walked out?"

Ida nodded. "I know Jeff was turned inside out by a lot of things. The fact that he wasn't Yvonne's protector any more was hard for him to let go of. As I said, he takes his responsibilities very seriously."

"What about his responsibility to me?" Angela asked before she could stop herself. "Wasn't I important enough? Didn't I count?"

The older woman fixed her with a stern glare. "If Jeff had asked you to marry him after Yvonne had the twins, would you have said yes?"

"No." There was no point in denying it.

"Why?"

Angela fought not to squirm beneath Ida's piercing gaze. "Because I wouldn't have known if he was asking because he wanted me or because Yvonne was taken. I didn't want to be runner-up."

"Don't you think Jeff knew that?" his mother asked. "Can't you believe him when he says that's part of the reason—the biggest reason—why he had to leave?"

Angela rubbed a fist against her forehead, the strain catching up to her in the form of a blistering headache. "I don't know. I want to trust him. I want to believe in him, and in myself. But I've got much more at stake now, and I can't risk it. I don't want to lose everything and get hurt again."

She broke off, suddenly realizing whom she spoke to. "I'm sorry, Mrs. Maxwell. I shouldn't be talking about Jeff like that. Especially to you."

Ida reached out, taking her hand. "It's all right. Mothers will protect their children, but if they're wrong, they're wrong."

"You think it was wrong for Jeff to leave?"

"No I don't. In fact, I suggested that he leave."

Stunned, Angela could only stare at the older woman. In that moment she didn't know whether to shriek her head off or just leave. This woman bore the responsibility for a great deal of Angela's heartache over the past year. "You told him to leave?"

"I thought he needed to get away for a while," Ida confessed.

When Angela turned away, unable to hear anymore, she added, "He came here the night you walked out on him. I've never seen my son so...lost as he was then. So yes, I suggested he take time off, to clear his head and find his way again. But he'd already made up his mind to go. He told me that he'd hurt people long enough, and he didn't want to hurt any of you anymore."

Angela closed her eyes in pain, her fingers digging into the dishcloth she held. She knew Jeff had told Yvonne and Mike the same thing when he came back. To hear it from his mother was unnerving.

The idea that she'd behaved unfairly towards Jeff was difficult to accept. Was it possible what he felt for Yvonne stemmed from his deep-seated need to protect? Angela knew enough to know that when the two first met, it had been just two years after the accident that claimed Yvonne's parents and twin sister and left her temporarily paralyzed. Knowing everything that Yvonne endured, Angela could understand why Jeff would want to protect her and continued to do so against any threat, even his best friend.

Ida's soft voice intruded on her thoughts. "You were married before?"

How could Cassie have passed that bit of trivia on so fast? "Yes. I got divorced seven years ago."

"Did you want it? The divorce, I mean."

Angela should have walked out then. She would have if she had been able. But Ida's reassuring presence kept Angela rooted. No one had ever asked her about her divorce, and she'd never brought it up. "Sometimes it's not a matter of wanting, but whether it's necessary or not."

Ida's gaze held hers. "Does Jeff remind you of your ex-husband?"

"No. They're miles apart." Thank God.

"It's natural to be cautious after a relationship ends," Ida said quietly. "You think of what you've lost, of what you'll miss, and you think about the mistakes you made and how you wish you could undo them. Hindsight is a necessary thing, but it can also cripple your heart and your future."

"So what are you saying?" Angela asked, feeling her throat tighten. "That I should throw caution to the wind and jump off the cliff, pretending that everything is all right?"

"Of course not. Relax and take each day as it comes, without over-analyzing and overdosing on the hindsight. You just might discover that the cliff isn't as high as you thought it was."

Angela sighed, hanging the dish towel on a hook. "You've given me a lot to think about."

"That's all that I ask," Ida replied, standing back with a satisfied air. "Don't you worry about anything or anyone else. It will work out whatever way it's supposed to."

And what way was that? As far as Angela was concerned, her relationship with Jeff couldn't go much further. Not when it seemed that the only thing it was based on was sex and Jeff's desire to be forgiven. "I'd better check on Kayleigh."

Ida nodded. "She's probably with Trina in the TV room. I don't suppose you know how to play spades?"

"I love that game, but it's been a while since I played."

Ida draped an arm over her shoulders. "Don't worry, we'll have you up to speed in no time. Come downstairs when you're done. You'll be on my team. I'm actually looking forward to trouncing Julian and Justin."

Angela's mood lightened. "Now that sounds like a good idea."

Fifteen

Jeff's mood headed for the toilet, and there was nothing he could do about it.

Between Jonathan's ignorant comment, Justin's continued ogling, and Julian's unspoken disapproval, Jeff's temper simmered like a pressure cooker, needing just one little thing to set it off. And he really, really hoped Julian would provide the one little thing.

Angela had become more withdrawn with every passing moment at dinner. If not for Cassie, he didn't think Angie would have said a word throughout the meal. Yet she volunteered to help his mother put everything away. They were still upstairs in the kitchen while everyone else, knowing the drill, trooped downstairs to the game room in the finished basement.

He couldn't settle the unease that threatened to upset the gorging he'd done earlier. His mother and Angie had been ensconced in the kitchen for almost half an hour. He knew his mother, knew she'd get Angela to spill her life history with just a few questions. And Ida Maxwell would be just as forthcoming about him. Maybe even too forthcoming.

"Jeff, stop that before you drive us crazy!"

Lyn's outburst caused him to pop the deck of cards he shuffled, sending cards flying. "Sorry."

"Hey man," Jonathan said, "relax. There's no screaming, no blood dripping from the ceiling. Everything's fine."

"If you say so." Jeff wasn't convinced.

"You were with her before?" Julian asked, gathering loose cards.

"Yeah. Right after Yvonne and Mike got married."

"Then she's the one that sent you around the world for a year?"

Jeff sat back, reluctant to air too much with his siblings. Being the oldest gave him the prerogative to interfere in their lives, not the other way around. "She was part of the reason."

The sound of shuffling pierced the silence. "Seems to me if you broke up with her, you must have had a good reason."

Surprised, Jeff frowned at his brother. He'd noticed Julian's lackluster welcome and continued coldness to Angela, but he had no idea why. "Jules, you got something to say, you need to spit it out."

"Okay, I'll tell it to you straight. I don't like her."

"Jules!" Natalie's shocked gasp spoke for all of them.

"I'm not taking it back," his brother said. "There's something about her, like she's got secrets or something."

"Angie doesn't have secrets from me," Jeff declared through clenched teeth. At least he didn't think she did. "And as for my ending up in New York, she wasn't to blame. It wasn't her fault."

"I think you're defending her a little too hard, bro."

Jeff felt his hands clench into fists. "I appreciate your heads up, bro, but I know Angie. She's not hiding anything from me."

"Maybe not." His tone unconvinced, Julian leaned back in his chair. "I mean, what do you know about her? What do you know really?"

"I know enough. Enough to know she's not playing games with me."

"Maybe she just wants someone to take care of her and that baby."

"And maybe you weren't listening to the conversation upstairs," Jeff retorted. "Angie doesn't need anyone to take care of her. She's got plenty of money, she doesn't need mine."

"Then you have nothing to worry about. Just make sure you use your head with her—and I'm not talking about the one in your pants."

In all his years looking after his siblings, Jeff had never reacted out of anger with any of them. Yet he found himself losing his temper with one of his brothers for the second time in a day.

He rose to his feet, leaning over Julian and everyone else gathered nearby. "I think the smartest thing you can do right now is to shut your face."

The warning in his voice effectively ended the conversation. Cassie placed a hand on the bunched muscles of his arm. "Why don't we take a walk, just you and me?"

"Fine." With one last venomous look at his brother, Jeff followed Cassie up the stairs and to the front door. They grabbed their jackets and headed into the night.

Gulping in the cool air, Jeff tried to ease his anger and his apprehension. Julian's reaction surprised and bothered him.

"He's just like you, you know."

"Julian?" He snorted. "Please."

"You don't see it?" Cassie asked. "No, I guess you wouldn't. You have always been the protector of the family, and Julian knows that. So he took the role of protecting you."

"Protect me?" He wanted to laugh. "From what?"

"Yourself."

Jeff froze in his tracks. "What're you talking about?"

Cassie sighed. "Sometimes, when your protective instincts are in full effect, you tend to do first, think later. Like when you tried to give up your scholarship to stay home and take care of us."

"But-but you guys needed me. I couldn't just go off and leave you without support."

"We know. That's why Julian got us together to vote you off to college."

"That was Julian's idea?" Somehow, he'd always thought Cassie had come up with that.

"Yeah. He had a whole plan mapped out." She threaded her arm through his and they started walking again. "He's as protective of you as you are of us. We all are."

He could understand it, but he didn't like it. Not when

it came to Angela. "Y'all don't have to protect me from Angela."

Cassie didn't answer, just stared at him with a look he'd seen once too often growing up. As happy-go-lucky as she was, Cassie also had a habit of seeing more than people wanted her to see. He never liked that look.

Unease rifled through him and he stopped again, disentangling his arm. For a moment the unease came close to pain. If Cassie didn't support him in this... "Are you warning me off her too?"

"Of course not." She pushed her braids over one shoulder. "I like her. She's doing a fine job with her cousin's daughter, she's successful, and she's not blinded by what a fine catch you are."

"Thanks. I think."

Cassie laughed. "I was complimenting her, not you. If you need a compliment, then I'll tell you I'm glad your tastes have improved. She's a definite improvement over those vacuous women you used to date."

"Gee, I feel so much better now," he said, his voice dripping with sarcasm.

His sister sobered again. "You did know that she was married before?"

His stomach gave a savage leap before dropping to his knees. "She talked to you about it?"

"No, I think it just slipped out." She gave him a worried glance. "I take it she hasn't talked to you about it either?"

"No." He fought to keep the frustration from his voice.

"Whenever it comes up, she just shuts down, like it's still too painful to talk about."

"Maybe for her it is."

"Why would it be?" Nerves stretched tight, he began to pace. "She was divorced before I met her. That was what? Almost seven years ago. Why would it bother her now?"

"I don't know," Cassie sighed. "How long was she married?"

"Four, five years—I'm not sure. She got married during college. But I do know she's been divorced longer than she was married."

"It can't be easy, having a marriage fail, no matter the reason. I'm sure it takes a while to get over it."

"I thought she was over it." He hunched his shoulders deeper into his jacket. "She didn't have any problems being with me last year."

"Well..." Cassie's voice faded.

"What? Did she tell you something?"

Cassie touched his shoulder. "She seemed to think there can't be anything more than friendship between you two."

Jeff closed his eyes in an effort to stem the pain his sister's words caused. If Angela could just come right out and say it to Cassie, did that mean there really wasn't any hope of moving forward?

"Hey, calm down. For what it's worth, I saw the way Angela looked at you. What she's saying and what she's feeling are two different things. I think she's just confused. Don't jump out of your skin."

"I can't help it, this whole night has been like a roller-coaster," he admitted. "And God only knows what Angie and Momma are talking about."

"Whatsa matter, big brother? Scared Momma's gonna reveal all your dirty laundry?"

"No." His voice was rueful. "Unfortunately, Angie's already seen me at my worst."

"So she won't think less of you if I tell her how you beat up Tyler Caldwell?"

"Tyler was a bully. No one picks on my sisters."

"You're right about that," Cassie chuckled. "After you boys beat up everyone who poked fun at us, no one even said hello to me. I'm surprised I had a date for the prom."

"Hey, I can't help it if Jules and Justin kept up the family tradition after I left."

Cassie leaned her head against his shoulder, giving his arm another squeeze. "I love you, you know."

"Uh-oh." He froze. "When you start being affectionate like that, I know you want something."

"Who me?" his sister asked, all wide-eyed innocence.

"Yeah, you." He clasped her hand and started walking again. "What do you want now?"

"Just information."

Here we go, he thought. "Okay, shoot."

"How serious are you about Angela?"

Cassie didn't believe in beating around the bush. How could he have forgotten that? "I brought her to meet you guys, didn't I?"

"That's wonderful!" She threw her arms around his neck. "So when are you gonna pop the question?"

"I already did," he confessed. "She told me no."

She broke away from him. "What do you mean, she told you no?"

Shrugging his shoulders in instinctive habit, he explained, "The first night I came back, I went to see her. I saw Kayleigh, assumed she was mine, and asked Angela to marry me. Her exact words were 'Hell no. Not now, not ever.' Something like that."

"Well, I can't blame her, especially if she thought you were only doing the honorable thing," Cassie retorted, instantly outraged. "I guess you haven't asked her again?"

"No, and it'll be a while before I do."

"Why? I know Momma already likes her."

"Not because of Momma. Because she thinks I'm in love with Yvonne."

"Good Lord!" Cassie's hand went to her mouth in shock. "That's why she went all strange when we started talking about Yvonne."

"Yeah. It's the main reason we broke up in the first place. It took me a year to realize how much I need her. Now I'm just trying to take it slow, convince her to trust me and allow me to prove to her that she's the one. I don't know what else to do or say besides what I'm doing now."

"God, what a mess," Cassie breathed.

"That sums it up. So it takes as long as it takes. She said she'd loved me before. I'm hoping she can love me again."

"You really do love her, don't you?"

"She's my everything," he said quietly. "When I'm with her and Kayleigh, I feel like I've come home."

"That's beautiful," Cassie said, her eyes bright under the glow of streetlamps. "You know I'm behind you."

"Thanks." He gave her a hug. Cassie was always the cheerleader of the family, encouraging and inspiring from the time she could talk. Her support meant as much as his mother's.

"You're welcome. Now let's head back. I want to make sure no one's spilled any blood."

Sixteen

"Out like a light," Jeff announced, setting the baby monitor on the end table before joining Angela on the couch. "Told you the ride home would do it."

She turned, putting her back to the armrest so that he could settle with her, his head resting on her chest. The ride home had been a quiet one. She hadn't known what to think when she emerged from the kitchen with Ida to discover that Jeff and Cassie had gone for a walk. Julian looked more pissed than he had before, and no one would look her in the eye. She felt as if she'd failed somehow, and had no idea why.

"She had a full day. So did I."

"But you survived."

Her hands paused in their journey across his chest. If making it out of the house without bursting into tears meant that she'd survived, then yes, she deserved a prize. "I thought I wouldn't when I lost that first round of spades. You weren't kidding when you said your family was vicious about the game."

"I know." He took one of her hands, kissing the inside

of her palm. "We Maxwells tend to play as hard as we work, but at least we leave the animosity at the table."

Most of them did. As they were sorting the decorations for the massive Christmas tree, Julian had warmed up to her some, probably thanks to his wife and Cassie. That only meant that he'd gone from outright hostility to mistrust. It bothered her more than she cared to admit.

"Do you like them?"

"Huh?"

"My family," he clarified, placing light kisses along her wrist. "Do you like them?"

"They're nice people," she replied, knowing it was a non-committal answer. "Is it important to you that I do?"

He tensed against her, silent. "I forget how we can get when we're all together," he said at last, his voice heavy with apology. "You don't have to do this again if you don't want to."

She didn't, but she couldn't tell him that. "You don't have to apologize," she whispered. "They weren't expecting me and Kayleigh and I didn't know what to expect from them. It'll take some getting used to, that's all."

"But you wouldn't choose to do this again, would you?"

"It's not that I don't like your family," she hastened to say, massaging the tension from his shoulders. "I do. Especially Cassie. Everyone is gorgeous and successful and funny. It's obvious that y'all love each other."

"We do."

"I just..." she paused. "Our house was always quiet, cause

my mother didn't like the noise. I just can't imagine what it must have been like, having so many people in one house."

"Loud," he said. "Somebody was always having an argument with somebody else. Mike had a hard time adjusting to it at times too. But he always came over when I invited him."

"You wanted to make sure he wasn't lonely," she guessed, and knew she was right when his shoulders tightened again.

"Well, my house was a lot easier to hang out in," he explained with a shrug. "Not so many antiques to break."

"Your mother said it was more like the Ark, and you were Noah. Take off your shirt."

He complied, then lay back again. "I don't think I was that bad. I was just popular, that's all. Everybody hung out at my house."

She smoothed her hands across the packed muscles of his shoulders then down to his biceps before reversing the process. "And yet you still found time to beat up bullies who picked on your brothers and sisters."

Silence, then, "What else did Momma tell you about me?"

Instead of answering, she concentrated on the sinfully pleasurable experience of feeling him up, skimming the palms of her hands over the hard definition of his chest. He relaxed further, head resting between her breasts, limbs heavy with quiet.

"Your mother told me you were going to give up your college scholarship."

He was silent so long she wondered if she'd offended

him. Finally he said, "My family needed me. Dad had just died, and Momma was still recovering. I felt it was what I needed to do."

"But you didn't."

"No." He shifted, as if uncomfortable with the memory. "They held a family meeting and voted unanimously to send me to UNC. They did everything but tie me up and ship me off, and for a while I hated them for it."

That surprised her. "Why?"

"Because I felt guilty. When Dad died, I became head of the family, and it was my responsibility to take care of everybody. We weren't poor, but we weren't exactly rolling in it either. I still felt guilty about leaving them behind, like I was abandoning them. I made as much cash as I could between schoolwork and basketball, tutoring, typing term papers, whatever I could do. I wanted to make enough money to take care of my family. And if that meant turning pro, I planned to do it."

"But you didn't," she said, keeping her voice quiet so as not to spoil his openness. "What happened?"

"I busted my knee in my junior year." His voice was ripe with bitterness and regret. "I thought I'd failed them again, but I was able to convert to an academic scholarship and got my finance degree. After I graduated I came home and began brokering and planning. The rest is history."

Nonchalance seasoned his tone, but Angela realized now how agonizing it must have been for Jeff to believe he couldn't fulfill his duty to his family. She knew now just how seriously he took his responsibilities. All his life, Jeff had protected those he loved and cared about. But who protected him? Who did he turn to when he needed shelter?

"Angie." He sat up, reaching for his shirt. "I'd better go. Between the meal and the massage, I'm about to drop off. I want to make sure I make it home in one piece."

"Stay here."

Sitting up, she put one hand on his chest to keep him from pulling on his shirt. "Unless one of the stores has a crisis, I have the entire weekend off. I—that is, Kayleigh and I—would like you to spend it here, with us."

A smile lit his eyes and dimpled his cheeks. "I'd like that, too."

"Then let's go to bed."

Once upstairs, Angela continued her gentle attentions, the desire to administer comfort a growing need in her. Without a word spoken, she undressed him, laid him across her bed, and continued the massage begun downstairs.

What wonderful skin, she thought, her hands gliding from his shoulders to the small of his back before returning. Smooth as silk and the color of henna, his skin flowed like a river of melted chocolate over sculpted muscles. Sensuous, alluring. Addictive.

Continuing her tactile and visual exploration, her hands swept across his buttocks to his thighs. Lord, he had a beautiful butt. She'd always been an eyes and smile woman before, but she'd changed her tune the first time she saw him in a pair of jeans. She actually felt faint.

Very much wanting to linger, she forced herself to continue down his legs. He hadn't moved or spoken since lying down. "Are you asleep already?" she asked.

"No," came his mumbled answer, "but I think I'm dreaming."

She smiled at the huskiness of his voice. If he thought he was dreaming, then he hadn't seen anything yet. Feeling wicked, she flipped him over.

The first thing she noticed was that he stood at attention, full and proud. The second thing was that he seemed quite relieved not to be lying on it anymore.

"I'm surprised you weren't doing a push-up with that thing," she remarked, kneeling beside him to massage his shoulders.

He opened one eye. "Well, I think I put a hole in your comforter and mattress."

"I think I can live with that."

"I'm glad. And I'd be ecstatic if you were naked too."

Laughter spilled from her. "Sorry, babe. This is your time. Relax and enjoy it."

"Enjoy it, I can do. Relaxing is something else."

Leaning over, she closed his eye with a gentle kiss. She pressed kisses across his forehead and cheeks, avoiding the sensual call of his lips to brush the strong chin and vulnerable spot beneath it. She swept her tongue along the line of his jaw to his ear, pleased with his answering rush of breath.

Knowing how much he enjoyed it, she took her time on his throat, moving across with measured portions of lips and tongue. He was far from relaxed now. She could tell by the deepened breathing, the tightening of muscles beneath her lips as she charted a leisurely course across his chest to one flat nipple. When she nipped it with a light touch of teeth, his breath left him in an explosion of air.

"Angie?"

"Hhm?" She switched to the other side.

He made a gargled sound. "I don't know what I did to deserve this, but could you please tell me so I can do it again? If I survive this, of course."

"I'll think about it."

She grinned against the scattering of crisp hair leading down his abdomen, a dark arrow pointing the way to glory. His stomach muscles clenched and his hips flexed, causing his penis to bounce in impatience.

In due time, my friend, she thought as she teased his navel with swirling sweeps of tongue. *I promise you'll get all the attention you deserve.*

Shifting lower, she bypassed the obvious, to Jeff's moaned disappointment. It became a sigh of pleasure when she trailed her kisses from his thighs to the smooth globes beneath his jutting erection. He shifted, giving her better access, and she took full advantage, laving the delicate spheres until he groaned constantly.

Then and only then did she move upward, giving suckling kisses to the underside of his throbbing manhood. He flinched and, unbelievably, swelled further, hard and hot and insistent. It amazed her, the contradiction of the male anatomy, hard yet soft, strong yet vulnerable, a pipe of velvet.

With meandering nips she reached the tip, which glistened with pre-release. The swirl of her tongue nearly lifted him off the bed.

"God! Angie..."

His voice was hoarse with a plea she couldn't resist. In one long smooth motion, she drew him in.

The force of his moan caused his entire body to shudder, his hands moving at last to rest on her head. She pleasured him to the best of her ability, sucking gently then insistently as his hips pressed and retreated. She could only take half his ample length, and had to content them both with sweeping tongue-kisses before returning to her sensual feast.

Much too soon, his hips increased the tempo. "Angie."

"Hhm?" She hummed around him.

A strangled sound tore from him. "Jesus, if you don't stop, I'm gonna—"

She didn't stop.

With an explosive breath he convulsed, arching off the bed as his orgasm erupted from him. She waited until he collapsed back against the mattress before retreating to the bathroom. Gathering a towel and a warm washcloth she returned to her bedroom.

Jeff lay as she left him and for a moment she thought him unconscious until she realized he was still very much aroused. "Hey! Didn't I just take care of him?"

"God yes," he breathed. "Maybe it's shock, but you made us both so happy he's too excited to sleep."

"Oh." She sat beside him, handing him the washcloth. "I don't think I can go another round right now," she admitted, massaging her jaw.

"You're not. It's your turn to lay back and relax."

Heat pooled within her at the soft words and the intent behind them. Still, she offered a token protest. "I didn't do this for it to be reciprocated."

"I know." He slid off the bed, steadied himself, then reached for her. "I want to do this for you, Angie."

"Okay." How could she refuse? She couldn't. On a slow simmer for the last half-hour, her body screamed its demand to be satiated.

His gaze hooded with desire and concentration, he unbuttoned her jeans just enough to pull her shirt free. He pulled the garment over her head, leaving her arms trapped and her breasts thrust forward like an offering. Which they were.

Still unhurried, his fingers caressed her from her temples to her cheeks. They traced the outline of her lips before flowing down her throat to rest on the scarlet silk and black lace that restrained the upturned slope of her flesh.

Lord, she could feel heat emanating from his hands, filling her breasts with a fevered excitement that tightened her nipples to the point of pain. Only one thing could alleviate it.

As if reading her mind, Jeff lowered his head, taking one silk-covered bullet into the heat of his mouth. The sweet pull gave her a pleasure so intense her knees threatened to give way. His arm snaked around her, anchoring her as his mouth continued to burn her through the silk.

He relented long enough to blow across the distended peak, the resulting chill after so much heat leaving her gasping. Then he turned his attention to the other crest, nipping her lightly. A shard of delight stabbed her to the core and she moaned again, eyes sliding shut against the pleasure-pain. A distant thought came to her, something about freeing her arms, but it burned to nothingness as sparks of passion shot through her.

At long last he freed her arms, sending the turtleneck to the floor. Her bra soon followed, and she was free. He pulled her closer, chest to chest, skin to glorious skin, before claiming her lips. Drunk in an instant, she clutched his shoulders to keep from falling, drinking from his mouth, quenching her thirst with his tongue.

A whimper tore from her as he abandoned her mouth. It deepened to a groan as he returned to the rise of her breasts, feeding on one dusky tip, then the other. Heat, pure delicious warmth, pulled at her center, stoking the flame of her desire, her hunger for him.

He stepped back, his gaze a physical touch on her skin. "You are so beautiful," he whispered in amazement, and at that moment she felt like the most beautiful woman in the world.

Unhurried, his hands went to the waist of her jeans, unbuttoning them. He knelt to help her with shoes and socks and denim, sliding the jeans down her legs. He returned the erotic torture she'd given him earlier by trailing kisses from her knees to her thighs, his fingers stroking sedately upward until coming into contact with the scrap of material she called panties.

When he kissed her through the thin layer of silk and lace, she had to clutch his shoulders to keep from falling. His breath hot against her center, he hooked his fingers into the strappy waistband, tugging gently until it pooled at her ankles.

Oh please, she thought to herself. Please.

"I intend to," he said. She realized she'd spoken her wish aloud an instant before he blessed her with an intimate kiss.

Her knees did buckle then. The world fell away—she fell away, collapsing back onto the bed. He guided her descent, positioning her so that he could kneel between her thighs beside the bed.

With his arms beneath her thighs, he lifted her, positioning her for his questing mouth. Boiling, reduced to nothing but flames, she stirred restlessly on the bed, needing, needing...

He stroked her once and she froze, unable to breathe, to sense. Then he lowered his head and she knew he wasn't kissing her.

He devoured her.

All at once she exploded, a shriek tearing from her, her climax violent, deep—and over all too soon.

"Damn, damn, damn!" she cried, slamming her fists into the mattress with each utterance.

"What is it?" he asked, resting his chin on her still-quivering belly.

"I finished too fast!" She felt like crying.

He laughed, low and seductive. "You don't think that's all, do you?"

"Ah...oh." She felt a blush creep up her cheeks.

He gave her a grin, his thumb making a light pass over the ridged crest of her desire. Just like that, she simmered anew.

The hot length of his arousal just pressed against her entrance as he rose above her, his hand bracketing her face. "I love to watch you come," he whispered. "Seeing you enjoy what I do to you, knowing that I pleased you—that's a huge turn-on."

She couldn't speak, couldn't do anything but lie there, mesmerized by the fire she saw in his eyes.

"I love how your eyes widen just before the moment," he continued, his husky tone skimming over her heated flesh. "I love the way your lips part, the little noise you make at the back of your throat. I love the way your pulse beats like a drum solo at the base of your throat."

The blunt tip of his arousal just brushed against the flooded rise of her center, the slight movement combining with his voice to enchant her. "I love the way your nipples harden when you're excited, the way they brand my hands when I touch you. I love the way your stomach clenches when you push against me, when you call out your pleasure."

He pushed slowly, oh so slowly, eyes-rolling-into-the-back-of-your-head-slowly into her. "And I love the way you melt for me, the way you open up for me then hold me close inside and out."

She closed her eyes against a fulfillment so perfectly exquisite that tears formed behind her eyelids.

"Look at me, sweetheart," he urged gently, rolling until she was atop him. She forced her eyes open. The look he gave her stole her breath, stopped her heart, righted her world.

He bracketed her cheeks with trembling hands. "Being with you is like coming home. Thank you for giving me that."

Tears broke free of her control, her senses overloaded. "Jeff..."

"Ssh." He kissed her deeply. "Don't say anything. Just come with me."

She straightened, settling him deep, so deep she could taste it. He flexed his hips and she echoed his groan. Throwing her head back in abandon, she rocked against him, yielding gladly to the perfection of it, setting the rhythm that would send them to the door of heaven.

His fingers found her pleasure-center as he surged upward, matching her stroke for relentless stroke. Straining against him, she reached for the shimmering prize, so close, so very close...

She rocked forward with a strangled gasp, colliding against him, and shattering with ecstasy. Seconds later she heard him call out, felt him tense, felt the storm of his coming rain deep inside her.

Seventeen

Jeff whistled as he started up breakfast, feeling happier and lighter than he had in months. Soon he and Angela would be together forever. Maybe the perfect time to ask her to marry him would be Christmas. He could imagine the huge bay window in her living room dominated by a giant tree, presents scattered everywhere, Kayleigh gurgling happily on the carpet beside them. Imagine the expression on Angela's face as she opened the tiny box, as he knelt on one knee, as he pledged himself to her forever...

"Hey, big boy. Whatcha cookin'?"

He turned to find Angela standing in the doorway leading from the dining room, her short turquoise robe opened slightly to reveal a honeyed swath of skin from neck to navel. The necklace he'd given her gleamed in the hollow of her throat. It took him a moment to remember that she'd asked a question. "Wh-what? Oh yeah—pancakes. I'm cooking pancakes. Are you hungry?"

"Yes." She loosened the sash on her robe, letting the garment fall to the floor. "But not for food."

Whatever he held in his hands he simply let go of. He

couldn't think of anything but reaching her, being inside her. His t-shirt went flying, then his sweats as he stalked toward her. Like an ebony Venus she watched him, the hazy, hungry look in her eyes making his entire body throb with want.

They collided in a crash of desire, melding tongues, lips, limbs. She all but leapt into his arms, wrapping those long legs around his waist, pressing her moist heat against his erection. The sensation nearly buckled his knees before he managed to make it to the counter, balancing her on its edge.

Hunger pulsed through him, urging him to put his mouth to the curve of her neck, to run his tongue across the expanse of skin from her pulse to the rise of her breasts. He had to get inside her. He'd die if he couldn't get inside her.

"God, I need you," he breathed, shaking with the overpowering truth of it. "I can't breathe for needing you."

With a rush, her breath caught in her throat. "I..need you too," she sighed as he entered her.

No other encouragement proved necessary. A groan pulled from him as he pushed into her sweetness. He wanted to savor it, wanted to prolong the magic, but the desperate need to make her his own drove him.

Pulling her closer to the edge of the counter, he surged in and out of her, creating a mutual wave of pleasure. With a gasp she tightened around him, arms and legs and inner walls as her release stole her breath. With a shudder and a hoarse shout he followed her, embedding deep one final time.

For a long moment they remained connected, heartbeats

and breathing joined. He didn't want to move away from her, didn't want to disturb the purity of the moment, the absolute perfection of being with her and in her. If he remembered nothing else, he would remember this.

Her head fell to his shoulder. "Don't, move," she breathed. "Just let me—feel this."

Glad she felt the same, he continued his light touch on her back, enjoying the sensation of the aftershocks that rocked them both.

Finally she sighed. "My parents came back home this morning. I have to take Kayleigh to see them." Her voiced filled with an obvious reluctance.

"Would you like some company?"

She turned her head until her lips brushed against his neck. "I would love some company."

Just like that, he began to harden again. "When would you like to go?"

With a low laugh she straightened until he could see her face. "I'd love to go right now."

It didn't take a genius to realize she wasn't talking about visiting her parents. "I think that can be arranged."

"Good," she smiled as she shifted against him. "Do you mind if I drive?"

Still deep inside her, he lifted her off the counter and headed for the living room. "Not at all."

Even the fantastic morning she'd spent with Jeff couldn't squash the dread gathering in Angela's stomach as they neared her parents' Grant Park home. Her mother hadn't been exactly thrilled with their relationship two years ago and had been less than sympathetic when it ended. Angela had no idea what would happen when she arrived with Jeff in tow.

Given how vulnerable she felt after meeting Jeff's family yesterday, she didn't think she could handle facing her mother without him, even with her father there in his perennial role as referee.

A hand covered hers on the steering wheel. "Come on, it's not going to be that bad, is it?"

"I wish I could say of course not, but I can't promise you that." She sighed. "This won't be like your house, full of love and laughter and noise. My mother and I don't exactly have a close relationship, and these visits can get a little strained."

"Doesn't matter," he said, his voice soft with reassurance. "I'm looking forward to meeting your parents."

Unable to do anything else, she turned her hand to squeeze his. "I think you'll like my Dad, for the most part. My mother is a different story. And if you don't mind, when it's time to escape I intend to use you as an excuse."

"All right." She could feel his curiosity, and she realized that they'd never talked about her relationship with her family. Such a huge part of her life, of who she was, and she'd never shared it with him.

Fear knotted her stomach. She hadn't told him before

because, despite her dreams to the contrary, their relationship had never been deep enough. Now she could feel the depth, feel the closeness they shared becoming truer. She loved him, and began to entertain the possibility that he could love her too.

But there was still her mother to consider. Her mother, for whom she had done nothing right. Her mother, for whom she always reverted to the skinny nine-year-old watching her cousin be lavished with the affection denied her. Her mother could make a perfect spring day seem cloudy with just a word.

Angela pulled into the driveway of her parents' Grant Park home and shifted the gear into park. For a long time she sat, staring at the weathered wood and stone exterior, the repository of so many memories, so many hopes. So much heartache.

Her parents were one of the few couples who'd managed to stay together. Of her friends, Angela knew some never knew their fathers, some had mothers walk away from them, some lost their entire families. In high school, she'd been the envy of kids in her neighborhood, having both mother and father in her life.

She would have traded lives with them in a heartbeat.

Her father and Shayla were the only reasons Angela lasted at home until she graduated from high school. Eric Davenport was the perfect counterpoint to her mother, warm and affable, and as free with his praise as Marie was stingy with hers. Because of him, both Angela and Shay had pursued business degrees. Angela had often spent late nights with her father when he brought work home, helping him go over figures and plot charts, totaling numbers on a calculator.

Though he'd worked long and hard until his retirement last year, Eric Davenport was glad that he was able to put her and Shayla through college, and that they hadn't "done anything stupid," as he'd said on more than one occasion.

But she had. She'd let Richard Giles sweep her off her feet, let herself believe he was her prince, let herself be trapped for nearly five years before she broke free. And her mother had blamed her for the demise of the marriage.

"Are you okay?"

The concern in Jeff's voice steadied her. "I'm fine," she reassured him. "It's all part of the process."

Part of that process included bringing Jeff to meet her mother. It was a test, to see his reaction to this part of her life. To see if he would still want to be a part of her life after this visit.

She took a deep breath. "Are you ready?"

For answer he leaned over, kissing her long and sweet. "Now I am."

The smile remained on her lips until she reached the front door. It opened and her mother stepped out, taking Kayleigh from her arms. "There's my princess. How are you today? My goodness, why are you dressed like it's a warm summer day instead of the day after Thanksgiving? Come on in, Nana's got just the thing to take care of you."

Without so much as a nod in her daughter's direction,

Marie Davenport turned and entered the house. Angela caught Jeff's stunned expression and felt an embarrassed remorse at what she was asking of him.

"If you want to cut your losses and run, I won't hate you," she told him, forcing her lips to twist into a smile.

"Nope," he said, giving her a quick peck before steering her through the door. "I kinda like the idea of being your knight in shining armor."

Her breath stuttered in her chest. How many times in her dreams had she cast Jeff into that role? Even as a child, she'd dreamed of it, dreamed that someone would ride up and carry her away. Then she'd put Richard into that role, shattering that dream forever.

"Don't try to be a white knight," she whispered. "A friend's what I need the most right now."

"You got it. Just so you know, I put the armor in the trunk."

With that final reassurance, she led him into her parents' home. Her father came up the hall, still larger than life as he'd been in her childhood. "Hey, there's my pumpkin." He engulfed her in a bear hug.

"Hey, Dad. I want you to meet someone." She squeezed him once before breaking away. "Dad, this is Jeff Maxwell. Jeff, this is my father, Eric Davenport."

She watched the two men size each other up the way only men could do. Jeff stuck out his hand. "It's a pleasure to meet you at last, sir."

"Hhm," her father said. "You the same Jeff Maxwell that

broke my baby's heart last year?"

"Dad!" Heat flushed Angela's cheeks.

Jeff didn't flinch. "Yes I am, though I'm trying to make up for that now."

"Good." He took Jeff's hand, shook it once, then released it. "I hope she's not making it easy for you."

"Dad!" she wailed again, then said, "of course I'm not."

Her father gave her a wink. "Come on in then. There's at least one game on."

Angela followed her father down the hall, her shoulders tensing with every step. These occasions never worked out right, no matter how positive she tried to be. Maybe this time would be different. Maybe, just maybe, she could end this visit without resorting to arguments.

Jeff watched Angela move through her parents' house as if she were a stranger come to visit. Tension radiated off her in waves. Even her father seemed to be gathering himself like a defensive tackle ready to make a block. Surely Marie Davenport wasn't that bad?

She was. He sat with Angela and her father, trying to watch the college football game. Her mother kept up a constant stream of talking as she fussed over Kayleigh. It seemed like innocent baby talk, until he listened to the actual words.

"How's my baby girl? You're looking thin! Must be that cheap baby formula you're being fed. Well, don't worry, Nana's got the good stuff, she'll take care of you, just like she's supposed to. And is that a rash? What sort of diapering is this? Lord only knows how long you've been forced to wear it."

Shocked, Jeff turned to look at Angela. Her eyes were fixed to the television, but the hands resting on her knees clenched into fists.

The snide verbal assault continued. The more Angela and her father sat silent, the more enraged Jeff became. When the game went to commercial, he rose to his feet. "I think I need some fresh air."

Eric rose to his feet as well. "I think I'll join you."

Angela gave him an apologetic smile, her expression hardening as she returned her gaze to her mother. Marie Davenport continued to be oblivious to everyone but Kayleigh.

Jeff followed Angela's father to a side porch just off the kitchen and next to the living room. A pair of wicker chairs crowded under the overhang, but Jeff was too keyed up to sit. Keyed up and insulted on Angela's behalf. "Is it like that every time?"

"Sorry about that," Eric Davenport said, fishing a cigar out of his shirt pocket and lighting it. "I guess that can be a little disconcerting to someone who hasn't witnessed it before."

"Disconcerting?" Somehow Jeff swallowed the urge to snort with derision. "Forgive me for saying so, sir, but it seemed to be more than a bit disconcerting for Angela too."

"I know," Eric Davenport sighed, for a moment looking every one of his fifty-eight years. "Lord knows I tried with them two, but they were always at odds with each other."

"It's always been like that?"

"Since Angela's childhood."

Jeff didn't try to hide his indignation. "Why didn't you take your daughter away from all that?"

"Selfishness. I love them both. My wife and daughter are my whole world. I can't be without either one."

He puffed his cigar in silence, sending blue smoke rings into the crisp afternoon air. "I taught Angela as best I could, shielded her as best I could. And when she met Richard during college, I let her go as best I could."

"Can you tell me about him? Angie's ex-husband?"

Eric looked at him solemnly through a haze of smoke. "She hasn't talked to you about Richard?"

"No."

"It's not my place to tell. All I can say is that she still blames herself for what happened."

"You mean the divorce?"

"The divorce, and everything that happened before the divorce," Eric said heavily. "My little girl tends to blame herself first, seek answers later."

Jeff shifted again, the truth of Eric's words seeping into his skin. He knew for a fact that Angela tended to blame herself for any and everything that went wrong, whether it was a downturn in sales, a corrupted file, even her cousin's death.

Was she right in blaming herself for the divorce? How could he know, since they'd never talked about it? She'd been married for five years; obviously there had been something between her and her husband to keep them together at least that long. What had Angela done—or thought she'd done—that she'd blame herself for the end of her marriage?

He turned to press her father for answers, then stopped. Raised voices sounded from the other room. Eric sighed again. "Well, the arguing started later than I thought it would. Maybe that's a sign of improvement."

Hearing the anger in the voices coming from the other room, Jeff had his doubts. "Well, we have somewhere else we need to be, so I think I'll go get Angie now."

"Probably a good idea," Eric agreed.

Leaving the older man behind, Jeff returned to the living room, pausing just outside the doorway.

"So you can give this man a second chance, but not your own husband," he heard Marie Davenport say. "Do you think you're going to do any better with him than you did with Richard?"

"Do you have to keep throwing Richard in my face?" Angela asked. "Don't you think I regret everything that happened?"

"He tried to give you everything, but you were too spoiled to be happy with that, weren't you?"

"What would you know about what makes me happy? You don't know the first thing about what makes me happy. You never did."

"You should be glad you had a roof over your head and clothes on your back, you ungrateful little—"

"Angie." Having heard enough, Jeff barged trough the

doorway. Angela and her mother stood on opposite sides of the room, facing each other like combatants in a coliseum. "It's time for us to go."

"You just got here and already you're taking my grand-niece away from me?" Marie's face twisted with disdain.

"I told you we wouldn't be able to stay long," Angela reminded her, her voice filled with long-suffering.

"Fine. Get on with you then." She turned her back to them.

Angela stared at her mother for a moment, then threw up her hands. "Fine, Mom. Have a good weekend."

She retrieved Kayleigh while Jeff grabbed the diaper bag then headed for the front door. Eric Davenport was already there, waiting.

"'Bye, Dad," she whispered against his cheek.

"'Bye, Pumpkin. You know I wish things could have ended different. I thought this time, the season—"

"It's all right, Dad. I've stopped asking why. Maybe that's a good start."

Her father's embrace tightened. "I'm proud of you. Never doubt that, not for a minute."

"I don't." She stepped quickly away from him. "I'd better get Kayleigh to the car and out of the chill."

"Mr. Davenport." Jeff shook the older man's hand. "It was good to meet you."

"I'm reading you, son. Just take care of my little girl."

"I intend to, sir. Thank you."

Awkward silence dominated the ride home, just as it had

the previous night. Jeff did what he could to lighten Angela's mood, his heart bleeding at the resignation in her face. She remained withdrawn, giving him monosyllabic answers when she answered him at all.

Back at the townhouse, they played with Kayleigh until the little one fell asleep, then watched a couple of movies over pizza.

As the night lengthened, so did Angela's silence. Finally he couldn't stand it any longer. "Baby, talk to me. Don't keep this locked up inside you."

She remained silent, looking down at their clasped hands. "You know, you'd think I'd be used to it," she finally said with a half-laugh. "You'd think after all these years I'd be immune to it, and wouldn't let her get to me. You'd think that when she starts that list of all my failures, I'd just say 'have a nice life' and walk away from her. But I don't. I keep going back. Like a fool, I keep on going back."

She released a shaky sigh. "And through it all is the fear that one day I'll actually become her."

Surprise had him staring at her, open-mouthed. "Why do you say that?"

Anxiety drove her to her feet, away from him. "What you saw today was the tip of the iceberg, Jeff. Being ignored by her is actually better than having her attention. When she pays attention to me, it's only to tell me what I've done wrong. I hope to God that I never put a child through what I went through growing up. No child should feel less than special, like a second-class citizen. A child should never feel like it was a mistake that she was born. A child should never be taught that love is something that has to be earned. And she never will earn it because she'll never do or be good enough for anything but occupying space."

God, her mother had dumped that on her as a child? Anger boiled in him. The urge to drive back over to Grant Park and give the old biddy a piece of his mind seethed through him. Angela's ramrod-straight back betrayed the hurt that she'd endured and continued to feel.

He crossed to her, moving up behind her and wrapping his arms around her. Words eluded him, and honestly he didn't know if he'd be able to keep the anger from his voice if he did speak. All he could do was hold her tight, his chin resting on top of her head, trying to communicate silently that she was special and necessary and loved.

"I would have run away," she said into the silence. "Used to dream about it all the time, about going to New York or California, and just getting lost. The only reason I didn't was because of my Dad. And Shay of course."

He turned her around. Her features were forced into a semblance of indifference, but he could see the glitter of pain in the depths of her eyes. He stroked her hair, her cheeks, her shoulders. "Sweetheart, if there's one thing I'm certain of, it's that you're in no danger of becoming your mother."

"Maybe. Maybe not. But I intend to make sure that I never do."

The harshness of her voice surprised and embarrassed her, he could tell. She slid her hand over his, keeping it in place against her cheek. "I'm sorry."

"Don't be," he suggested quietly. "It's been a stressful couple of days. You should try to get some sleep while you can, though. Kayleigh won't stay asleep forever, you know."

"You're right," she admitted, shaking her body as if to rid herself of dark thoughts. "Will you stay?"

He studied her silently. The armor she'd carefully erected about herself had begun to erode, and he didn't know if she'd want him to be there to witness it. "I want to, but if you'd rather be alone—"

"No," she cut in, her voice just above a whisper. "I need to feel your arms around me, just for a little while."

He obliged immediately, squeezing her tight. "Angie, you're not in any danger of becoming your mother. Please believe that. You have more compassion and care and love than she ever could."

One tremor, just one, shook her body. "Thank you," she breathed in his ear. "I needed that."

He held her tighter, the need to protect her and keep her safe raging through him. He couldn't believe the cruelty Marie Davenport showed her only child. If it were up to him, he'd make sure that the woman never got the chance to hurt Angela again.

This time, he led her upstairs, helping her undress before putting her to bed. He undressed, then slipped in beside her, fully intending to just hold her until she drifted off to sleep. Yet when she moved against him, pressing her lips against his throat, he couldn't deny them the comfort they both sought.

Treasuring each moment, he made love to her, really made love to her, worshipping every curve and valley of her body. Each strand of hair, each dimple, each pore, none escaped his ministrations. Her sighs of satisfaction blessed him as he poured his offering on the altar of her pleasure, poured his heart and soul into her.

Afterwards, he held her cradled in his arms. He was thankfully exhausted but sleep eluded him. Anger still crawled through him, thanks to Marie Davenport. Listening to the woman spouting venom at her only child had angered him as few things had done. And he couldn't forget Julian. Julian, as protective as he himself ever was, questioning Angela's motives, casting doubt on her. Saying she had secrets. Which immediately made him think about her ex-husband, and the marriage she was so reluctant to discuss. Happy Freakin' Thanksgiving.

She stirred beside him. "You're not asleep."

"No. Maybe I should go, so you can sleep."

Her arms tightened around him. "I want you to stay."

It must have cost her a great deal to admit it. He knew she didn't want to be vulnerable to him, knew that she was afraid he'd hurt her again. But she had the power to hurt him just as deeply, even if she didn't know it

"Hey, why aren't you asleep?"

She sighed. "Too busy thinking to sleep."

"What are you thinking about?"

Her body tensed against his. "Our families."

Of course. If they were all he could think of, why would he think it was any different for her? "What about our families?"

Silence filled the room. "I guess it's a good thing I wasn't trying to impress them," she confessed at last. "If it were a contest, I'd definitely be on the losing end."

Simple as the words were, they cut him nevertheless. "Angie, that's not true. My family likes you."

"Julian doesn't."

Denial sprang to his lips, but he said, "I know."

She pressed her face against his chest, lying still. "Did he say why?"

The calmness of her tone convinced him to continue even though he knew he'd regret it. "He thinks you're keeping secrets from me."

Stiffening further, she lay silent for a few moments. "What secrets does he think I'm keeping from you?"

Needing to feel the beating of her heart, he pulled her closer, caging her in with his arms. "He didn't say, and I didn't ask. I went for a walk with Cassie instead."

Her hand began a slow trail across his chest, but he knew it for an absent gesture. Sudden anger had him gritting his teeth. Damn Julian!

"I'm sorry Angie," he whispered against her hair. "You don't have to see him again."

She moved apart from him, distancing herself. Those few inches felt like a thousand miles, causing his gut to clench. "It's okay—after all, it's not like I'm trying to join the family or anything."

It took everything in him not to roar in denial, to tell her in no uncertain terms that she would join his family. She belonged to him, now and always.

"Maybe it's not secrets," she said. "Maybe he just doesn't think that I'm good enough for his big brother. Maybe he thinks that I'm using you, taking advantage of your generosity."

"Well, he's wrong," he growled, pulling her closer to him. "If anything, you're too good for me. Which you've told me on more than one occasion."

He felt her flinch and mentally kicked himself. "I was mad," she confessed in a small voice. "I think you're a good man, Jeff Maxwell."

"Just not good enough to marry. Unlike your ex-husband."

Once more she tried to pull away from him. He cursed under his breath and tightened his hold on her. Since he'd started it, he might as well finish and totally muck up the remainder of the night.

"Tell me about him."

"Why?"

The rawness of her voice clawed at him, but he steeled himself in determination. "I want to know about the man who was able to get you down the aisle."

Stiffness tightened her body against his, whether from anger or sadness he didn't know. She remained silent, and he felt he owed her enough to let her have it for a moment.

"I'm surprised my father didn't fill you in," she finally said. "I met Richard Giles in college. He swept me off my feet. We got married, it didn't work out, and we got divorced after five years. That's all there is to it."

That most certainly wasn't all there was to it. Any idiot could sense that. His mother and sister had both told him that Angela still had strong feelings where her marriage and divorce were concerned. Now he knew what they meant. God, she still felt the pain of that divorce seven years later—it translated itself to him through every rigid muscle in her body.

The abject misery in her voice hammered at his resolve to get the full story from her. Did she not want the divorce? Did she fight against it? If she had a choice, would she go back to her husband?

Did she still love him?

He decided he didn't want to know, didn't want the gash in his heart to bleed any faster. "You should try to get some sleep now. Kayleigh will be awake soon."

She drew a shaky breath. "I'm sorry, Jeff, I didn't mean—"

"Ssh," he whispered, cupping her face in his hands. "It's okay." He kissed her cheeks, her tears, her sweet mouth. They made love again, with a quick, quiet desperation. Afterwards he held her close, soothing her as she slipped into sleep.

He lay awake for a long time afterward, his mind churning. Julian was right, he thought. She was keeping secrets.

Maybe not deliberately, maybe not because she wanted to deceive him. After all, he knew some about her past, just the glimpses she'd given him over the past few days. But it wasn't enough. He had to know more.

He just hoped the knowledge wouldn't be his undoing.

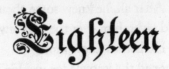

Eighteen

Angela looked out her office window, not seeing the bustling microcosm twenty stories below. The holiday season had revved into high gear, but she found she couldn't enjoy it. Decorating the townhouse seemed like too much of an effort. Besides, Kayleigh wouldn't be aware of the meaning, so why go through all the drama?

She knew the reason for her ambivalence. Jeff Maxwell. As soon as she'd let him back into her life, as soon as she started gathering the courage to let him into her heart, he backed off.

And it was her fault.

The Thanksgiving weekend had strained the fragile bounds of their relationship. Neither mentioned the conversation they'd had in bed, but she knew they both thought about it. Saturday morning he'd left before breakfast, saying he had things to attend to. She'd accepted it, and even believed it for as long as it took him to pull out of her driveway. But it was an excuse to get away from her, and she knew it.

Why didn't she just tell him what he wanted to know?

So he wanted to know about her ex-husband. Why did she have to make it out as a big deal?

Because her failed marriage was her most glaring failure. She couldn't tell Jeff how stupidly naive she'd been, believing that Richard embodied the fantasy of her Prince Charming. That he would take her away from the pain she'd endured in childhood, that he actually wanted her.

She couldn't tell Jeff that the fantasy had been real until they'd come back from their honeymoon and Richard revealed his true nature. Couldn't tell him that for five years she'd actually tried to make it work, actually contorted who and what she was to please her bastard of a husband. Couldn't tell him that her mother had called her spoiled the one time she'd tried to confide in Marie Davenport about her marriage difficulties.

Couldn't tell Jeff that the day she'd tried to leave him, Richard had surprised her by coming home early and proceeded to beat her until she couldn't stand. Shayla had to come get her after Richard left, informing her that he was going to visit his "real woman."

No, she could never tell Jeff the truth. Knowing how he viewed responsibility, he would blame her for her failed marriage, even more than she blamed herself. He'd lose all respect for her, would never want to be with her again. Or worse yet, his protective instincts would kick in and he'd treat her like a victim in need of being saved.

Her hands tightened into fists. No longer did she need or want a prince to ride to her rescue. She'd survived on her own. She'd succeeded in her own right, with her own talent and blood and sweat. Her victimization had ended the day she agreed to testify against her husband in federal court.

With a sigh she rested her head against the window. Maybe it was for the best that Jeff withdrew now. Even if she could finally accept that Jeff had never fallen in love with Yvonne, the fact remained that Angela would never know if he stayed with her out of love, out of a sense of responsibility, or because he believed Kayleigh needed a father.

He'd begun slipping away from her already. In the three days since their disastrous Thanksgiving weekend, the only time they spent together occurred during strained business meetings working on the stupid operational review. No personal conversation, no hint of the passion they could evoke in each other. They treated each other as strangers, people who wanted nothing more than to finish their project and get on with their lives.

A knock on her door interrupted her reverie. "Angela?"

Wiping at her leaking eyes with a surreptitious hand, she turned to face her assistant. "Yes, Janice?"

"There's a courier here with a package for you. He says yours is the only signature he can take."

She followed her assistant into the outer office and signed the proffered clipboard. Taking the flat manila envelope, she thanked the courier and retreated to her office.

Curious, she sat in her chair, turning the envelope over in her hands. No postage, no return address, just her name, title and business address printed in familiar but unidentifiable bold writing

It couldn't be a bomb, she thought in mock seriousness. Too flat. Maybe Jeff had sent her something as a peace offering. The thought made her smile. A certificate for another trip to the spa? That had been such a magical rejuvenating outing that she'd scheduled a recurring appointment.

What had he send her? Once their relationship had become sexual again, he'd enacted his fantasies, sending her chocolate sauce, champagne, edible underwear. He'd broken a speed record to get to her that day when she called to tell him she put them on after lunch. And what fun they'd had on top of her conference table when he had her for dessert.

Her mood lightened, Angela ripped open the envelope and spilled the contents into her hands.

"Oh God." The smile died on her face and her hands began to tremble so violently the photo fell to the desk. She closed her eyes, not needing to see it longer to know what it was—not wanting to see it ever again.

Forcing herself to take a deep breath, she opened her eyes and stared down at a copy of her wedding portrait. It had to come from Richard. Who else would have sent it?

A twelve-year-old memory swam to the surface of her consciousness. Her wedding day had been full of sunshine and hope and promise. They'd wed in the chapel on campus, and even now she could remember pink and white blossoms everywhere, from dogwoods to azaleas, and dappled sunshine peeking through the oak trees. How happy she had been, so sure her dreams were becoming a reality. Believing that with

Richard she would leave the pain of her childhood behind, start a family of her own, raise children who would always know that they were loved, no matter what.

Richard had shared those views. At least he'd seemed to during the heady days of their courtship. Only after the honeymoon had she realized that her future held pain and despair and deceit.

The phone beeped, startling a shriek out of her. "I'm busy, Janice," she snapped when she caught her breath.

"I'm sorry, Angela. There's a caller on the line."

"Then take a message."

"I-I tried, but he identified himself as Richard and insisted I interrupt you.."

Ice slid down her spine as memory and dread pressed in on her. "I-I'll take the call, Janice. Thank you."

Calming herself proved difficult, but she managed by affirmation. She'd reclaimed her life after their divorce. Success belonged to her. She was beyond him. He could not hurt her.

Empowered, she lifted the receiver and pressed a button. "Angela Davenport. How may I help you?"

"Hey now." The husky voice oozed with familiar charm. "Is that any way to greet the husband you haven't seen in seven years?"

She refused to react to his barb. Well, almost. "Did you enjoy your vacation?"

"That's cold, coming from you. Even if I deserve it."

She didn't argue. By being cold she'd survive the nauseating task of talking to him again. "I can think of better ways you can spend your money than sending me junk photos. Like taking a slow boat to China."

Richard's voice lost its affable edge. "I don't think it's junk, Angela. I sent that picture because I figured it was the only way I could get you to talk to me."

"What makes you think I want to talk to you?"

"Oh, I think you will, especially when you hear what I have to say."

The tone of his voice had her pausing. "You've got two minutes. Talk."

"I am out of jail. Been out for about a month, trying to get my life back together. But there's some unfinished business between us."

Don't ask, she thought to herself. If you don't ask him, you won't know. "All your assets were seized, Richard. I have nothing of yours. What unfinished business could there possibly be between us?"

"How about the fact that we're still married?"

Jeff sat at Angela's desk, unable to believe what he held. Her wedding photo.

Why would it appear now, seven years after her divorce? She didn't have one displayed in the townhouse, nor in any of her photo albums. Never once in the time that he'd known her had he ever seen mementos of her wedding, as if she'd excised those years from her past. So why had this photo suddenly appeared?

More and more every day he regretted pushing Angela to answer his questions about her marriage. Obviously she'd begun reminiscing, pulling out old photos from somewhere. Maybe she was thinking of the good times as opposed to what she had now.

Hell, she probably wanted to reunite with the man she'd dedicated five years of her life to, hoping to rekindle whatever had been good and forgive whatever had gone wrong.

"Oh!"

Janice stopped in the doorway in surprise. "I'm sorry, Mr. Maxwell. I didn't know you were here."

Jeff turned the photo face-down on the blotter. "I dropped by with the final draft of the report and thought I'd see if Angela wanted to get a bite."

Janice's pale face paled even further beneath her glasses. "I don't think she's coming back today, sir," the assistant admitted.

"Really?" Jeff kept his voice light, but he knew something was up. "Why do you say that?"

Reluctance highlighted Janice's features as she said, "She was fine until a courier delivered a letter and then she received a phone call. Shortly afterwards she came out, asked me to clear her calendar for the rest of the day, and left. Just like that."

Just like that. Jeff felt his stomach drop like a forty-floor free-fall. "Did she say where she was going, who she was meeting?"

Janice hesitated, and Jeff had his answer. Angela had gone to meet her ex-husband. Still, he held to a minuscule shred of doubt. "Janice," he put on his most charming smile, "if there's some crisis, Mrs. Benjamin will want to know. I can tell her when I drop off the report."

"All right. Her last call was from the gentleman who couriered over the letter. He asked if Angela had received it, then asked to speak to her. He said his name was Richard."

Bile rose in Jeff's throat, and it was all he could do to keep from smashing his fist against the desk. So her son-of-a-bitch ex-husband had contacted her, and she'd gone running like a bitch in heat.

"Thank you, Janice." How he managed to keep his voice level, he had no idea. "If you don't mind, I'm going to use the phone, then I'll be out of your hair."

She smiled. "No trouble at all, sir."

Jeff settled deeper into the executive chair after the assistant left, trying with little success to rein in his temper. His carefully constructed plans for the future were beginning to crumble around him, and he didn't like it one bit.

For years, he'd given freely of his heart to his family, to his friends, but he'd always kept his soul reserved, thinking that all he needed, all he wanted rested in protecting those he cared about. He'd never had the opportunity to ponder the loneliness of his soul—until Yvonne got married and the last of his self-appointed responsibilities was resolved.

Thick as he was, it had taken him a year to realize how

much he needed Angela, had always needed the sight of her, her smile, that wicked laugh. Now it looked as if he'd reached his epiphany too late.

The idea that Angela didn't want him was hard to accept. Having her throw him over for someone she hadn't seen in seven years struck at his ego, but most especially at his heart.

So many things made sense now. Why Angela had avoided talk of the future like politicians being questioned about their interns. Why she'd refused to discuss her marriage.

"Mr. Maxwell?"

He gave a cursory glance to the door, then did a double take as he caught sight of Janice's worried face. "What is it?" he asked, half-rising.

Something in his expression caused her to back up a step. "It-it's Kayleigh, sir."

He felt the hairs on the back of his neck rise. "What about Kayleigh?"

Janice looked as if she'd rather be anywhere other than in the room with him, and he couldn't blame her. "The nursery just called. Kayleigh's still there."

Blood rushed to his ears, colored his vision. "Angela left without taking Kayleigh?"

The quiet menace in his voice had the admin assistant backing up again. "I'm sure she thought she'd be back before the nursery closed for the day, sir. I tried to call, but her mobile phone went straight to voice mail."

Probably because she lay holed up with her ex-husband in a hotel somewhere. "I'll get Kayleigh," he said, doing nothing to control the anger in his tone. "Since I've picked her up before, I'm on record. Call them and let then know I'll be down in five minutes, and I'll try to call Angela."

"All right, sir." Janice left.

Jeff forced himself to sit in the chair, his movements exaggerated by his anger. He'd known on some instinctive level that Angela hadn't told him the whole truth when it came to her marriage; now he knew why: she still loved her husband, and apparently would do anything to get back with him.

Yet her apparent betrayal of him paled in comparison to leaving Kayleigh behind. The baby girl had been given into her care by her dead cousin, an obligation she'd accepted completely—even to the point of fighting her mother for custody. Yet when her ex-husband showed up out of the blue, everything else got kicked to the curb.

Fury settled deep in his veins as he pulled his cell phone from his pocket. He flipped the tiny device open and pressed a single digit, speeding-dialing Angela's mobile.

It rang four times before going to voice mail. He waited ten excruciating seconds before dialing again. If he had to, he'd dial every five seconds until she answered.

On is third attempt she answered, her voice clipped. "Angela Davenport."

Jeff knew her phone would display his number, so why the businesslike tone? "Janice told me you left the office in a hurry, clearing your calendar for the rest of the day," he said, struggling to keep his tone casual. "Is something wrong?"

"N-no. Something unexpected came up that I have to deal with." Her voice grew stiffer with each word.

"I see. I suppose that's why Kayleigh is still at the daycare?"

"Kay...? Oh, Lord. I forgot to make arrangements for that."

His hands trembled with the desire to curse her out and disconnect. God, he didn't want to believe that she'd forgotten the baby, but she'd just admitted that she had.

"Shall I pick her up for you?" How he maintained the casualness, he had no idea.

"That's a perfect solution," she answered in clipped, impersonal tones. "Let me consult my schedule, and I'll call you back with details to meet. If that's all, I really must get back to my meeting."

If that was all? The attempted brush-off incensed him more. That most certainly wasn't all. "Fine," he said, just as clipped. "I'll take care of Kayleigh. See you later."

He disconnected, unable to be on the phone with her one minute longer, and pocketed his phone with exaggerated care. He really wanted to throw it across the room.

Angela had brushed him off in a hurry. She obviously didn't want him to know who she'd met—and didn't want her guest to know whom she spoke to.

He knew, however. She was with Richard. From the background noise, it seemed as if they were in a bar or a restaurant. A nice, intimate dinner for two following a romantic rendezvous? His imagination dramatized his thoughts in vivid detail.

It didn't take a rocket scientist to know that Angela had loved her ex-husband. That came through loud and clear in the photograph. Maybe Richard had been the first to capture her heart. First loves were hard to let go of, hard to ignore. Did Angela regret letting Richard go? Was she even now trying to recover the good old days?

Of course she was. What other reason could she have to throw off her current life to reclaim her former one?

He headed for the elevator, and the nursery five floors below. He'd give her a chance to explain. One chance. If she didn't, there would be hell to pay.

Nineteen

Angela placed her phone on the table, amazed at the steadiness of her hand. The palpable anger in Jeff's voice had unnerved her. What would he do, she wondered, if he knew this wasn't a business meeting but instead a reunion from hell? Suddenly she dreaded going home to face him almost as much as she dreaded the present set of circumstances.

Almost.

"Another client?"

Instead of answering, she sat back in the booth, staring at the man she'd once loved enough to marry. Even in the dim light of the sports bar she could tell that the last seven years hadn't been gentle to him. New lines sliced into his nut-brown face, and most of the weight he'd carried from living the good life had disappeared, whittled away to a muscled wiriness. It gave him a look of debonair dangerousness she could have found attractive if she didn't know his true nature—or have Jeff.

"I'm not here for conversation, Richard," she said evenly. "You call out of nowhere with this cockamamie story—"

"It's the truth."

"Then I need proof."

He sat back with a sigh. "We don't need to be enemies, you know. There was a time when we weren't."

"There was also a time when I didn't know that two and two equals four," she retorted. "That was a long time ago, and I'm no longer naive."

His eyes raked her, and she forced herself not to pull her jacket tighter about herself. "What happened to the sweet little woman I married?"

"You happened, or don't you remember?" she asked, her voice filled with acid. "I left that sweet innocent woman on the steps of the federal courthouse, and I never looked back."

Memories beat at her. She'd actually done some work for Richard's firm, not realizing that there were two sets of bookkeeping records. Then came the day that she'd been approached by federal agents, asking questions about the firm's activities.

In her admitted naiveté, she'd mentioned the interview to Richard. He'd assured her it was standard procedure for a company seeking government contracts. The very next day he'd started setting her up to take the fall for bilking hundreds of people out of their life savings. Only her business skills, learned at her father's knee and honed in college, had proved her innocent. Richard's act of violence against her when she'd tried to leave him had sealed her decision to contact the FBI again.

The trial had literally been a trial by fire. Richard's lawyers had tried to color her as a spoiled vindictive woman seeking revenge for driving her husband into another woman's arms. She'd had indisputable evidence and several other witnesses, but having her private life aired like that had humiliated her. Never again would she be put into that position.

"You lied to me, cheated on me, and abused me. We may not be enemies, but I'll never be your friend."

The charming smile vanished. "What's with all the hate, Angela?" he wondered. "I made my mistakes. I paid for them—"

"After a jury found you guilty."

"I paid for my mistakes," he said again. "Seven long years, I paid for them. Now I'm out, and I want to reclaim my life. But I discovered that our divorce wasn't finalized."

Her heart leapt to her throat. "What?"

"Our divorced was never finalized. We're still married."

Oh my God. "You're wrong," she said, feeling her world tilt. This could not be happening.

"Sorry, Angela, but it's true."

"It can't be." She felt her hands ball into fists as her stomach gave a sickening lurch. "After the trial, I had my lawyer send yours the papers. He said everything was taken care of."

"My lawyer apparently never finished the process. Didn't you even ask your lawyer to follow up with mine?"

Angela felt her face flame. She'd been so ready to have that part of her life over and done, she'd taken her lawyer at his word when he'd told her she didn't have to go to court.

Apparently he'd been eager to take his money and run on to the next high-profile case. How could she have been so stupid?

"Where's your lawyer now?" Richard asked.

"I-I don't know. I didn't keep up with him after the trial."

"Since he obviously collected his fee and jumped ship, we are, for all intents and purposes, still bound in holy matrimony."

Her stomach roiled at the thought. "There was nothing holy about our matrimony, Richard. You put me through hell."

"Hey, don't be acting like it was all one-sided," he shot back. "You were always the perfect little princess, wanting a prince to ride to your rescue and do your bidding. You made it impossible for a normal man to love you!"

The accusation struck home. She rose. "I'll have my current lawyer look into this debacle first thing in the morning. I want you out of my life."

"Angela, wait."

He made a grab for her arm, but she pulled free of his grasp. "Don't you ever touch me again," she hissed, conscious of other patrons looking at them in curiosity. "If what you say is true—and I find that hard to believe—my lawyer will take care of this. And then we are done, do you hear me? Done!"

"How will I get in touch with you?"

"You obviously know where I work and what my number

is. Have your lawyer call me there. Goodbye, Richard."

She threw some money down on the table and stalked out, grateful when the chill evening air hit her flushed face. Why did this have to happen? She'd reconciled her past and moved beyond it. Just when she thought herself ready for her happy-ever-after, the past came back and bit her in the butt. How could fate be so cruel as to bring Richard Giles back into her life? What had she done so wrong in a past life to merit the trouble she had now?

More unnerved than she cared to admit, she forced herself to develop a plan of attack. She'd have her lawyer look over the divorce paperwork tomorrow. If her worst nightmare revealed that she still was tied to Richard, she'd bribe heaven and hell to have the bond severed as quickly as possible. She didn't belong with Richard; she knew now that she never did. Her body and her heart belonged to Jeff.

Oh Lord, Jeff. She groaned aloud, pausing as she started the engine. What would she tell him? What could she tell him? "Honey, I know we've got issues we're working through, but guess what? Not only are we having an affair, but I'm committing adultery too."

No, she couldn't tell him about this. If she told Jeff Richard was back, she'd have to tell him the whole sordid history. How she'd been a fool for love, then a scapegoat, then a witness for the prosecution. If he were unsure about her now, how much worse would it become if he knew her whole history?

Darkness had settled fully by the time she pulled into her

driveway. She sat there a long moment, trying to control the racing of her heart, the unrelenting feeling that disaster loomed nearby. Her hard-won self-confidence rocked precariously on the edge of a cliff. She suddenly, desperately, needed to feel Kayleigh in her arms, to feel Jeff's protective embrace encircling them both. Needed the feeling of security that her facsimile of a family gave her.

No light illuminated the interior as she stepped inside and locked the door. For a moment a frisson of fear went through her. Jeff's car sat next to hers; where was he? "Jeff? Kayleigh? Are you guys here?"

"Rough meeting?"

Startled, she shrieked and dropped her belongings, sending her briefcase and purse and unmentionables spilling across the tile foyer. Jeff materialized out of the darkness of the living room. Arms folded across his chest as he leaned against the doorframe, studying her.

"You scared me," she accused, stooping to scoop up her belongings. He didn't offer to help. Obviously, he was still angry with her. "Where's Kayleigh?"

"Do you care?"

She straightened, staring at him in surprised hurt. "That's not fair, Jeff. Of course I care."

"I'm sorry." His lack of sincerity translated loud and clear in his angry stance. He relieved her of her briefcase and returned to the living room. "She's not here."

"What?" His response halted her frenetic movements. "What do you mean, she's not here? Where is she?"

"I dropped her off with Yvonne. I didn't know how long you were going to be, and I didn't plan to stay here long waiting for you, so I thought that was best."

She groaned inwardly, feeling a stress headache march up her neck. Knowing Yvonne, she'd have a lot of explaining to do. "Thanks, I'll go get her after I shower and change." Just talking to Richard had made her feel dirty.

"The meeting was that bad?"

"What meeting?" she asked, flipping on the light-switch to illuminate the room.

"The meeting I interrupted when I called you earlier. The meeting you cleared your schedule for."

"A minor crisis, but I can handle it," she said, trying to convince both of them. Her nerves stretched tighter. "You know how hectic it can get, especially this time of year."

She would swear she saw fire blazing in the dark depths of his eyes. "Must have been tough, though," he murmured, coming close. He reached up, removed her blazer, then tossed it over the arm of the couch before gently pushing her down. "Janice said you were very upset when you left today."

Janice's helpfulness would be her undoing. Angela made a mental note to draw and quarter her admin assistant in the morning. "You know me," she finally said, shifting as he sat beside her. "If I'm not stressing out over something every day, then something's wrong."

His hands began a slow massage of her shoulders. "Do you want to talk about it?"

"No." Her answer was quick, too quick, and her shoulders tightened anew. She didn't want to expose Jeff to this, not now, not ever. "I can handle it."

"Okay." His voice softened, but his hands tightened on her collarbone. "No need to mix business with pleasure."

Pleasure. Just the distraction she needed. "That's a good rule of thumb to live by," she murmured, forcing herself to relax under his ministrations.

His hands shifted, spreading open the collar of her blouse, fingers brushing against the lace covering her breasts. She felt his breath on her neck a split-second before his lips descended, the gentle pressure dispelling her earlier horror. Tilting her head to give him better access, she closed her eyes and gave in to the soothing sensation.

"Let's talk about your ex."

"What?" Her eyes flew open and she turned to face him, shocked. If he felt anything remotely sensual, she couldn't tell by looking at him. His jaw set firmly as his eyes bored into hers, demanding answers.

Did he know? The question snaked into her mind unbidden. How could he? Janice knew nothing about her ex-husband. Only Yvonne did, and Angela knew her friend wouldn't betray her like that. Would she?

"Why do you want to talk about him?"

"You never said much about him when I asked you at Thanksgiving."

And look how that weekend had ended, she thought to herself. Why ask now, for the love of God? The last thing she wanted to do was spoil a potentially beautiful evening of kiss and makeup by interjecting talk of her soon-to-be-again ex-husband.

"There's nothing to talk about," she finally said. "It was a long time ago."

"Hhm." The non-committal noise sounded unconvinced. "Where is he now, do you think?"

She looked him in the eye and told him the truth. "I don't know, and I don't care."

He cupped her cheek. "You haven't seen or heard from him in seven years?"

Why question her like this? Angela felt her stomach bubble in unpleasant heaves. "I certainly didn't go looking for him," she answered when all she wanted to do was scream. "Can we talk about something else? That's ancient history."

His stare, heavy with intent, almost touched her skin. "Really?"

He was jealous. The realization hit her without warning. That's what this was about—Jeff was jealous of her ex! The knowledge made her want to laugh, but his expression made her wary.

Wanting to prove his jealousy unfounded, she rose to her feet. With a deliberate swing of her hips she turned to face him. "I'd rather talk about the way I feel when you touch me," she said, unzipping her skirt and sending it cascading to the floor.

With smoldering eyes he stared at her, not moving a muscle. "And how do you feel?"

Music filtered through her imagination, a soft sensual beat. Swaying, she slowly undid the buttons on her blouse. "I don't know. Do you think you could remind me?"

Sparks lit the depths of his eyes. He licked his lips as she opened her blouse, causing her stomach to clench against a sudden hunger. "Maybe I could remind you," he said, his voice husky. "Maybe I need reminding."

Never taking her eyes from his, she sashayed closer. She slid her hands over the peacock blue lace of her bra, down her stomach to the scrap of fabric that served as matching panties, resting at the tops of her stockings. A daring, enticing smile floated to her lips. "If I have to do this myself, why are you here?"

Like a shot he came off the couch, stalking to her like a panther stalking prey. Realizing she'd pushed him too far, she backed away until she was stopped by a wall.

Hands slapped the wall on either side of her shoulders. Excitement pooled in her womb as he leaned closer, his lips just brushing her ear. "Didn't anyone tell you that you shouldn't play with fire unless you want to get burned?"

Don't push him, girl, she thought to herself. But his dangerous mood and her own desire made her reckless. "Maybe I want to get burned," she purred, brushing against him. "Are you hot enough?"

"Obviously you don't know when to stop teasing a man," he growled against her ear. "Guess I'll have to show you."

His lips settled in the hollow of her throat, sucking voraciously. One hand held her upright by teasing her breast, the other threatened to unhinge her by teasing her through her panties.

With a moan, she reached for the buttons on his shirt, needing his skin against hers. Impatient, she yanked, sending buttons flying. He lifted his head to stare at her. "Oh, so that's the way you want it?"

She didn't blink. "Yes."

Without another word his lips assaulted her, a driving, dominating kiss that drugged her senses and had her moaning. She kissed him back just as hard, her nails scoring his back, needing his passion, needing his anger, needing his care. Needing to forget.

In a fist, his hand bunched around the fabric that covered her secrets and pulled. The fabric capitulated without a fight, sliding down her legs to the floor. His fingers delved into her heat, filling her, stroking her, driving her over the edge until she began to chant in one succinct phrase what she wanted him to do to her.

Then it happened. He cupped her buttocks, lifted her, then slammed into her. She wrapped arms and legs about him, her teeth sinking into his shoulder as she met each violent thrust with a savage move of her own.

"Is this what you want?" he asked, his voice rough. "Is this what you want from me?"

Passion and ecstasy and lust collided in her. All she could answer was "Yes, yes!"

Incredibly, his pace quickened, his fingers digging into her buttocks as he plunged into her over and over. She screamed as her climax crashed violently through her. Her muscles contracted in rapture as she felt him pour deep inside her. "God, oh God."

"Dammit!"

She must have blacked out for a moment, for the next thing she knew, he was setting her back on her feet. He pushed away from her, his movements violent and angry as he righted himself. "Dammit," he said again.

Angela clutched her blouse about her. His still-smoldering anger made her suddenly aware of the lewdness of her state. Lord, she even still had her heels and stockings on, just like a porno movie. "Jeff, wh-what's wrong?"

He laughed, and the coldness of it chilled her. "There's so many things wrong right now, I don't even know where to start! I mean, what the fuck just happened here?" He laughed again. "Never mind, I just answered my own question."

Stung, she crossed the room, reaching for her skirt. "You don't have to cheapen it."

"Why not? Isn't this what you wanted?"

She couldn't look at him. It was what she wanted, but not in a sordid way. "Jeff, I—"

"What do you want from me, Angie? Cause I got to tell ya, if it's just stud service, you can forget it!"

He'd moved beyond anger into fury. She fumbled with the buttons of her blouse, anything to keep from seeing his fiery expression. "What do you want from me?" she forced out.

"You know what I want, Angie." He closed the distance between them, his hands settling on her forearms. "I want this—you, me, Kayleigh."

"Why?" she asked without thinking, barely holding back a sob. "Because Mike and Yvonne have it? I'm not Yvonne, Jeff. I never will be. If that's what you want, you're going to be disappointed. I will fail you."

The clench of his jaw didn't conceal the flash of pain in his eyes. Seeing the shocked pain on his face made her regret her words.

"That wasn't fair, Angie." He pushed away from her. "Then again, maybe it was."

Lord, she shouldn't have done it, shouldn't have voiced her fear aloud like that. She could feel failure rearing its ugly head, preparing to strike. "Why can't we just go on the way things are?" she asked, her voice cracking in sudden fear. "We can be happy with that."

"You think I want you just for nights, just for sex?" he asked. "If that's all I wanted, I could be with anybody."

That hurt. She could barely force her lips to move. "Then why aren't you?"

The softness of her words froze him. She could read the surprise in his eyes a moment before he shut down completely, withdrawing from her.

"I guess that's something I'll have to think about. You certainly aren't the person I thought you were."

Her heart hitched in her chest before dropping. "What do you mean by that?"

The glance he gave her filled with derision. "I had this image of you, so caring, giving up your life to take care of your cousin's child. You put her first in everything. That's what I thought anyway."

"What are you talking about? I do take care of Kayleigh!"

"Bull!" he snarled. "You've been entrusted with that baby's life and you just took off without looking back!"

He released the full force of his anger. "You dropped everything—including your panties—when your ex-husband called."

Air rushed from her lungs as if she'd just been kicked in the stomach. "Oh my God. You know?"

"God, you've got the balls to admit it?" he thundered. "You think I wouldn't figure out why you can give me your body but not your heart? It was so easy to forget everything we have when your ex made his booty call, wasn't it? You forgot about me, your job, your responsibilities—I could care less about that. But forgetting Kayleigh, forgetting the promise you made to your dead cousin to take care of her daughter—that's too much! I can't be with someone who'll put some man above a child."

She stumbled back from him as if he'd slapped her. "Oh God," she whispered, horror filling her as she realized what he thought. "Oh God, I didn't—I wouldn't—"

"But you did," he retorted, anger flattening his voice to the consistency of gravel. "When I called you earlier—from your office, by the way—it was like you didn't even know who Kayleigh was. All because you were wrapped up in that son-of-a-bitch ex-husband!"

"It's not like that, Jeff!" Desperation crawled through her as she took a step toward him, stretching out her hand. "You've got to believe me."

"I don't think I can believe anything you have to say, ever again. Your actions speak a helluva lot louder than your words."

She ruined it. One look at his face told her that she'd messed up for good. "Jeff, please, if you'll just let me explain—"

"It's too goddamn late for explanations!" He spun back to her. "I want to be a part of your life and you won't let me. Fine. I can deal with that. You want to end this, go back to what you had before? Fine. We end this. I can deal with that too. But I don't need a farewell fuck before you shove me out the door."

"That's not what this was!"

"Oh wasn't it? Then what was it?"

Words refused to form in her throat. What could she say anyway? That the reason she'd made love to him was because she needed to purge the sight and sound and smell of Richard from her senses? That she needed to know that he cared for her and loved her, despite her failures? That she wasn't just some responsibility of his? That he would still want to be with her even when he knew everything about her?

But she didn't know. She'd never known how he felt. Looking at him now, she wondered if he ever had cared for her, despite what he said.

Pain kept her silent and it only infuriated him. With vicious movements he grabbed his coat from the recliner. "I don't know what kind of game you think you're playing, but I'm not going to be a part of it. I just feel sorry for Kayleigh, having to depend on you to take care of her."

With that final arrow he left, slamming the front door behind him. Angela sank onto the couch, drawing her knees to her chest in an instinctive protective gesture. "It's not like that," she whispered. "It isn't."

The utter oppressive silence of her house pressed in on her, mocking her. The poison of her failure seeped into her veins, draining her thoughts, her heart, her soul.

Zombie-like, she stared straight ahead, trying not to visualize the shambles she'd made of her life. Numbness settled into her hands, clenched into fists about her legs. Numbness was good; it indicated a lack of sensation, lack of emotion. She willed it to spread faster, to drive out the pain that threatened her sanity.

Suddenly she rose to her feet, moving like a robot through the eerie silence that layered her home. She had to force her fingers to close around the phone, to lift the receiver. Be calm, a thought came to her. If you don't, Yvonne will want to know what's wrong.

No, she couldn't tell Yvonne what had happened. Couldn't tell her happy and successful friend how she'd failed once again.

A sob tore from her, quick and brutal, startlingly loud

and discordant in the quiet. She swallowed it with effort, then held the receiver up for the difficult task of dialing her friend's number.

"Hello?"

"I need to come get Kayleigh."

"Angie? Are you feeling okay? You sound like you have a cold."

She's giving you an out. Just take it. But she could only handle repeating, "I need to come get Kayleigh now."

"She'll be fine if you want to leave her here. You know I always keep extra supplies on hand."

Angela closed her eyes against a fresh wave of pain. Yvonne meant the words as reassurance, but after Jeff's condemnation it felt like battery acid being poured into her wounds. Yvonne had to keep supplies at her house because who knew when Angela was going to flake out and forget her responsibilities?

"I don't want to leave her," she ground out. "I need to come get Kayleigh. Now."

Silence. Then, "All right. I'll have everything ready when you arrive." The line went dead.

It took several tries before Angela's attempt to replace the receiver came to fruition. She'd just alienated her best friend, a friend who had done nothing but help her.

She pushed the grief away. It didn't matter. Nothing mattered except Kayleigh. Regardless of what anyone said or believed, she would do right by her niece.

Twenty

Thank God for her palm organizer.

Angela's life had become a series of well-ordered check-lists, each completed task a cause for celebration. By concentrating on the minutiae, she could ignore the big picture, ignore the glaring hole where her heart had been.

Three days. Three days of frantic work, of meeting with her lawyer, of pretending that nothing was wrong. Three days to progress from misery to anger, and she'd progressed with a vengeance.

Jeff in his righteous anger hadn't even given her the courtesy of allowing her the opportunity to defend herself, to explain that he'd misunderstood. Even now she could correct his stupid mistake with one phone call. But she didn't. If he could believe the worst of her so easily, she didn't need to be with him anyway.

So why did she still hurt like hell? Why did she still feel guilty?

Because he was right about one thing. She had left Kayleigh to chase after Richard, just not the way Jeff believed. She should have hung up with Richard and called her lawyer, should have started the investigative process immediately. Maybe then she wouldn't be sitting at her desk trying for the umpteenth time not to cry.

No, better for Jeff to show his true colors now, before she'd gotten too far. If not this, there would have been something else she would have failed to do, something else he would have disapproved of. As if he embodied perfection, as if he'd never done anything wrong.

Well, he wouldn't get the chance to hurt her again. No one would. The lesson was learned. From now on, she would be devoted to Kayleigh and focused on her career. Sure she'd be alone, but no one would ever accuse her of not putting Kayleigh first ever again.

"Angie?" Lawrence called. "Janice said you wanted to see me?"

She looked up, then smiled for the first time in three days. Only Law could make a red suit look good. "I do. Close the door behind you, will you?"

As he complied, she left her chair and moved to the couch. "I probably should wait until after work to discuss this, but I want to give you plenty of time to think about it."

"Think about what?" he wanted to know. "How you need a major 'tude adjustment? It's the holiday season—you need to lighten up."

So her mood had been less than stellar, but as long as people thought it was work-related, she could handle it. "I'll lighten up in time to spread holiday cheer when I hand out the bonus checks."

She turned to face him on the couch. "I want you to talk this over with Jaime, of course. I don't expect an answer right away."

A shadow of concern crossed his honeyed features. "What's this all about? You know if it's not illegal, immoral, or gonna cost me money, I'm there for you."

This time her smile came easier. "It shouldn't cost you too much money, thanks to the trust fund, but it will cost you a lot of love."

"Angie." He took her hands. "I won't say you're making me nervous, but if you don't come right out with whatever this is, I'm gonna have a fit."

Inhaling a deep breath, she looked at him and said, "I want to make you Kayleigh's guardian, if anything should happen to me."

Lawrence just stared at her, causing her to wonder if she was the first person to ever render him speechless. A flush of what she took as pleasure blossomed in his cheeks, and his lips worked as if he wanted to smile, but he looked as if he edged toward an asthma attack instead.

"Oh my God." His hands tightened around hers. "Are you serious? Really serious?"

"Of course I am," she replied, her smile growing as the knowledge that she'd chosen right spread through her.

"B-but what about Yvonne?"

Angela knew Yvonne would take Kayleigh and willingly, but she also knew Law would cherish Kayleigh as much or even more than any mother could. "You're my first choice,

Law, and my best choice."

She'd struck him speechless again. Another smile dusted her lips. What a relief to feel something other than heartache and failure.

"Oh my God." He splayed one hand across his heart. "We'd be honored, of course. Absolutely honored!"

He threw his arms around her neck as she wrapped her arms around his waist, appreciating the gesture more than he knew. "I'm so glad you want to," she mumbled into his shoulder. "That's just such a big relief knowing that if something happens to me, Kayleigh will be with someone who'll love her and cherish her like she deserves..."

One minute she spoke calmly, the next tears choked off her words and streamed down her face. Lord, she'd thought the pain was behind her, thought she'd managed to get over it. But denial only prolonged the anguish.

"Lawrence, what in the world have you done to her?"

Angela groaned through her tears. Yvonne would walk in on her breakdown. She needed her perfect, successful, and loved best friend to witness her sorrow like she needed a hole in her head.

"H-he didn't do anything to me," she finally said, accepting the tissue Lawrence offered as Yvonne sat on her other side. "Except agree to become Kayleigh's guardian."

"Terrific!" Yvonne said, obviously pleased. "Not that I want anything bad to happen to you, but Law's an excellent choice. I just thought, well I thought that maybe you and Jeff would officially adopt Kayleigh when you two get married."

Somehow she found the ability to calmly state, "Jeff and I broke up."

"What?"

"When?"

"What did he do?"

"Jeff and I had an argument, three days ago. It's as much my fault as it is his, but he didn't give me a chance to explain."

Law set the box of tissue on the table. "Okay, girl. Spill."

With her two, best friends flanking her, Angela spilled her story—every horrible detail of it. She held nothing back, not even her own shortcomings. Maybe if she let it go, excised the pain, maybe then she could heal and move on.

"Oh my God," Yvonne whispered. "Richard's back? And he thinks you're still married?"

"There's no thinking about it," Angela said, reaching for another tissue. "My lawyer has the paperwork now. Seems my old attorney neglected to follow up with Richard's to make sure he signed and filed the papers."

"Jesus," her boss said. Lawrence said something less holy. "Well, all you have to do is explain to Jeff, and everything will be all right."

"I know you want us to work, Vonne, but I just don't think we're meant to. First I thought he was in love with you, then I wondered if he wanted me because of Kayleigh. But it doesn't matter now. He thinks I'm irresponsible."

"That can be explained—"

"He said that he can't be with a woman who'll put a man above the needs of a child. He said he feels sorry for Kayleigh, depending on someone like me to take care of her."

"He's an idiot," Yvonne declared in heated commiseration.

"He's a bastard," was Law's assessment. "I can't believe he said that."

"It doesn't matter," Angela said, finally tired of the whole thing. "At least I found out now how little he thinks of me. I'm just glad I didn't do something stupid—like say yes when he asked me to marry him. Course, thanks to Richard, I wouldn't have been able to do it anyway."

"So what are you going to do?" Yvonne asked, taking her hand.

"What do I want to do? I'm going to get my life back. My lawyer should have this debacle with Richard finalized by the weekend. Then I'm going to give Jeff Maxwell a piece of my mind. And then I never want to see either one of them again."

"I had her. I had her then I lost her."

Jeff sat in a club chair in Mike's office, torn between hurt and anger. He actually felt beyond anger, beyond hurt. He felt as if Angela had betrayed him.

"Or maybe I never really had her at all, not if she could go back to her ex-husband so easily."

Christ, that hurt. The idea that she'd been playing him, that she had never loved him, cut him to the core.

"Are you sure that's what happened?" Mike asked. "That doesn't sound like the Angela I know."

"Yeah, well, maybe she held out on all of us." Bitterness ran rampant through him, but damned if he could curb it. "I was there, at her house. I asked her about it. At first she denied it until I called her on it."

"Then maybe you got it wrong."

"What makes you think I'm wrong about this?"

Mike sat on the edge of his desk. "Think about it, man. If she wanted to get back with her ex, she wouldn't have waited for you to come back. She could have done that as soon as you left town."

Maybe she had. The thought snaked through his mind, and he voiced it to Mike. "Maybe she's been trying to get back with him, and then I showed up, messed it all up. It explains a lot."

Mike gave him a look, brows raised in a you-got-to-be-kidding-me expression. "You really don't have a clue, do you?" he asked, surprise filling his voice. "You have no clue how Angela feels about you."

"She feels about me the same way I feel about her now," he retorted. "Nothing."

"I thought you loved her."

"I thought I did too. Now I don't."

Jeff watched his friend's pale skin suffuse red. "Thought? You thought you loved her?" he repeated, anger lining every word. "If you don't know how you feel, how can you expect Angela to know? And let me tell you, if you can turn it off that easily, you were never in love. And if you don't love her then you're the one playing games, not the other way around."

The vehement criticism stung. "I'm not playing games."

"Do you love her?"

"What does it matter now?"

"Do you love her?" Mike asked again, spacing each word.

"Yeah." It hurt like hell to admit it, but he still loved her.

"Why?"

"Why what?"

"Why do you love Angela?"

"Jesus, man," Jeff exclaimed, hunching his shoulders in a defensive gesture. "Why the hell are you putting me on the spot like this?"

Mike folded his arms, his expression implacable. "When I married Yvonne, Angela pretty much became my sister. I'm as protective of her as you are of yours. And despite how close you and I are, I'm not going to let you hurt her again."

"I don't want to hurt her."

"Then tell me the truth." Mike's expression didn't yield an inch. "You've had a year away, then you come back and you claim you love Angela and want her back. I want to know why."

Jeff exploded from his chair. "Because I need her, all right!"

Agitated, he crossed to the window, searching for words.

"I'm a selfish son-of- a-bitch. I want a family, I want to be happy. And when I'm with Angela, all of that seems possible. I feel lighter and freer than I ever have, and I get this—this sense of peace that I don't get otherwise. I feel like I can do anything, be anything, or just be me. And when she smiles...God, when she smiles at me, it's like sunrise on a world of darkness. I'd do anything to make her smile."

He sighed, his anger evaporated. "I love her, Mike. I love her so much it hurts. But I never told her. I could never admit it, thinking she'd refuse me. Where would I be then? Exactly where I am right now—without her."

"Talk to her," Mike urged. "Apologize for being an ass and let her into your head and your heart. Give her the words. I think you'll find out this was all a misunderstanding."

"That doesn't make sense," he dismissed. "She's still hung up on the man. Why else would she change the subject whenever I press her about it? Why else would she keep holding me away?"

"Because you're an idiot, that's why."

He looked up as Yvonne stalked into the office, looking primed for murder. "Vonne, I don't need this from you right now."

"Too damn bad, you're going to get it anyway." She stopped in front of him, hands to her hips. "Did you even bother to ask Angie why she went to see her ex-husband out of the blue?"

"No," he admitted, feeling like a toddler caught with his

hand in the cookie jar.

"You know how determined she is to keep Kayleigh and raise her right. Did you even wonder what in the world could happen to make her fly out of the office without Kayleigh?"

"I didn't have to wonder," Jeff replied, feeling the anger once more. "I went to visit her that same day, and I found a copy of her wedding photo. Janice told me that someone named Richard had sent it over. Besides, she looked so guilty when she found out I knew she saw her ex. I just assumed she went to reconcile with him, to have make-up sex."

"You're an idiot!" Yvonne said again. "Why do men think it's always about sex?"

He could feel the defensive hairs rise on the back of his neck. "You weren't there, Vonne, you didn't see her face. Every time I've asked her about her ex she's pushed me away. What else am I suppose to think besides the idea that she still has feelings for him?"

"That's not what it was. Angela can't stand her ex-husband."

"Then what is it? What else would make her forget Kayleigh and run off to see him?"

Yvonne crossed to him. "I think you should sit down for this."

An invisible hand crept into his chest and gathered his heart in a cold fist. "What? What is it?"

With a light touch, she pushed him down in a chair and took the one opposite. He realized Mike had walked over to join them, a reassuring shadow. "What is it, Vonne?"

She reached out, taking his hand, but he didn't feel it. "Angela flew out of the office because Richard told her their divorce wasn't final."

Jeff leaned back in the chair, gripping the arms because it suddenly felt as if the world had fallen away. "Sh-she's still married?" He could barely speak over the pain that blossomed in his chest.

"She didn't know that the divorce had never been finalized," Vonne said into the too-loud quiet. "She thought everything was finished when Richard went to prison."

Prison. The word stuck in his throat, rough as sandpaper. "Yvonne, if this is some kind of joke, it's in very bad taste."

"I wish I was joking." Yvonne's eyes watered, and Mike perched on the arm of her chair, rubbing his hand on her back. "Angela told me everything just a little while ago. Richard has been in prison for the last seven years, for money laundering and fraud among other things. Angela's testimony put him there."

This sounded like some movie of the week, not Angela's life story. "And she's really not divorced?"

"She's got her lawyer looking at everything now. She should be able to get the decree official by the end of the week."

"So she doesn't love him?" It seemed that way, but he wanted, needed, to be sure.

"Angela doesn't love Richard. From what I understand, it wasn't ever a happy marriage."

"Why wouldn't she tell me this? What did she think I'd do? Leave?"

"Isn't that what you did?"

Mike's quiet question hit him like a truck. He sagged against the back of the chair. That's exactly what he'd done. He'd let his own anger and insecurities cloud his judgment. The things he'd said to her that night...

"Damn." He covered his face with his hands. "First I try to ruin your life then I ruin Angela's—twice. I suck at this! She's better off without me."

"So that's what you're going to do, leave her alone?" Yvonne asked.

"Of course not." He dropped his hands. "I'm going to find a way to earn her forgiveness-again. I know I need her a helluva lot more than she needs me, but I want to help her through this. This thing with Richard must have knocked her for a loop. All I did was make it worse."

With perfect hindsight he could recall how upset she'd been. Frantic, even. Almost afraid.

"Wait a minute." He turned to Yvonne, his protective instinct rising like a tidal wave. "Angela testified against her husband, putting him in prison. That was seven years ago. So you're telling me that as soon as he gets out he sends that photo to make sure she'll see him, then he tells her they're not divorced and it's supposed to be all good?"

"What are you saying Jeff?"

"I'm saying that a man who neglected to sign papers to free the wife who put him behind bars is up to no good.

That's what I'm saying."

"Oh God." Yvonne stared at him in surprise. "You don't think he'd try to hurt her, do you?"

Jeff shot to his feet. "I don't know. All I can tell you is that this doesn't feel right. Maybe it's just me, needing to redeem myself by protecting her. I don't know. But even if she doesn't forgive me, I'd feel a lot better if I know for sure that he stays away from her."

Yvonne glanced at her watch. "I think she's on her way home now."

Mike crossed to his desk, lifted the receiver on his phone, and dialed a number. "Hi, Janice, Mike Benjamin. Is Ms. Davenport available? Okay, thanks."

He turned to face them. "She just left for the nursery."

Jeff pulled out his cell phone and tried her, but it went to voice mail. "I guess she's in the elevator," he said, heading for the door. "I'll try to catch up with her."

Anxiety he couldn't shake had him quickening his pace. He couldn't escape a feeling of impending disaster. Whether it was his making or not, he didn't know. All he knew was that he had to get to Angela. Now.

Twenty-One

Angela walked through the parking deck, Kayleigh securely tucked in the sling across her chest. Ever since her fight with Jeff she'd eschewed the stroller, needing to feel the reassuring weight of the baby in her arms.

If she knew Yvonne at all, her friend had gone straight to look for Jeff when she left Angela's office. Yvonne had this image of the four of them—herself, Mike, Jeff, and Angela—happily ever after, and she refused to let it go.

It needed to be let go. Angela realized that now. Wishful thinking and hoping and dreaming for someone to be a white knight had proved to be a child's fairy tale. She'd have to rescue herself, she thought, then realized she didn't need rescuing at all. She had a career she loved, a child she adored, friends who'd stand with her no matter what. Her life would be what she made of it, and she had no intention of making it an ode to a broken heart.

"Hey, Angela."

As the familiar voice reached her she gasped and spun around, clutching Kayleigh tighter. "Richard! What are you doing here?"

He shoved his hands into the pockets of his coat. "I came by to see you."

"What for?" she demanded, stepping back from him. Kayleigh began to squirm and fuss.

"Hey, what's this?" He pushed open her coat. "A baby? So the princess ain't a goody-two-shoes after all, huh? You been holding out on me, committing adultery and having a bastard."

"If that's what you came to say, you can leave now," Angela retorted, shushing Kayleigh as she backed away from him again. Where was Ernie, or any of the other security guards who roamed the parking deck? "Anything you want to say to me from now on, you can say to my lawyer."

"Oh, I don't think you want me to say this to your lawyer," he said with an easy smile, pulling a gun out of his pocket. "I think this should stay just between the two of us, don't you?"

Oh my God. Angela felt her heart seize in her chest as she stared at the gun he held so casually for her to see. "What do you want?" she stuttered.

"See, it won't kill you to be polite." He smiled again. "I figure you owe me, being all big money while I rotted away in prison."

The smile slipped from his face. "You owe me for putting up with you the first few years we were married. You owe me for putting me in jail. And you owe me for living it up when I had to deal with all that bullshit in prison. You couldn't even come to see your dear old husband, not once in seven years. I thought for sure you'd realize I didn't sign the divorce papers."

"You did that on purpose?" she whispered, shocked.

"Of course. It was the easiest way to get back at you. I wanted you to come to the prison, see where you put me. I wanted you to have to come to the hellhole you put me in and beg me to sign the papers. I wanted to see your face when I told you no."

His lips curled in derision. "How stupid could you be, not checking to see if the divorce was finalized? But then, you had no reason to, did you? In seven years, no one came close to asking you to marry them, did they? Why doesn't that surprise me?"

Angela blocked out his words in an effort to stave off the feelings of worthlessness and failure that threatened to consume her again. She wouldn't give in to pain, she wouldn't give in to panic. She had to try to get away from him, had to save Kayleigh.

"Don't even think about it." Richard's harsh voice, and the looming presence of the gun, forced her attention back. "Where's your southern hospitality? You haven't even invited me back to your place, so we'll do that first, after we make a stop at an ATM. Then we'll have a real reunion, won't we, sugar? You and me, we got a lot of reminiscing to do."

Acid rose in her throat, causing her to gag. No way in hell would she let Richard into her car, into her house, into her body. She'd rather die first. But she had Kayleigh to think of. Kayleigh had to be protected at all costs. Once they got into the car, however, she would be at his mercy.

She licked her lips, thinking fast. "Maybe you're right, Richard. Maybe I do owe you. But you're going about this the wrong way. You don't have to resort to violence. Let me just write you a check, I'll make it out to cash—"

It happened so fast, she didn't realize that he'd hit her until pain blossomed in her jaw. "You just don't get it, do you?" he snarled, grabbing the collar of her coat. The cool barrel of the gun pressed against her burning cheek in an obscene dichotomy of comfort and terror.

He pushed her up against her car, unmindful of Kayleigh smashed between them. "I ain't gonna be bought off, baby girl. You got seven years of pain to make up for, and I intend to make you feel every single day of it!"

Kayleigh wailed, protesting the press of bodies. Richard stepped back slightly. "Now shut that kid up or I'll shut her up for you."

Something unhinged in her at that moment, suspending thought and goading her to action. With all her might she kneed him in the groin, and when he bent over double, she kneed him again, catching him square in the face. As he went down, a dark shape came at them like an avenging angel, and landed on Richard. Jeff. "Angie, run!"

She didn't need to be told twice. Clutching a squalling Kayleigh, she dashed through the maze of parked cars, bent over double to be less of a target. Any moment now she expected to hear a blast of noise, expected to feel pain blossom as a bullet slammed into her.

Two sharp cracks, like backfire, shattered the tense quiet. Angela froze behind an SUV, knowing in her heart of hearts that the sounds had nothing to do with backfire. With trembling fingers she fumbled the pacifier back into the screaming infant's mouth. "You have to be quiet now," she whispered. "Please Kayleigh, shush up now."

As if understanding the danger of the situation, the baby settled down. It didn't matter; Angela's blood pounded so heavily through her ears she couldn't hear anything else if she wanted to. And she really wanted to.

With her heart thumping loudly in her chest, Angela fumbled into the pocket of her coat and pulled out her cell phone to dial 911. "My name is Angela Davenport, I'm in the parking deck of the Twin Towers office building in Midtown on Peachtree Street. My ex-husband just tried to kidnap me and my niece—h-he had a gun, but my friend surprised him and told me to run and I did and oh God, I just heard two shots fired, and now it's quiet, it's so quiet right now..."

"Ma'am? Ma'am are you hurt?"

Trying to stop the tears from overpowering her, Angela took in great gulps of air. "F-fine, but Jeff, I have to make s-sure he's all right..."

She could hear the person on the other end saying something, but it didn't matter. Two shots fired. She had to make sure Jeff was all right.

Expecting the worst, she straightened enough to peer over the hood of the SUV. The silence and stillness pressed in on her. Looking back in the direction from which she'd come, she saw two shapes lying still, so still, by her car.

"Oh God, Jeff!"

She didn't think, didn't feel, she just ran, Kayleigh clutched close. Now that it was over people appeared everywhere—the elevator, cars coming up the ramp, people walking through the crosswalk. Flashing orange lights signaled the late but welcomed arrival of a security guard.

Unable to breathe, Angela skidded to a stop before the two men. The acrid smells of gunpowder and blood assaulted her. Richard lay face down on the concrete, unmoving, a dark stain spreading around him. Jeff lay face up, eyes closed. With a trembling hand, she reached out, touching his shoulder. "Jeff?"

He groaned, the sweet sound unhinging her knees. As she dropped to the concrete beside him his eyes flicked open. "Are you...Kayleigh...all right?"

"W-we're f-fine, the police are coming, security just got here."

Ernie, the guard, knelt beside them. "Ms. Davenport, what happened?"

Angela explained quickly and brokenly, then, realizing she still held her mobile phone, passed it to the guard. "I called 911." She turned back to Jeff. "Are you hurt? Can you sit up?"

"Richard. Where's that son of a bitch?" Jeff hissed, struggling to sit up.

"He's not going anywhere," the guard said. "Are you

hurt?"

"Yeah," Jeff answered, closing his eyes with another hiss of pain. "Side...hurts like a bitch."

"Okay, don't try to move. The paramedics are on their way up."

Angela noticed for the first time the way he clutched his left side, the dark stain on his fingers. Blood. His blood... "Oh God, he shot you."

Ernie pressed something into her hands. "Hold this against the wound, tight as you can. I'm going to make sure the ambulance gets through."

"O-okay." She took the diaper and pressed it against Jeff's side. "Oh God, Jeff, I'm sorry, I'm so sorry."

"He hurt you," Jeff growled, staring at her face. "The son-of-a-bitch hurt you."

"Don't worry about me," she managed to say, his words making her conscious of the pain that still radiated through her cheek. She deliberately averted her face. "I'm all right."

"I can't help worrying about you," he managed. "Y-You should have told me about him, should have told me the truth."

"I know," she cried, fear and guilt vying for the shattered remains of her composure in an emotional tug of war. "I thought I could handle it, and he'd be gone."

"I would have...protected you," he said, his voice fading under the shrieks of the arriving ambulance and police. "I can't protect you if you're not straight with me."

"Jeff, I—"

"Ma'am, you need to move back so the paramedics can see to him," Ernie said, pulling her away.

Reluctantly she went, standing in numbed silence as paramedics treated Jeff. Everything took on a blurred, nightmarish quality as she suffered through the sight of Jeff being loaded into an ambulance, Richard being zipped into a black bag.

It could have been minutes, it could have been hours. She had no idea, no concept of anything. Dimly she wished she could be one of those women who fainted, whose minds decided that enough was enough, and shut the body down. Obviously she had a high threshold for pain and suffering; despite the numbness that slowed her senses, she was aware of everything that occurred around her.

A female paramedic stepped up to her. "Ma'am, why don't you let me take your baby while my partner takes care of you."

Panic had her clutching Kayleigh tighter. "No. I can take care of her. I can."

"It's all right. I just want to make sure that she's okay, that you're both okay."

"I'm fine," she insisted, taking a step back.

"Ma'am, you're bleeding from a cut on your cheek and your eye is swelling shut. Let us help you."

"All right." She let herself be led to another ambulance, let Kayleigh be taken from her. "Jeff, is he gonna be okay?"

A police officer appeared beside her. "Which one is Jeff?"

In a dull tone, she answered police questions as the paramedics patched her bleeding cheek. The past came roaring back, stealing the happiness she'd carved out over the last seven years as she revealed to the police all the sad, sordid details of her penchant for failure.

"Angie? Oh God, Angie."

Lights blurred and danced before her eyes. It took a moment for her brain to process that Yvonne stood in front of her, with Mike standing protectively behind her.

"The police said that Richard's dead," she informed them, her voice sounding distant and strange. "He wanted to, he wanted—"

Her voice cracked as she choked on the tears that hadn't stopped since she'd heard the gunshots. She forced herself to swallow and continue. "I kneed him in the crotch, then Jeff slammed into him and told me to run and I did and, oh-my-God, Jeff got shot and it's all my fault."

"Angie, don't say that—"

"It's true, though," she insisted. "And now I have to tell his mother. How am I going to be able to look her in the eye and say, 'My ex-husband shot your son because he was trying to protect me'? How can I face her and tell her that?"

"You don't," Mike said. "I'll call Ida. You concentrate on talking to the police and avoiding the media."

"Media?" She suddenly noticed the crowd gathered, held back by police and the obscene yellow crime scene tape. Bright lights gave the parking deck an unnatural glow, lights from the various news outlets. How had they found out so fast?

"Oh God, I have to call my parents," she managed to say. "If my father sees this on TV..."

"Don't worry about that," Yvonne said, embracing her. "We'll take care of it. Everything's gonna be fine."

She was wrong, Angela thought, allowing Yvonne to lead her away. Nothing would ever be fine again.

There were Maxwells everywhere.

Thanks to Mike's phone call to Ida, they'd beaten her and the Benjamins to the hospital. They dominated the waiting room, clustering together, shutting her out. Even Yvonne and Mike made it into their inner circle, both giving Ida Maxwell an encouraging hug before sitting off to one side of the waiting room, arms about each other for comfort.

Intentional or not, the slight cut Angela to the core, forcing her to make herself unobtrusive. She sat in the seat farthest from the family, the bandaged side of her face out of view, arms wrapped tightly about Kayleigh in a quest for comfort. It took everything in her to resist the urge to curl up in the chair and hide. In silence she waited for someone to realize she sat there, waited for someone to point out her failure and place the blame squarely where it belonged.

Shock had finally ebbed, leaving reality in clear, cold focus. Jeff could have died. Those four words reverberated in her mind, in her heart, in a horrid litany. Jeff could have died, and it would have been her fault.

Guilt swamped her, consuming her. There was no way to sugarcoat it. Because Jeff felt the need to protect her, he'd placed his life in jeopardy.

"Angie?"

She lifted her head to see her father coming down the hallway, her mother close behind. Impending dread kept her rooted in place until her father pulled her to her feet and engulfed her in an encompassing hug. "Daddy, oh Daddy..."

"It's all right," her father's voice rumbled with reassurance. "Everything will be fine."

"Let me see Kayleigh," her mother said, reaching into their embrace to lift the infant.

"She's fine, Momma," Angela said, keeping a firm hold on her niece. Something told her that if she let her mother take Kayleigh, she'd never get her back. "We both are."

"I want to see for myself," Marie insisted.

"Leave it, Marie," her father said, loosing his hold.

"You always did take her side." Her mother's voice took on the sharpness that constantly flavored their conversations. "Even when she's at fault."

Angela felt tears prick her eyes, but she'd be damned if she'd give her mother the satisfaction of seeing them fall. "Richard was an evil man, Momma. He always was. He deliberately failed to sign our divorce papers, he deliberately pulled a gun on me tonight. He deliberately hit me before he threatened Kayleigh. No matter what, I wasn't about to let him hurt her."

A horrible thought slammed into her, one she hadn't considered before. "It was you, wasn't it?" she asked her mother, horror stealing the volume of her voice. "You told Richard where I was. You gave him my office number."

"Like he couldn't have found you anyway, after you flaunted yourself in the newspaper in those fashion shows your so-called business does," her mother shot back. "He told me he'd kept track of you all these years. He knew a lot about you, more than I told him."

Angela took a step back, clutching her niece tighter. "You never believed me, what I told you about Richard. You never believed he was bad, never believed he deserved to go to prison."

"Angela—"

"Just when I think you can't hurt me anymore, you one-up yourself. This is it, Momma. I can't take anymore. As much as I love you, I can't keep doing this to myself or to Kayleigh. I won't."

"Angela?"

Ida's voice startled her, choking off her tirade and prompting her flight response. Instead, she turned to face the Maxwell matriarch, prepared to endure the censure she would see in the older woman's eyes. Ida stared back at her with concern, sadness, and understanding. "Momma, Dad, this is Ida Maxwell, Jeff's mother. Mrs. Maxwell, these are my parents, Eric and Marie Davenport."

"It's good to finally meet you," Ida said, shaking her parents' hands. "I wish the circumstances were different."

"I'm sorry that your son was injured," Marie said stiffly. "He shouldn't have been dragged into this."

Mortified, Angela stared at the floor, wishing for the umpteenth time in her life that her life could have been different.

"Well, Jeff loves Angela, and Kayleigh," Ida said in her unruffled voice. "He wouldn't let anything happen to either of them."

Surprised by the statement, Angela raised her gaze to Ida's. The older woman gave her a soft smile before turning back to her mother. "You've raised a wonderful daughter. Both of you must be very proud of everything that she's accomplished."

"We are," Eric Davenport said, giving Angela a smile. Her mother remained silent, save for a non-committal grunt.

"Dad, why don't you guys go on home?" she asked, wanting nothing more than to get them gone. "Kayleigh and I are fine. Yvonne and Michael will give me a ride home after we hear what the doctor has to say. I'll talk to you tomorrow."

"Okay, pumpkin," her father answered. "Let me know if we need to do anything, all right?"

"Sure Dad," she said, watching her mother move down the hall without a word. "Bye."

As her father left she turned to Ida. "I'm sorry, Mrs. Maxwell," she whispered. "I'm so sorry. For my mother, for what happened to Jeff—"

"It's not your fault, Angela," the older woman said, laying a hand on her arm. "I want you to stop blaming yourself.

Come over and sit with the rest of us."

With automatic movements, she allowed Ida Maxwell to guide her back to the family. She kept her eyes to the floor, but she could feel their stares, feel Julian's harsh accusing glare.

She didn't belong with them and she knew it. She'd known it at Thanksgiving, but she'd wanted to believe, needed to believe, that it was possible, that one day she'd have a family that loved her and accepted her. She did have a family, with Kayleigh. And that would be enough.

The doctor came in, interrupting her morose reverie. Everyone rose, the silence thickening the air in the waiting room. "We removed the bullet and repaired the damage, which was minimal to begin with. We'll want to keep Mr. Maxwell at least a day to make sure everything is fine, but I foresee a complete recovery."

Cheers rocked the waiting room and the doctor gave them an indulgent smile. "He's still groggy from the anesthesia, but you can see him for a few minutes."

Angela stood back as Jeff's family moved out of the waiting room and followed the doctor down the hall. "Are you coming?" Yvonne asked, leaning against her husband.

"Of course," Angela replied, giving her a reassuring smile. In reality she didn't know if his mother would let her see Jeff or not. "Go on ahead, I'll catch up with you in a moment."

They left, and she sagged against the wall, closing her eyes in sweet relief. "Thank you, God," she whispered.

"Thank you."

"This is all your fault, you know."

She opened her eyes. Julian lounged beside her, his relaxed posture a stark contrast to the anger on his face. "My brother could have died because of you."

"I know that," she whispered, guilt clawing at her. "I'll go to my grave knowing that, remembering that, and seeing that. Does that make you happy?"

"What will make me happier is if you'll stay out of my brother's life," he retorted. "Jeff's spent his whole life being responsible and it's held him back. The only thing that's holding him back now is the guilt and responsibility he feels towards you."

Julian's words slithered through her consciousness and took root. He was right. Jeff hadn't returned home from New York because he wanted to, because he wanted her. No, what drove him, what had always driven him, was his sense of duty and responsibility.

Not love. It never had been love.

She knew that now, at long last. He only felt responsibility towards her. Maybe because he'd hurt her once before and still felt guilty over it, maybe because she now had Kayleigh and he thought her incapable of raising the baby alone.

It didn't matter. She'd heard from his own mouth that he wanted to protect her. It seemed to be all he wanted. Never once had he mentioned love. She'd promised herself that she'd never lose herself to someone who didn't love her.

She intended to keep that promise. Better heartache now than heartache later.

"If you think I want Jeff to feel responsible for me, you're mistaken," she said, her voice even. "What I want from Jeff is something he can't give me."

"What? Money? A father for that baby?"

"I don't need Jeff's money. And I turned down his offer to be Kayleigh's father. All I want from Jeff is his love, and he can't give me that. So nothing you say or do can hurt worse than that."

The surprise on Julian's face would have been laughable if she'd been capable of humor at the moment. "We were already broken up before this happened, Julian. I just want to make sure he's all right, and then I'm out of your family's life."

Turning heel, she stalked away from Julian, following the path everyone else had taken. Given the number of people who cared for him, it was easy enough to discover where Jeff was.

Hoping to check on him and be gone quickly, she walked up to Yvonne and Michael. "Is he okay?"

Yvonne wiped at her red-rimmed eyes. "Yeah, he's tired and he's not talking much, but he-he—"

She turned her face into her husband's chest. "He's fine," Mike said, holding his wife close. "He even cracked a smile when Vonne told him she was going to kill him when he got better."

Angela believed him, but she still wouldn't be able to

accept it until she saw for herself that he was okay. Yet she couldn't make herself turn to the door. What would she say, what could she say? Maybe it would be better if she didn't try to see him. Maybe it would be better if she just walked away now...

"Jeff's asking for you."

She turned at the sound of Ida's voice, fighting the instinct to turn and run. "Why don't you let me hold Kayleigh for you?" the Maxwell matriarch suggested, already lifting the baby away. "Go on, he's waiting for you."

Seeing no reason to delay the inevitable, Angela nodded, then threaded her way through the knot of Jeff's siblings to enter his room.

His was a private room, spacious and airy, but the beeps and clicks of the monitoring equipment served as constant reminder that this was indeed a hospital. He lay facing her, seemingly asleep, and the tears that hovered just below the surface welled up again.

She walked to the bed, her feet dragging with the leaden weight of her emotions. He opened his eyes as she approached, giving her a tired, drug-induced smile. "Hey, I thought you weren't coming."

Taking his outstretched hand, she drew closer but resisted his silent entreaty to sit beside him. "Well, you had a lot of people—family—wanting to see you."

"They could have waited." His eyes roamed her face, lingering on the bandage on her left cheek. "What happened with your husband?"

She flinched at his use of the word. "H-he was pronounced dead on the scene. The police will probably come talk to you tomorrow."

"How are you? And Kayleigh—is she okay?"

"Kayleigh's fine. Me, I'm still scared to death."

His fingers tightened around hers. "You don't have to be anymore."

"It'll be a long time before I'm not," she confessed.

"I'm sorry, Angie."

Surprise caused her to stare at him. "You're apologizing to me? Why?"

"I shouldn't have come off like that at your house a couple of days ago. But when you didn't tell me the truth about seeing Richard, I stupidly assumed the worst—that you still loved him and had gone to rekindle your relationship." He squeezed her hand, his grip weak. "Why didn't you tell me the truth about your marriage?"

She closed her eyes, a sinking feeling gathering in her stomach. "So Yvonne told you about that?"

"Yeah, this afternoon."

"That's why you came looking for me in the parking deck?"

"Yeah," he said again, his voice slurred thanks to the medicine. "Once she told me that, I wanted to apologize, and I wanted to make sure you were all right. "

He only wanted to help her, she knew that, but his words still hurt. "I thought I could handle it. I didn't have any intention of seeing him again. I gave the papers to my lawyer and I thought that would be it."

With a sigh he settled back against the pillows, his eyes sliding shut. "I wish you would've been straight with me from the beginning. I would have been able to protect you better."

The last words she wanted to hear vibrated in the air between them. Angela felt her fingers go numb in his light hold and she extracted them. "I'm not your responsibility, Jeff. I don't need you to protect me."

"I want to protect you, Angie. You and Kayleigh."

For a moment she couldn't speak, so many things were shooting through her. He still hadn't mentioned love. All he wanted was to protect her, like she was some prized object instead of a lover.

"I told you once before, you're not Superman," she managed to say. "I don't need you to protect me." I need you to love me.

He sighed again. "But if I hadn't been there today to protect you, it could have ended up a lot worse. You could have been hurt, or Kayleigh."

She closed her eyes against a fresh onslaught of pain. Nothing had changed between them. He would still see her as incapable of caring for herself and Kayleigh, still see her as a failure.

"You're right," she whispered. "I endangered you and I endangered Kayleigh. You have no idea how sorry I am that it came to that. If I could make it turn out differently I would. All I can do is promise that it will never happen again."

"Of course it won't," he said, pushing back against the pillows. "It's over now."

"You're right," she answered. "It is over."

"Ma'am?" With quiet, efficient movements, the nurse entered the room. "I'm sorry, but you have to leave now."

"Okay." Angela rose to her feet as the nurse entered the room. Jeff's hand tightened on hers. "I'll see you when I blow this Popsicle stand, right?"

One last lie wouldn't hurt. "Sure."

"Okay." His eyes slid closed.

Stifling a sob, she loosened her fingers from his then leaned over to press a kiss against his forehead. "Goodbye, Jeff," she whispered.

One last caress of his cheek and she turned away. She walked out the door without looking back, leaving her heart behind her.

Twenty-Two

He'd lost her.

Jeff stared at the enormous Christmas tree that dominated his mother's living room, its blinking lights doing little to cheer him.

I need some time to deal with everything that's happened with Richard and with us. I'll never forgive myself that you got hurt because you felt the need to protect me. I don't want you to feel that way about me. I'm not your responsibility. I never was.

The unsigned note had arrived at the hospital with a bouquet, just after he'd been cleared by doctors and interviewed by police. Simple lines that seemed to spell out a dismal future.

Still, he had to know for sure. With his arm strapped to his chest to prevent stretching his wound, he was forced to have Julian drive him by Angela's townhouse, only to find it deserted. Every phone call he'd made to her went unanswered. Even Yvonne didn't know where Angela was. She'd disappeared.

The gunshot, painful as it was, served as a blessed distraction to the ache in his heart. The horrible words he'd said to Angie when he accused her of getting back with her husband burned like acid in his stomach.

He needed to apologize. He needed to beg her forgiveness, beg her to give him another chance. If he had to walk on hot coals, he'd do it. He had to prove to her that he felt more than responsibility for her. He had to.

His cell phone rang, shattering the quiet. He snapped it open, hissing against the stab of pain in his side. "Angie?"

"It's me."

A sigh of relief shook him to the core. "Thank God. Angie, please, we need to talk. Where are you?"

"I'm taking some time off. The police finished questioning me, so it was okay to leave for a while." Her breath trembled through the phone. "I called because I wanted to talk to you about the note I left."

His stomach tightened into knots. "You need some time. I can understand that. I'll give you all the time you need."

"I can't see you again, Jeff," she whispered. "I can't do this anymore."

"Don't say that." His grip tightened on the phone. "I said some awful things to you. I know that and I'm sorry. I swear to God I am. But we can do this. We can be together. We can be a family, you and me and Kayleigh."

"No, we can't."

"We can," he insisted, forcing the words past the lump in his throat. "We can do whatever we want—if you love me like I love you."

Silence. He waited a pain-filled eternity for her response. "You don't love me, Jeff," she whispered. "Not the way you think. I'm just another responsibility, like Yvonne and your sisters. Somebody for you to protect. You've done that, and I'm so grateful to you for doing that. But I know there's something in me that keeps people from loving me. Richard didn't, and Lord knows my own mother doesn't."

"Angie." The matter-of-fact tone of her voice chilled as much as the words themselves. "You're wrong. There's nothing wrong with you. It's not your fault that people, including me, are too blinded by their own hang-ups to see how special you are."

"Maybe, maybe not. Either way, it doesn't matter. I can't go through the trying and failing again. I can't. I'm sorry."

Too late. He'd told her how he felt too late, and now she didn't believe him.

"Come on, Angie." He knew he was begging, but he didn't care. "Don't do this. Not like this. Not over the phone. Let me see you."

Her breath stuttered again. "I don't think that would be a good idea."

"I just want to talk to you, that's all."

"I'm not going to change my mind," she warned him.

"I understand." I just don't accept it. "When can I see you?"

Another long silence. "We'll be back the day after

tomorrow," she finally said. "You can come by the town-house around six."

"Thank you, Angie. I'll see you then."

He sat for a long time after she disconnected. Two days. He had two days to come up with something, anything, to convince Angela to change her mind.

"I want to help."

He looked up as Julian entered the room. "Don't you think you've helped enough?"

His brother grimaced. "Yeah, the wrong kind of help. So I've got to make it right."

"You want to make it right." Jeff couldn't keep the sudden anger at bay. "You did your level best to make Angie feel uncomfortable and now you want to help?"

Julian had the grace to look repentant. "I saw her at the hospital. I talked to her while we were waiting to hear about you. I learned two things about her."

"What?"

"That she loves you, I mean really loves you. She told me that she only wants one thing from you, but it's something you can't give."

Jeff felt his heart plummet. He knew the answer, but he asked the question anyway. "What's that?"

Julian sat beside him on the couch. "She told me that you guys broke up before you were shot and that you wouldn't get back together because you felt more responsibility for her than love."

Pain blossomed in his chest, and he had to close his eyes

against it. "I do love her. And I feel responsible for her. All my life, I've protected the people I love. How am I supposed to separate the two?"

"You don't," Julian said. "That's part of you. What you have to do is convince her that you love her more than you feel responsible for her."

"And I've got two days to come up with something that will convince her." He sighed, placing his head in his free hand. "What can I do in two days?"

"I don't know, but we'll think of something," Julian said. "After all, this is the season for miracles."

Every mile the taxi took her closer to home, the more Angela regretted her decision to meet with Jeff.

She knew he deserved a face-to-face breakup. It had killed her to leave a note. It was the coward's way out, and she'd taken it because she knew he'd try to persuade her otherwise.

How many times was a person supposed to put her heart on the line, she wondered. How long could she keep trying and hoping and praying before enough was enough? She couldn't do it. Couldn't take another emotional failure.

She'd reached a turning point in the last few days, she realized. Sorrow for Richard's death balanced the relief she felt at finally being free of him. Confronting her mother in the hospital had relieved the need to continually throw herself on the rocks of her mother's favor. Enough was enough.

"It's just you and me, kid," she whispered to Kayleigh, sleeping peacefully beside her. "We'll do just fine, you'll see."

One day she'd actually believe it.

"Here you are, ma'am."

She looked up as the driver slowed to a stop. The town-house in front of her glowed and shimmered with an abundance of holiday decorations. "Driver, this isn't my house."

"It's the address you gave me," he returned, pointing to the mailbox.

Frowning she looked at the number on the holly-drenched mailbox. "This is my address. Who in the world...?" Her voice faded as her front door opened and Jeff stepped out into the late afternoon sun, his left arm in a sling. "Oh my God."

"Looks like your Christmas present got here early," the driver said with a laugh, popping the trunk before leaving the taxi.

With nerveless fingers, Angela fumbled the door open and stepped out, reaching back in to retrieve Kayleigh's carseat. Jeff was at her side when she straightened. "Hi."

"H-hi." She barely had enough breath to form the word. This had to be a dream. This couldn't be reality.

He wore a dark sweater, the pale sling on his left arm a stark contrast. His eyes seemed darker than she remembered, and she realized that he'd shaved his mustache. She also realized that it would take a long time to become immune to him.

Inhaling deeply, she found the means to say, "Did you do all this?"

"I had some help," he admitted, taking a suitcase in his right hand and leading them all up the sidewalk. "Law and Jaime, Vonne and Mike. And Julian too."

"Julian?" Now she knew she was dreaming. "Julian helped?"

"It's his way of apologizing to you," he said, setting the case down before pulling out money to pay the cab driver. "And mine too."

Her mouth dropped open as she stepped over the threshold. The inside of her house looked like a department store. Poinsettia, pine garland and lights dominated every wall, nook, and cranny. "Oh my God."

"Wait until you see the tree."

"You got a tree?"

With a grin, he led her into the living room. "I got you a tree."

What a tree. It was the biggest tree she'd ever seen, filling the bay window and jutting into the living room. Lights and decorations glimmered at her, and presents already nestled among the lower branches.

"Oh my God." Tears pricked her eyes. "I can't believe you did this for me."

"I'd do anything for you, Angie," he said, his voice quiet with conviction. "Don't you know that by now?"

She knew. Of course she knew. The proof of it glared back at her in the form of the sling on his arm.

"I told you once that I wanted to give you Christmas and your birthday all wrapped into one," Jeff said, gently lowering her into a chair before placing Kayleigh's seat on the floor beside her. "I had this all planned for Christmas Eve, but I think I want to give you your presents now."

"Jeff, I—"

"Five minutes," he interrupted, laying a finger across her lips. "Just give me five minutes. That's all I ask."

Unable to speak, she could only nod. He crossed to the tree, then returned carrying a large crimson and gold gift bag. "It's been said that I feel responsible for you. I'm guilty as charged. I feel responsible for everyone that I love. But what I feel for you goes far beyond that."

She watched as he reached into the bag and retrieved something that looked like a rolled up mat. When he shook it out, she saw that it was actually a rug, shaped and shaded like the earth.

"Because I love you, I want to lay the world at your feet," he told her, laying the rug in place, "so that you never want for anything."

He reached into the bag again, pulling out a bowl. Upending it, he sent rose petals cascading through the air. "Because I love you, I want to lay you down on rose petals, so that you'll never feel hurt."

Angela felt tears spill down her cheeks as he pulled a red cashmere wrap from the bag and settled it around her shoulders. "Because I love you, I want to wrap you in my heart so that you'll never be cold."

Kneeling before her, he reached into his shirt pocket. "Because I love you, I want to give you the sun and moon. But I want to start with this star, so you can make a wish."

Her heart thudding in her chest, she watched him open a tiny blue velvet box to reveal a brilliant-cut diamond solitaire. "Make a wish, sweetheart. But don't wish for my love and devotion, because you have that already."

Shocked, she could only sit there, one hand covering her mouth, staring at the most beautiful diamond ring she'd ever seen. "Oh Jeff."

"Angie, you are my heart. When you smile at me, I feel invincible. When you touch me, my heart literally skips a beat. And when you love me—" his voice roughened— "And when you love me, my soul is at peace. You are everything I ever want, need, or love. And I will continue to protect you with my life, because I never want to be without you. Will you do me the honor of marrying you and letting me love you?"

"Oh." She found it difficult to catch her breath. "Oh."

"Angie?"

"Th-the world," she managed to say. "You gave me the world."

"Angie..."

"And roses, and your heart and a star..."

"Angela, it's damned hard for a man with a trick knee and stitches in his side to kneel for long."

Blinded by tears, she slipped to the floor, kneeling in front of him. "Because I love you, I want to share my world with you because it's empty without you in it. Because I love you, I want to be your bed of roses to comfort and support you. Because I love you, I want to wrap you in my love because you've made it burn bright."

She smiled through her tears. "Because I love you, I want to give you the moon and stars because being with you is heaven."

"Angie." His fingers trembled as he pulled the ring from the box. "Is that a yes?"

She held out an unsteady hand. "It most certainly is."

The ring slid into place where it belonged. "When would you like to get married? Is New Year's Day too soon?"

New Year's Day. A time of new hopes and new beginnings. She lifted her eyes from the ring to regard the man she loved. "I think New Year's Day would be perfect."

"I love you, Angie." His eyes shimmered with the truth of his words. "I've always loved you. It just took me too long to realize it. I'm so sorry I wasted the last two years, sorry that I didn't—"

She put her fingers to his lips. "No apologies, sweetheart. Not anymore."

INDIGO

Winter & Spring 2002

🕮 March

No Apologies	Seressia Glass	$8.95
An Unfinished Love Affair	Barbara Keaton	$8.95

🕮 April

Jolie's Surrender	Edwina Martin-Arnold	$8.95
Promises to Keep	Alicia Wiggins	$8.95

🕮 May

Magnolia Sunset	Giselle Carmichael	$8.95
Once in a Blue Moon	Dorianne Cole	$9.95

🕮 June

Still Waters Run Deep	Leslie Esdaile	$9.95
Everything but Love	Natalie Dunbar	$8.95

Indigo After Dark Vol. V		$14.95
Brown Sugar Diaries Part II	Dolores Bundy	

OTHER INDIGO TITLES

The Price of Love	*Sinclair LeBeau*	*$8.95*
The Reluctant Captive	*Joyce Jackson*	*$8.95*
The Missing Link	*Charlyne Dickerson*	*$8.95*
Truly Inseparable	*Wanda Y. Thomas*	*$8.95*
Unconditional Love	*Alicia Wiggins*	*$8.95*
Whispers in the Night	*Dorothy Love*	*$8.95*
Whispers in the Sand	*LaFlorya Gauthier*	*$10.95*
Yesterday is Gone	*Beverly Clark*	*$8.95*
Yesterday's Dreams, Tomorrow's Promises	*Reon Laudat*	*$8.95*
Your Precious Love	*Sinclair LeBeau*	*$8.95*

*You may order on-line at www.genesis-press.com, by phone at
1-888-463-4461, or mail the order-form in the back of this book.*

Love Spectrum Romance

Romance across the culture lines

Forbidden Quest	Dar Tomlinson	$10.95
Designer Passion	Dar Tomlinson	$8.95
Fate	Pamela Leigh Starr	$8.95
Against the Wind	Gwynne Forster	$8.95
From The Ashes	Kathleen Suzanne Jeanne Summerix	$8.95
Heartbeat	Stephanie Bedwell-Grime	$8.95
My Buffalo Soldier	Barbara B. K. Reeves	$8.95
Meant to Be	Jeanne Sumerix	$8.95
A Risk of Rain	Dar Tomlinson	$8.95

Indigo After Dark

erotica beyond sensuous

Indigo After Dark Vol. 1		$10.95
In Between the Night	Angelique	
Midnight Erotic Fantasies	Nia Dixon	
Indigo After Dark Vol. II		$10.95
The Forbidden Art of Desire	Cole Riley	
Erotic Short Stories	Dolores Bundy	
Indigo After Dark Vol. III		$10.95
Impulse	Montana Blue	
Pant	Coco Morena	

ORDER FORM

Mail to: Genesis Press, Inc.
315 3rd Avenue North
Columbus, MS 39701

Name _____

Address _____

City/State _____ Zip _____

Telephone _____

Ship to (if different from above)

Name _____

Address _____

City/State _____ Zip _____

Telephone _____

Qty	Author	Title	Price	Total

Use this order form, or
call
1-888-INDIGO-1

Total for books _____

Shipping and handling:
   $3 first book, $1 each
   additional book _____

Total S & H _____

Total amount enclosed _____
      MS residents add 7% sales tax

ORDER FORM

Mail to: Genesis Press, Inc.
315 3rd Avenue North
Columbus, MS 39701

Name _____

Address _____

City/State _____ Zip _____

Telephone _____

Ship to (if different from above)

Name _____

Address _____

City/State _____ Zip _____

Telephone _____

Qty	Author	Title	Price	Total

Use this order form, or call
1-888-INDIGO-1

Total for books _____

Shipping and handling:
$3 first book, $1 each additional book _____

Total S & H _____

Total amount enclosed _____

MS residents add 7% sales tax

ORDER FORM

Mail to: Genesis Press, Inc.
315 3rd Avenue North
Columbus, MS 39701

Name _____

Address _____

City/State _____ Zip _____

Telephone _____

Ship to (if different from above)

Name _____

Address _____

City/State _____ Zip _____

Telephone _____

Qty	Author	Title	Price	Total

Use this order form, or call 1-888-INDIGO-1	**Total for books** _____ **Shipping and handling:** $3 first book, $1 each additional book **Total S & H** _____ **Total amount enclosed** _____ *MS residents add 7% sales tax*

ORDER FORM

Mail to: Genesis Press, Inc.
315 3rd Avenue North
Columbus, MS 39701

Name _____

Address _____

City/State _____ Zip _____

Telephone _____

Ship to (if different from above)

Name _____

Address _____

City/State _____ Zip _____

Telephone _____

Qty	Author	Title	Price	Total

Use this order form, or call
1-888-INDIGO-1

Total for books _____

Shipping and handling:
$3 first book, $1 each
additional book

Total S & H _____

Total amount enclosed _____

MS residents add 7% sales tax